BITTER ROOTS

BITTER ROOTS

Ellen Crosby

**SEVERN
HOUSE**

First world edition published in Great Britain and the USA in 2022
by Severn House, an imprint of Canongate Books Ltd,
14 High Street, Edinburgh EH1 1TE.

Trade paperback edition first published in Great Britain and the USA in 2022
by Severn House, an imprint of Canongate Books Ltd.

severnhouse.com

Extract from *Winegrowing in Eastern America* is reproduced by kind permission
of Lucie Morton.

British Library Cataloguing-in-Publication Data
A CIP catalogue record for this title is available from the British Library.

ISBN-13: 978-0-7278-9102-0 (cased)
ISBN-13: 978-1-4483-0807-1 (trade paper)
ISBN-13: 978-1-4483-0806-4 (e-book)

All Severn House titles are printed on acid-free paper.

Typeset by Palimpsest Book Production Ltd.,
Falkirk, Stirlingshire, Scotland.
Printed and bound in Great Britain by
TJ Books, Padstow, Cornwall.

To Lucie Morton, with grateful thanks for sharing your knowledge, expertise and, especially, your friendship.

God grant me the serenity to accept the things I cannot change, the courage to change the things I can, and the wisdom to know the difference.

– *The Serenity Prayer*, Reinhold Niebuhr

Wine is the most inspiring and mysterious agricultural commodity on earth. Such a religious and romantic aura surrounds wine that it has always occupied a place apart from other farm products. Indeed, tractors and hoes rarely come to mind when we think of wine. Rather, we have visions of good food, friends, and happy times.

– *Winegrowing in Eastern America*, Lucie Morton

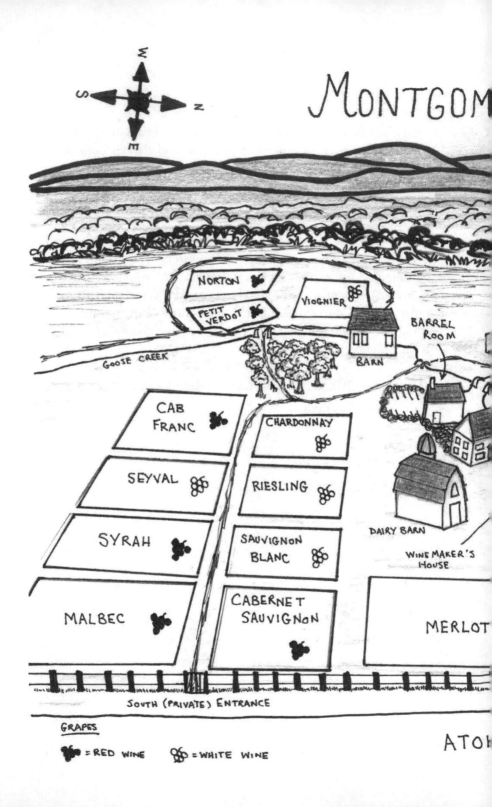

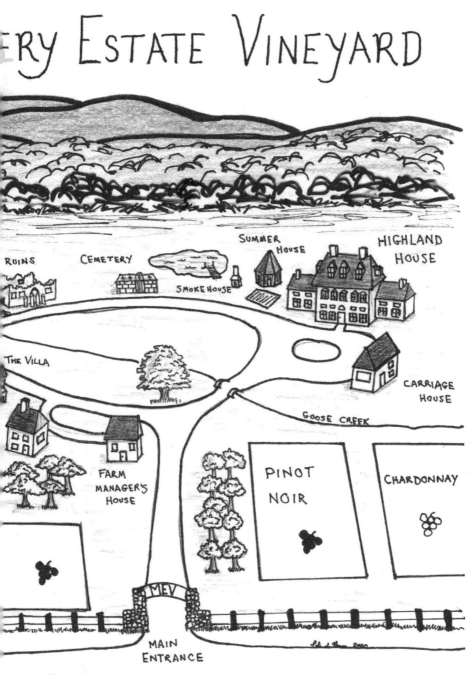

ONE

J ulia Child once said that every woman should have a blow-torch in the kitchen. To that I would add: and a chain saw in the garden. Or the vineyard, should you own one. Blowtorches and chain saws say you're a woman who means business. They say *don't mess with me*.

'These vines are going to *die*. They're not going to get any bigger.' I was stunned, but I was also angrier than I'd been in a long time. These vines had also been fine, just *fine*, for the first two years after we planted them.

The technical name for what my fiancé Quinn Santori and I were looking at said everything and explained nothing: *Failure to thrive*. What it meant was: *I have no clue what happened*.

'I know, Lucie.' Quinn sounded as upset as I was, but also weary. 'I know that.'

For three back-breaking years he and I had nurtured these vines, cared for them. *Loved* them like children. After lavishing money on their growth and development without making a dime off them so far, it was their turn to kick in and pay rent and expenses. This year these Cabernet Franc grapes should finally have been producing their first proper harvest so we could make wine from them. It was a grape that did well in Virginia soil and our wineries were known for making good wine from Cab Franc. So, when we planted these vines, we thought – no, we *knew* – we were backing a winner. Instead here we were standing in a field of stunted, sick-looking grapevines.

I scraped at the dirt at the base of the withering brown trunk with the tip of the cane I've needed ever since a car accident ten years ago. Was something in the soil causing this? Was it the rootstock itself? A parasite? *What was it?*

'I can't handle looking at this,' I said to Quinn. 'I'm ready to rip 'em all out right now.'

'Come on, not so fast, baby. We still don't know what caused them not to grow. And why this – disease or whatever – stops all of a sudden and the other vines are fine. We have to at least figure that out.'

'*Nobody* knows what's wrong,' I said. 'And it's not from lack of asking people to come out and take a look for themselves.'

It had been like throwing darts at a dartboard while wearing a blindfold. Everyone who came by to give us their considered opinion – and that included agents from the County Ag Extension Service as well as an expert in grapevine diseases from Virginia Tech – shook their heads and delivered the same verdict: 'Your guess is as good as mine.'

What were we supposed to do with *that*?

Truth be told, I knew Quinn was even more upset about what was happening than I was – and that's saying something – because he's our winemaker. It's part of the job – worrying all the time, second-guessing yourself when something goes wrong, figuring it's your fault. Convinced you could have prevented what happened. *Should* have prevented it, if only you'd known what to do or seen it coming. Or as Quinn – whose childhood home had a small altar in the linen closet where his devout Spanish mother prayed daily – told me, it was like Catholic guilt on steroids.

This time, though, I knew he was factoring in the other big event in our lives that was making me especially emotional and volatile: our upcoming wedding eight days from now. A wedding that would take place here at the vineyard where this blotch of ugly, shriveled vines among so much green stood out like the worst kind of eyesore.

We climbed back into the dark-green Gator, Quinn at the wheel, me taking pictures with my phone as we drove up and down aisles of what should have been lush, leafy vines. In mid-May, now that bud break had taken place and the other vines were flowering, you should already be able to see the promise of what was to come over the next few months until it was time for harvest. Instead we found only shrunken, wizened vines with anemic-looking leaves that barely reached the first trellis wire.

Elsewhere, though, the vineyard, with thousands of tiny white flowers just beginning to show under new spring leaves, looked spectacular. Vineyard bloom, as it's called, usually lasted a week, maybe two at most, and, regular as clockwork, it was something we never had to worry about occurring, because grapes are hermaphroditic, or asexual. They pollinate themselves, so there's no waiting for the birds and the bees or the wind to get the job done – or *hope* it happened. This year, fingers crossed, bloom would still be going on during our wedding. The fleeting, elusive scent – a sweet floral note with an underlying earthy tone – would be a faint, tantalizing grace note in the air. Some guests would recognize it, but others would swear they smelled *something*, or thought they did, if only they could put their finger on it.

'We need to get Josie up here,' Quinn said as we rounded a corner where an apricot- and peach-colored Sweet Fragrance rose bush marked the beginning of the Cab Franc block. 'Let her take a look before we rip everything out, see if she can diagnose what's wrong.'

Josie Wilde was the premier vineyard consultant on the East Coast. Let me amend that: she was the premier vineyard consultant in the United States, period. And because she'd studied winemaking and grape growing at the Université de Montpellier in France and spoke fluent French, she was also on speed dial at a number of prominent French vineyards. I had wanted to hire her to help us at Montgomery Estate Vineyard and advise us in the barrel room where we made our wine because – well, who wouldn't? Strictly speaking, you didn't *hire* Josie. *She* agreed to take you on if she thought you would be a worthy client. That you were serious about upping your game, that you would do the work, put in the time.

I convinced her we were, and we would.

In 1976, California moved out of France's shadow on a nothing-happening day in August when the British owner of a Parisian wine shop decided to do a blind tasting of French versus California wines because business and the city itself were about as dead as your proverbial doornail. An American reporter from *Time* magazine wrote about the little wine shop competition because, see above, nothing else was going on. To everyone's astonishment – *Zut alors! Ce n'est pas possible!*

– the California wines won, the story ended up in *Time*, and you would have thought the Californians changed the laws of gravity without telling the French. So I didn't see why history couldn't repeat itself and Virginia could emerge from under California's behemoth dominance and the breezy taken-for-granted assumptions that any wine made east of the Sierra Nevada couldn't possibly be that good. Instead we found ourselves backpedaling as we dealt with more and more problems with the grapes and vines that seemed to be the inexorable consequence of climate change.

Josie lived about two hours south of us in Charlottesville, where she had a sweet little laboratory behind her Craftsman bungalow. The first time I visited, it reminded me of a child's playhouse until I went inside and saw the state-of-the-art computer software she used and all her high-tech toys and equipment – including a drone for taking aerial photos of the vineyards and a badass power saw for cutting through thick grapevines to see what was inside. She had also rigged a trellis system in her postage-stamp backyard that looked like a life-sized game of cat's cradle where she grew and experimented with dozens of varietals of grapes.

To be honest I was surprised that Quinn was the one to suggest asking Josie to drive up here and survey the diseased grapevines. He hadn't been as gung-ho as I was to hire her – the alpha male thing about ceding some of his authority and being told what to do – but maybe he was coming around.

'I know Josie needs to see this,' I said. Next he'd be saying that Eve Kerr should get over here and take a look as well.

'Eve should probably come by, too,' he said in a bland tone. 'Since she's the one who sold us these vines.'

Eve Kerr could sell ice to Eskimos, especially if the Eskimo was male. She'd moved here from California three years ago, excited about the promise of Virginia evolving into a major player in the wine world after so many years of heartache and outright failure. Make that *centuries* of heartache and failure: we'd been trying to grow grapes and make wine in the Old Dominion since 1619 when the Virginia House of Burgesses passed a law that made it compulsory for every household to plant and maintain ten grapevines imported from Europe. A nice idea in theory, but a complete nonstarter in reality since everyone's vines ended up dying in the intolerant, pest-ridden climate of the New World. Then California blew past us in the 1800s and we chewed the dust of their lush vineyards. By the end of World War II, when American palates grew more sophisticated and we started drinking more wine, nearly everyone – even folks overseas – assumed that California wine was a tautology for American wine.

By the 1980s we tried again – Virginians are nothing if not stubborn – when we were done licking our wounds from the devastation of Prohibition. And before that, it had been the ruined farms and trampled landscapes of Civil War damage. But this time, *finally*, we started getting it right. Gaining a reputation, getting noticed on a national stage as a 'wine destination.' Becoming known as a place where you could experiment – grow Russian Rkatsiteli next to Italian Barbera next to southern French Tannat next to Portuguese Touriga next to you-name-it. In Virginia you could make your mark. Stand out. Get noticed.

Eve Kerr got noticed all right. She was stunning. When the Beach Boys wished they all could be California girls, they were channeling Eve. Long-legged, fit, toned, tawny blonde hair, cornflower blue eyes, perfect smile, a beach and surfer girl who went to UC-Davis and double-majored in viticulture and enology. Now she wanted to ride the wave that was Virginia's future, so she took a job with Landau's Trees & Vines, a family-owned business that had been around for sixty-five years. When Jackson Landau took over what had been a small but profitable mom-and-pop farm from his parents twenty-five years ago, he turned it into the largest commercial nursery, not just in Virginia, but on the entire East Coast. Conveniently, the farm was about twenty minutes away in Delaplane, which made it a local business for us.

So, yes, Eve Kerr – Jackson's right hand – was a knockout, but she was also smart, funny, and she knew her stuff. Plus she had that laidback California vibe that made her so easy to deal with. Or had been easy to deal with until recently, when more than one vineyard began complaining about problems like ours: grapevines that had been doing fine for a couple of years. Until they weren't fine. Until they suddenly started showing symptoms of disease and dying. And people started asking questions about the grower who had sold them to us: Landau's Trees & Vines. Maybe those vines had been diseased from day one and the problems were just now showing up.

Eve began pushing back, defending her boss, who, she said, would *never* do something like that. Landau's stood on their sixty-five-year reputation as a family business and guaranteed their products; there was no way *in hell* they'd sell anything that they believed was diseased or damaged to long-time clients, people they knew like family.

'You know what Eve's going to say when we call her,' I told Quinn, although I also knew he was probably going to say that he'd talk to Eve. One Californian to another, two UC-Davis grads, no less, who could communicate in fluent California-speak, a dialect that somehow eluded the rest of the country. 'She's going to say "After three years in your care, those vines are your responsibility. There are too many factors that we couldn't possibly control after all this time. I'm sorry they're not doing well, but it's not our fault."'

'Maybe so, but we still need to talk to her,' he said. 'I can handle her.'

As predicted.

'She's not going to budge.'

These days it felt like there was less paperwork involved to adopt a child than there was to buy grapevines from a nursery. First you sign a contract. Then there's a licensing fee. And a registry fee. Plus a whole heap of other little add-ons. By the time you're done being nickeled and dimed with all the extra charges tacked on like ornaments on an over-decorated Christmas tree, you've bought a two dollar and fifty cent grapevine for four bucks. Multiply that by a couple of thousand grapevines and you're talking about some serious money. Just how much money, you wonder? For an acre and a half of Cabernet Franc?

Thirty thousand, easily. And that's just to buy the vines. Then you have to hire folks to plant them. You also have to fertilize those tender new vines and spray them, so they'll grow and thrive, and you pay more folks to do those tasks. There's pruning and thinning, all work done by hand, so the canopy lets in enough sunlight for the grapes to ripen perfectly, or at least that's the plan. So you hire people to do that. All the while you sweet talk these vines, cajole them, love them. They *owe* you for three years of being coddled and nurtured while you worked your butt off for them.

Instead they don't do anything they're supposed to do – you know how teenagers can be – and even though you keep trying, one day you throw up your hands and face the harsh reality that you're out about a hundred and eighty thousand dollars, all told. You have the Come-to-Jesus talk with the recalcitrant vines that Quinn and I were having right now and, let me tell you, it's not pleasant.

And if you replace these wretched vines that let you down so badly, you know what?

You start the process all over again. If you have another hundred and eighty thousand to burn, that is.

We didn't. That's why God invented banks. And second mortgages.

'Let's go back to the winery,' I said. 'Nothing more to see here that isn't going to keep breaking our hearts.'

Quinn nodded and turned the ATV around. 'Why don't you call Josie and see when she can come by? You two get on better than she and I do.'

He had a point. Quinn had chafed at the iron-clad non-negotiable terms and conditions Josie had insisted on from all her clients. *Hire me and you do what I say. Full stop. Don't waste my time – and your money.* Fortunately I had been able to persuade her that Quinn would fall in line. And he had. Mostly.

So I would call Josie and he would call Eve. Josie and I would have a blunt, unvarnished pull-no-punches talk. Quinn was going to try to charm Eve based on the you-catch-more-flies-with-honey-than-vinegar theory and maybe salvage something out of an otherwise total loss.

I didn't want to burst my fiancé's bubble, but all the charm in the world wasn't going to change her sorry-but-no-dice answer.

'All right, I'll call Josie,' I said. 'But you know when Eve comes by, we won't just be dealing with her. She'll bring Richard and he's going to snow us with a bunch of facts that sound like a foreign language we're supposed to understand, and we don't. He'll back her up two hundred percent.'

Dr Richard Brightman, horticulturalist extraordinaire and professor at the University of Northern Virginia. Between him, Eve, and Jackson Landau they had been the Holy Trinity you wanted to deal with when you needed to buy grapevines. It had been Eve's all-in gung-ho enthusiasm that convinced Jackson his nursery ought to be a testing ground for Richard's research trials to clone rootstock that would be more resilient to climate change. First of all, it would put them on the cutting edge of the industry, promoting potential pioneering break-throughs. Second, they'd get noticed, written about, talked about – possibly even as competitors of her alma mater, UC-Davis, the premier research university in the US for anything to do with grape growing and winemaking. No small feather in the cap. Third, a few years earlier Richard had already perfected a brilliantly simple way after trial and error experiments to graft hardy, resilient rootstock to more disease-susceptible vines with the end result being a grapevine that was guaranteed to be disease- and pest-free. The quid pro quo was that Jackson – who supplied a vast network of East Coast orchards and vineyards – would use Richard's new graft with its By-God-Guaranteed-Good-Housekeeping-Seal-of-Approval assurance that the plants were in impeccable health. And the real pot-sweetener: Jackson voluntarily paid Richard a nickel for every vine and sapling he sold with the Brightman Graft because it was just such a brilliantly simple but genius innovation.

Which added up to a nice chunk of change for Richard. And a cozy relationship between him, Eve, and Jackson. In other words, how likely was it Richard was going to bite the hand that fed him, to rat out Jackson if he even suspected the vines might have been diseased from the get-go?

Quinn turned off the dirt-and-gravel road that ran along-side the vineyard onto Sycamore Lane, the pretty private road that meandered through our land connecting the winery, our home, the family cemetery, and the Ruins, a tenant house burned by Union troops during the Civil War. A number of years ago we'd renovated the Ruins, turning it into an outdoor stage. In eight days' time fairy lights outlining the shell of the old house would twinkle, a band would play, and we would dance under the almost-full moon – the Flower Moon, May's full moon, would appear two nights before our wedding – and celebrate with family and friends at our reception.

As Quinn and I pulled into a parking space behind the barrel room he said, 'Eve's a decent person. I think I can get some traction with her.'

I knew why Quinn had blinders on where Eve was concerned, but I also knew trying to get anything remotely resembling traction with her was like trying to push wet string uphill.

'If you do manage to extort something from her, everyone else with diseased vines is going to want in on it. Especially Otto and Ali. Look at what's happened to them.'

'I know.' He pursed his lips together and frowned. 'I know. Such a damn shame.'

Otto and Ali James, who owned Bacchus Winery nearby in Middleburg, had lost almost all of their tiny vineyard for the same reason we – and others – had. Dying vines. And, like all of us, they had bought their rootstock from Landau's.

But unlike most of us, the Jameses were going to lose everything. They had gone all in, played for all the marbles, and now they had nothing in reserve: nada, zilch, zippo, rien. Mortgaged to the hilt, retirement account and savings tapped out, a loan from Blue Ridge Federal that was probably going to be called soon. They were going to close the doors to Bacchus once they sold their equipment to the rest of us for pennies on the dollar – and then what?

Ali was devastated. Otto just lost it.

'It's even more of a tragedy considering what it's doing to Otto. Especially after his meltdown the other night,' I said.

According to my cousin Dominique Gosselin, owner of the Goose Creek Inn, the most romantic restaurant in the region and recent recipient of a Michelin star, Otto showed up in the bar and proceeded to get so stinking drunk the bartender refused to keep serving him. Someone took his keys and called a cab to take him home to Ali. On his way out the door he turned around and told the entire room, in a voice loud enough that everyone could hear, that he was damn sure Eve *and* Richard *and* Jackson knew the vines they were selling every-one were diseased but they'd formed a conspiracy of silence and were stonewalling.

He'd also announced in the same loud, angry voice that he was going to prove irrefutably that they did know and then sue their asses off.

Either that, or he was going to kill someone.

TWO

We climbed out of the Gator and Quinn passed me my cane. 'Everyone knows what Otto said when he got hammered that night,' he said. 'If you weren't there, you heard about it the next day at the General Store.'

From Thelma Johnson, the sassy octogenarian owner of said General Store, the pulsing nexus and beating heart of our little village of Atoka. You had to love the General Store. It had been an institution practically since God was a boy.

Thelma kept it well-stocked with the essential things we needed around here, from bait to ammunition to hoof polish for the horses, as well as the white stuff you had to have on hand when the other white stuff was falling from the sky. She received a daily supply of fresh croissants, muffins, and donuts from a bakery in neighboring Leesburg – the delivery guy climbed in through the side window to get the key if the front door was still locked – so it was an easy-going, well-established relationship. She also kept three pots of coffee labeled Plain, Decaf, and Fancy going, which meant her store was *the* place to congregate every morning.

But beyond the coffee and fresh-baked goods, what really kept everyone coming in was that you knew Thelma knew everything, and I mean *everything* that was happening in two counties – and that she was happy to . . . well, *share* her knowledge. Besides, her far-flung sources of information were unimpeachable: a coterie of collaborators known as the Romeos, which stood for Retired Old Men Eating Out. It was an august group of elders that whiled away the days at local restaurants hoovering up any tidbit of information that came along, which they then disseminated to the mother ship. In addition to holding court as habitués of the region's many dining establishments, they frequented their fair share of watering holes, meaning they were also Retired Old Men *Drinking* Out.

Which was how Thelma had learned from first-hand accounts about Otto's threats and the ugly scene in the bar of the Goose Creek Inn. And now everyone in Atoka and Middleburg knew about it as well.

'I feel awful for Otto and Ali,' I said to Quinn. 'Ali told me they're leaving town once they sell Bacchus and that Sloane Everett might buy the place since their land is adjacent to his. So maybe they'll come out of this with a little money after they pay off their debts.'

Sloane Everett, our newest neighbor, was a retired NBA legend who had recently moved from southern California to Virginia with his wife, three daughters, and six championship rings. Despite stepping away from basketball he was still a sought-after superstar: a smart, popular, good-looking businessman who had signed lucrative contracts endorsing everything from cars to dog food. The Sloane and Isabella Everett Foundation helped kids in poor neighborhoods by buying school supplies, providing tutors, sponsoring summer rec programs and providing college scholarships.

'That would be good for Otto and Ali if Sloane bought their place,' Quinn said. 'He's rich enough that he could easily afford Bacchus. Hell, he could afford two Bacchuses.'

'Yes, but he's also got dying vines, same as Otto and Ali. They were failing before he even bought his vineyard from Harry.'

'Harry Dye was completely upfront with Sloane about that when he sold him the place, so it was *caveat emptor*. Plus Austin made sure Sloane knew what he was getting into as well,' Quinn said. 'Austin said Sloane told him that it could have looked like something after the apocalypse, but he really didn't care about the vineyard and its problems. He bought the house and the stables because Isabella fell in love with the place and she wanted a home on the East Coast in addition to the palace they own in California.'

Austin Kendall, one of the Romeos, had come out of semi-retirement to handle the eight-figure Everett deal for Kendall Luxury Estate Properties and probably could now buy himself a private island with his commission. If that's what Austin said, his word was gold.

Plus there was the other story that had been going around. Not just that Isabella wanted an East Coast home because she'd grown up in D.C., but also because she wanted their three young daughters to be far, far away – at least geographic-ally – from a little scandal involving their father and a drunken hookup with a cocktail waitress at a ski resort in Utah. When the story got out, as of course it would, Sloane tried claiming the sex was consensual. The waitress had a different opinion and it involved a date-rape drug. Eventually enough money bought her silence and there was no trial, but nevertheless the salacious Internet stories – real and invented – did irreparable damage to Sloane's golden-boy reputation as an upstanding family man – not to mention his marriage. Isabella took him back, stood by him at a teary, penitent news conference where he professed to being a changed, humbled, and grateful man and talked about loving Jesus as his Savior, not to mention his wife, his daughters, his team, the NBA, motherhood, apple pie, the American flag and the kitchen sink. But after that, Isabella, who knew she'd saved her husband from a career-ending auto-da-fé, had kept him on a short leash.

'However bad the vineyard looked when Sloane bought it, I heard from Antonio who heard from Vance that Sloane changed his mind about not being interested. All of a sudden he's decided having his name on a bottle of wine is totally cool,' I said.

Antonio Ramirez was our vineyard manager. Vance Hall had been Harry's winemaker whom Sloane asked to stay on, initially telling him to do 'whatever' and send him the bill. The only thing Sloane had been interested in changing then was the vineyard's name to GSV for Golden State Vineyard, or more formally GSV Estate Winery, in honor of his career playing for all four California NBA teams. Now supposedly he was all-in with the vineyard.

Quinn shrugged. 'That's what he says *now*. I wonder how long until he gets bored or burned out and turns it all back over to Vance?'

It was a fair question. Because, sure, it is totally cool and even fun owning a vineyard, but it's also a hell of a lot of work. I mean, basically, we're farmers. Anyone who thinks we spend our days toddling around the fields, glass of wine in hand, admiring God's handiwork and waiting for those grapes to ripen to perfection so we can work our alchemy in the barrel room and, voilà, wave our wands and produce a wine to die for, is, frankly, delusional.

'I don't know how long he'll stick it out,' I said. 'But in the meantime, an NBA superstar like Sloane Everett taking charge of his own vineyard right here in Virginia couldn't hurt us.'

Media attention, more visitors, more visibility. In other words, one of Sloane's famous slam dunks.

And, God knows, more money as more people came out here to visit and find out about all of us. To buy and drink our wine, enjoy our Virginia hospitality.

Although there was already plenty of money in this region, which was why we were known as the tony, affluent heart of Virginia's horse and hunt country. A substantial amount of wealth was tied up in beautifully manicured estates with Old World names, some dating from the 1700s and evoking our English colonial roots. Our streets were named for the signers of the Declaration of Independence because they were friends of the man who founded the town in 1787, so we had a long and distinguished American pedigree.

Even more money was invested in horse farms that raised and bred thoroughbreds that one day might be winners of the Derby or at the Olympics or maybe even the really big prize: the Triple Crown. The town's annual Stable Tour, a fundraiser held every Memorial Day weekend, brought thousands of people out here to take a peek at the glamorous, rarefied world of steeplechase racing, fox hunting, and polo. Along with the chance to stroll through multi-million-dollar stables and training grounds or enjoy the picture-postcard view of future champions grazing in jewel-green pastures with the Blue Ridge Mountains as a backdrop.

We already had a number of celebrities who lived here before Sloane Everett arrived. Mostly they were attracted by the natural beauty of our rolling hills and winding country lanes lined with stacked stone walls and our old-fashioned small-town charm with its horsey, tweedy overtones and beloved traditions. But those folks who had settled here were pretty low-key and appreciated that no one went gaga or gawked if they were seen at the Cuppa Giddyup getting a latte or buying Cow Puddles at The Upper Crust, because that's how we were. No 'look who I just saw' photos posted on social media. Live and let live. Everyone was entitled to their privacy.

Sloane Everett was a whole different kettle of fish. A flashy, magnetic star who was not only buddy-buddy with basketball royalty, but also had A-list friends from Hollywood, not to mention an ex-president and a few Silicon Valley tech moguls who came and sat courtside to watch him play. No one had quite figured out yet how he was going to fit in here – or stand out.

And whether he was going to join what was becoming a louder and louder chorus from his neighbors: vineyard owners and winemakers who had the same problem he did with dying vines. All of which had come from Landau's Trees & Vines.

This evening Quinn and I were hosting a blending party for our new Chardonnay. It would be a gathering of staff, friends in the business, plus my cousin Dominique and my grandfather, who was visiting from Paris, all of whom would spend a couple of hours swirling, spitting, tasting, discussing and making notes to help us figure out what combination of flavors would make the best Chardonnay from the different barrels we'd been aging.

But while we were doing that, I knew the evening would almost certainly devolve into an informal discussion about

our options for getting some kind of retribution or remuneration – *anything* – from Jackson Landau as compensation
for our considerable losses. Which right now was about as
likely to happen as Dom Pérignon himself joining us for
the evening.

Decades ago in California a group of vineyard owners had
sued the pants off a nursery they claimed had been selling
diseased vines *for years*. It had been ugly and bitter, pitting
friends against each other and tearing apart a close-knit
community. Neither Quinn nor I wanted to see something that
savage happen here in Virginia. We were a whole lot smaller
than California and we didn't have the same clout. Our strength
came from banding together, from being united and helping
each other out. From remembering that we had a shared goal:
to make Virginia a winemaking region to be reckoned with.
But with Jackson not giving an inch, and Eve and Richard
digging in their heels as well, I knew a number of vineyards
– most notably Otto and Ali at Bacchus – were already at the
tipping point.

By tonight we'd probably know who was ready to get
out the long knives and who still wanted to try diplomacy. I
knew that Quinn – the Californian among us – would argue
for trying to work this out, make a deal, and find the middle
ground. No lawyers. No lawsuits. And, God knows, no airing
our dirty laundry for the rest of the wine world to see.

He would be in the minority.

Everyone else – from the beating war drums I'd heard – was
ready for a fight.

And if those who wanted to draw blood could get someone
like Sloane Everett on board, then, Jesus Lord, the fireworks
might be epic.

Sloane wasn't coming to tonight's session – frankly, he didn't
yet have enough experience or knowledge to be discussing
the finer points of taste, aroma, type of fermentation, all the
technical stuff – plus, and this was more to the point, it wasn't
clear whose side he was on. He could very well decide he
really didn't want to get mixed up in something that had the
potential to turn ugly since he hadn't bought diseased vines:
Harry had. Maybe, like Quinn, he didn't want to see another

California-type explosion that would take his newest interest – GSV Estate Winery – down with it. He could afford to turn a blind eye.

But Vance Hall, Sloane's winemaker, would be here. He'd know which way the wind blew with his boss.

As if he read my mind – which I often thought he did – Quinn said, 'Hopefully Vance will fill us in on just how committed Sloane is.'

'I hope so,' I said. 'Come on, let's go inside and make those calls – you talk to Eve, I'll call Josie – so we can figure out where we are.'

We were still standing next to the Gator, mostly because we didn't want to have this conversation in the wine cellar in front of Antonio and the rest of the crew. They didn't need anything else to make them more anxious and jittery these days. ICE was doing a bang-up job of that, swooping down and rounding up people they suspected were in the country illegally, making them disappear. Asking questions later.

Since everyone on our crew was Hispanic, just like every other vineyard around here, our guys looked over their shoulders every damn day. And each night when they left to go home, we never knew who wouldn't be back tomorrow because they or someone they knew had been whisked away. So they'd gone to ground.

But now Quinn's eyes skidded away from mine. 'I thought I heard you talking to Frankie on the phone this morning, something about meeting her later to talk about nail polish and what color will go with your dress *and* your shoes and that you two needed a big powwow. So I thought I'd give you . . . uh, space . . . to see her and discuss fifty shades of pink or whatever. And if it's all the same to you, I'd like to be as far away from that conversation as possible.'

He was smiling, but there was something a bit off in what he said, the way he said it. *Nail polish? Really?*

He wanted to call Eve privately. Without me around.

Was he going to give her a heads-up about just how bad it was, how angry some folks were? Or was it something else? I wanted to ask him why, but I didn't. Probably just more pre-wedding emotions creeping into everything, including a tiny twinge of jealousy because he wanted to talk to her exclusively and keep me out of it.

So I smiled back and said in my blandest way, 'Nail polish is *important*, in case you didn't know, buddy. And you do know Frankie wants our wedding to be perfect.'

Francesca Merchant, who ran the retail side of our vineyard with the military precision of a general organizing a multi-pronged campaign, had volunteered to be our wedding planner and I'd gratefully accepted. No detail was too small to miss her attention. It was a bit of overkill, if you asked me – and I knew it occasionally drove Quinn nuts – but, bless her, our wedding was going to be as close to perfect as it could possibly be. My grandfather, who had stayed on after he came over from Paris a few months ago, was going to give me away. My older brother Eli had applied for a license to marry Quinn and me. We would be surrounded by family, friends, and neighbors – the people we loved most.

That was all that mattered. Nothing else.

'And *you* know Frankie's going to call the National Weather Service and *tell* them what the weather has to be that day, right?' Quinn didn't mind needling me about Frankie's detail-minded overexuberance.

I laughed and refused to take his bait. 'She won't need to. I already know it's going to be perfect. It's an outdoor wedding in our garden. It *has* to be perfect.'

He leaned down and gave me a long, lingering kiss. 'I'm marrying you. That's as perfect as it gets.'

He was whistling as he walked into the barrel room, something pretty and tuneless, and that's when I told myself I was being an idiot. Quinn wanted the same thing I wanted: for Landau's Trees & Vines to do right by us over our dying vines. And OK, he thought he'd have better luck sweet-talking Eve than I would, which was probably a fair assessment. Maybe I shouldn't rule out the possibility that they'd work out something no one else around here could manage because of that California connection. At least he should give it a shot, right?

It was no more and no less than that.

Wasn't it?

THREE

The early-morning chill had evaporated, replaced by golden sunshine, a luminous blue sky, and a spring breeze as soft and sweet as a kiss. Quinn had gone inside to call Eve, but also to check in with Antonio since, in addition to figuring out the Chardonnay blend tonight, we were busy with the summer wines – making rosé and bottling Sauvignon Blanc and Viognier, the early season whites.

Harvest may be our busiest time when we work flat out for days and nights to get the grapes picked and brought in to be sorted, crushed, and fermented – our annual marathon race against Mother Nature and her mercurial ways – but there was always something going on, either out in the field or in the wine cellar. More often than not, in both places. Just now we were in the midst of labor-intensive projects in the field like thinning shoots, tying up vines that had come down, and suckering – which, as it sounded, meant removing the weaker grapevines so they wouldn't detract from the strength of the main trunk. We'd also started mowing the rows between the vines, known as the middles, and there were still repairs to be made to the trellises that had sustained winter damage.

I retreated to the courtyard – the large wedge-shaped space that connected the wine cellar where we made wine with the Villa where we sold it – to call Josie. On days like this it was a crime to stay inside if you didn't need to, since it wouldn't be long before the hammering heat and withering humidity of summer arrived even before the calendar made it official. And with it would come more and more energy-sapping days of temperatures in the 100s as each summer seemed to get hotter than the one before. It was a heat we hadn't been accustomed to, but I knew we'd better start learning to live with it. Because it wasn't going away.

Frankie had already worked her pre-wedding magic in the

courtyard, filling the halved wine barrels we used as planters with lacy red geraniums and variegated ivy which, by autumn, would be rioting like no one was minding the store. She had also hung mossed baskets filled with red and purple fuchsia or velvety multi-colored pansies from brackets attached to the portico columns that lined the perimeter of the courtyard on two sides.

I sat on the low stone wall where I had a sweeping view of the south vineyard and the layered Blue Ridge Mountains that framed it – including the ugly swath of brown, gold, and mottled green that used to be our Cabernet Franc vines. Which got me mad all over again.

Josie was blunt to the point of being terse – as expected – when I called her, but then she never messed around with her time and your money. She was a pretty redhead with an English-rose complexion, enormous green eyes, and a faint drawl – replete with Southernisms – that was more pronounced when she was upset or had had a couple of glasses of wine. You might be forgiven if you mistook her for a delicate flower that wilted easily based on her fragile-looking beauty, but you wouldn't make that mistake a second time once you dealt with her. You'd pull your hand back to make sure you didn't get bitten again.

'I meant to take a look at those vines when I was up there to see you last time,' she said. 'I'll bet you any money that what you've got is *Phaeomoniella chlamydospora*.'

A tongue-twister of a name, with a hell of a shorthand description. Something you didn't want to hear, even worse than 'failure to thrive.'

'Black goo,' I said, and my heart sank.

'Yup,' she said. 'Black goo. Has anyone brought that up yet?'

'No.'

Vines infested by black goo can appear normal for months or years. When the fungi start growing, however, they can kill the vines or just make them sickly underachievers. That's exactly what we had in the Cab Franc block.

But the way you find out for sure if it's black goo is by cutting open the vines to see what's running through the veins.

What you want to be looking at is clear sap. If you get a black, gummy ooze, it's over.

The symptoms of black goo are many and varied: stunted growth, grooved and asymmetrical trunks, graft unions that fail to callus over, leaves that prematurely turn yellow. But finding that dark sticky substance when you open up the vine is what seals the deal. And though black goo sounds almost like a bad joke, unlike its serious, complex-sounding Latin name, it is nonetheless an apt, unforgettable description. Coined by another top vineyard consultant, a woman named Lucie Morton.

Now maybe it was here. In Virginia. At Montgomery Estate Vineyard. *Damn damn damn.*

'If that's what it is, we'll have to rip those vines out, won't we?' I said.

'Probably. Especially if they've already developed into full-blown Esca disease and you have no replacement trunk,' she said. 'I'm driving up there tomorrow to see another client. I can stop by first thing in the morning, say around nine, so we can confirm it one way or the other.'

'Thanks; that would be great. Quinn is calling Eve. We want her to come by, too.'

'And do what? Take responsibility? Bless your heart.'

Which was a Southernism that covered a lot of territory, ranging from 'don't be so naive' to 'you're an idiot.' And a bunch of other things in between.

'Go back and read the contract you signed when y'all bought those vines,' she said. 'They're indemnified six ways from Sunday. Hell, *sixty* ways from Sunday.'

She thought I was naive. *And* possibly an idiot.

'Do you think she and Jackson knew they couldn't guarantee the vines were disease free?' I asked.

'I do, but so what? Right now I can't prove it.'

'*Could* you prove it?'

'I mean to. But in the meantime, may I direct your attention to Exhibit A? Cal-i-for-ni-a. That big state on the other coast. I'm sure you've read about what happened in the nineties with all the finger pointing, lawsuits, and everyone blaming everyone else – and how well that worked out for them. Being vindicated

– forcing the grower of the biggest nursery responsible for selling diseased vines to go out of business – was, in some ways, a pyrrhic victory. Because it just about destroyed a close-knit winemaking community, so the collateral damage was incalculable.'

Which is precisely what Quinn didn't want to happen here in Virginia.

'How do you plan to prove our growers are doing the same thing here? I don't want us to end up like California,' I said.

'Me neither,' she said. 'So that's why I'm going to be checking out vineyards that have diseased grapevines and see what's causing the damage. My hunch is that will give me the irrefutable proof I need to make a case that everyone's got black goo – but it's gonna take some time. I'll tell you this, though: I must be doing something right, must have hit a nerve somewhere, because all of a sudden I'm starting to get pushback.'

She had dropped it into the conversation casually, but she sounded . . . worried? Apprehensive?

Scared?

'What are you talking about? What kind of pushback?'

'Threats.' She paused. 'Maybe just folks blowing smoke. Or maybe not.'

Her words were clipped, succinct, but the hair on the back of my neck suddenly seemed to be electrified. 'Jesus, Josie. You mean threats that involve bodily harm?'

'I don't know. I didn't get a letter of explanation. I figure it's either that or else destroying my professional reputation. Which is sort of the same thing in my book.'

'What are you going to do?'

I could hear her shrug through the phone. 'There's nothing *to* do. A threat is just ugly talk, you know that. Someone has to actually *do* something, you know, kick it up a notch.'

'In spite of those threats you still plan to keep pushing?'

'If you mean am I going to keep trying to prove that nurseries are selling vines that already are, or could be, diseased, then yes. Specifically, Landau's Trees & Vines, but there are others,' she said, though Landau's was in her crosshairs. 'Whether they did it knowingly or not. Even if they *didn't* know at the time that the vines were going to die, they surely are well aware of it now. But since I can't climb into anyone's head and walk around to understand whether they were dumb, naive, or just plain greedy, I need to figure out another way to do it. And hope my reputation isn't in shreds when I'm through.'

'What can Quinn and I do?'

'Well, I hope you're in my corner. That would help. Though I suspect Mr California might not be totally on board. Considering one of the players is Eve Kerr.'

Mr California was her name for Quinn. 'He's still hoping that diplomacy works out and we get some kind of concession from Jackson and Eve.'

She made a tsk-tsk sound with her tongue. As in: 'Bless Quinn's heart, too.'

'Butter wouldn't melt in her little California mouth. And don't forget Richard. He's part of it, in bed with Eve and Jackson. You want my opinion?' she asked, going on before I could answer. 'You're not going to get anywhere trying to reason with any of them. They can't afford to admit they were wrong. It will cripple Landau's financially. The nursery in California – and they were one of the biggest – went out of business because of all the lawsuits. A lot of people lost a lot of money. So you can bet Landau's is going to fight back and do their best to smear your reputation in the process, discredit you every step of the way. "You guys don't know what you're doing and you're trying to blame your incompetence on us." Wait for it.'

'That's ugly.'

'Pick your battles, Lucie. You might not want to die on this particular hill.'

'Or I might. They gave their *word*, Josie. This is about more than just bad vines that are going to be a total loss. We *trusted* Landau's because of their reputation and the promises they made. All of us. It feels like a very personal betrayal. My mother did business with Jackson's father.'

'Let's talk tomorrow,' she said. 'I'll see you then.'

After we disconnected it was a toss-up whether to go find

Quinn and ask him how the charm offensive went with Eve, or see Frankie to discuss fifty shades of pink nail polish.

I chose nail polish.

Francesca Merchant's ring binder of information for our wedding had long ago gotten so thick and heavy that she now carried it around in an L.L.Bean boat-and-tote bag. When I walked into our tasting room in the Villa a few minutes later, she was standing behind the bar with the binder open, making notes.

The Villa had been designed by my French mother who had wanted it to look like a beautiful old *auberge* that could have twirled into Atoka like Dorothy's house landing in Oz, except it would have come from *la France profonde* – somewhere in the heart of France. Over the years the ivy-covered red-brick building had graced the pages of such magazines as *Travel & Leisure*, *Food & Wine*, even *Architectural Digest*, because it looked so beautiful and idyllic with its backdrop of rich greens from the vineyard bracketed by the variegated layers of the serene aptly named Blue Ridge Mountains.

Though we had enlarged the building a few years ago when we outgrew the space, my older brother Eli, who is an architect, had not only designed the addition but also served as construction supervisor making sure the new part fused so seamlessly with the old you wondered if we'd really done anything – especially on the outside once the ivy spread to the new walls.

Inside, my mother's paintings of the vineyard and the farm still hung on the whitewashed walls; the serpentine bar she had designed with its beautiful mosaic of twining grape-laden vines caught everyone's eye the moment they entered the room. If you happened to be there when the sunlight streaming through the French doors sparkled off the jeweled tiles, the vines and the grapes looked as if they had been lit from within by fire. It was this room, this place more than any other, that had so much of my mother's indelible, graceful stamp on it. Some days I felt as if she was still here with us – and not a day had passed since her death, after her horse threw her while jumping over one of the many stacked stone walls on our land, that I wished with all my heart that she was.

Especially now, on the eve of my wedding. When she wouldn't be the one to button the tiny satin-covered buttons on the back of my dress and make sure the delicate wreath of flowers I wore in my hair was secured with enough hair pins to keep it in place. Or fasten the pearl necklace that had been handed down in her family around my neck. Instead, my younger sister Mia, and Kit Noland, my best friend and matron of honor, would help me with my dress and the flowers and the pearls. And, of course, Frankie. Wedding planner extraordinaire.

Frankie looked up when she heard the front door close and smiled at me. Then she saw my face and her smile faded. 'What's up?'

When Frankie's kids were growing up, she could have won the 'Volunteer of the Year' award every single year they were in school, and even a few years after they graduated. She. Did. It. All. Head chaperone for the choir trips, recruiter of science fair judges, organizer of the All-Night Graduation Party, booster mom for the basketball, football, and soccer teams and, of course, president of the PTA. I asked her once if she'd ever kept track of how many cakes and cookies and cupcakes she'd baked over the years and all she said was, 'I went through three ovens in eighteen years.'

After her children left for college and she and her husband were empty nesters, she went stir crazy for about two weeks before showing up here and asking if we could use another person to help pour wine for guests on weekends when she wasn't at her day job. It wasn't long before I began relying on her more and more until one Saturday morning she told me she'd be willing to quit her other job if I'd let her run the retail side of the winery. I said yes before she could change her mind, realizing she was giving up a high-powered six-figure job in D.C. hobnobbing with hotshot influential newsmakers in exchange for far more modest pay hobnobbing with an eclectic laid-back staff who liked pouring wine. Plus she'd have to assert herself with Mosby, the territorial gray barn cat that acted like *he* owned the place.

Unsurprisingly our clients loved Frankie and the joke went

around that she heard more confessions – especially after someone had a couple of glasses of wine – than the priests at the Catholic church in Middleburg. Folks trusted her because she was discreet, but more importantly because they always found an ocean of compassion in her friendly, nonjudgmental blue eyes.

So now I told her about the dying vines, about Josie, and about Eve. I left out the part about my tiny twinge of jealousy over Quinn wanting privacy when he spoke to Eve, but Frankie being Frankie, she gave me a shrewd look and said, 'What are you not telling me? Come on, spill it.'

I spilled. 'It's stupid. Just pre-wedding jitters. I know he loves me, I know he's crazy about me.'

'But?' She had been aligning bottles of nail polish on the bar in a precise, tidy row like soldiers.

'But nothing. I'm fine. Good Lord, where did you get so many bottles of nail polish?'

Not fifty, but still . . . at least a dozen.

'From a friend who owns a salon in Leesburg,' she said. 'She loaned them to me for the morning so you could pick the color you want for your wedding day. I've got to get them back to her as soon as you choose. With a bottle of last year's Montgomery Estate Cab Sauv. She knew it won the Governor's Cup, so she was fairly specific when I mentioned I wanted to give her a thank-you gift.'

I couldn't remember the last time I'd worn nail polish – if ever – because it made no sense in my job.

'Help me out,' I said, examining the bottles. 'Who thinks up these names? Dew. Morning Mist. Bubble Bath. Pinkgasm.'

Frankie picked up a bottle that looked like the most delicate shade of pale pink. 'How about this one? Gossamer. It's sheer and pearly, plus it's pretty and feminine. And it'll look great with your dress, which has just a hint of pink in it.'

'Done.' That had been easy.

She shook the bottle. 'Want to try it, see what it looks like?'

'Sure,' I said.

I held out my left hand and we both looked down. Dirt under my fingernails after this morning's expedition to the Cab Franc block and my index fingernail broken off at a weird angle. Fortunately my beautiful antique diamond engagement ring, which had belonged to Quinn's Spanish grandmother, was on my dresser on a Waterford ring holder that had been my great-grandmother's.

Frankie coughed and said in her most diplomatic way, 'Why don't I schedule a manicure for you the day before the wedding? And then promise me you won't dig in the dirt or bottle wine until after you're married?'

I drew an X across my heart with my jagged index fingernail.

'Good.' She started painting a nail. 'By the way, you did confirm with David that he's coming by Sunday at four to check the wedding venues and what the light will be like next Saturday, right? I sent him an itinerary the other day, so he has the timeline.'

Planned to the last millisecond.

And . . . I'd forgotten.

'Right.'

She glanced up and took one look at my face, which gave me away totally. I got the 'Did you fake your mother's signature on that failed geometry test?' steely stare I remembered from a teacher long ago. Yeah, I know. The only thing she'd asked me to do when she was spinning plates *and* keeping juggling balls in the air.

'He'll come,' I said. 'Don't worry. He's incredibly conscientious. I'll call him to double-check. Word of honor.'

She gave me another look.

'Today. I'll call him today,' I said.

David Phelps was my brother.

To be precise, he was my bi-racial half-brother.

Last year on a whim I decided to spit into a vial and mail my saliva off to one of those laboratories that told you all about your family ethnicity and how much of your DNA was related to the Neanderthal cavemen 40,000 years ago, along with information about your current relatives, however distantly related they were.

I live in the house that my ancestor Hamish Montgomery built in the late 1700s, where generations of my family have lived before me. Everyone – all of us, including my mother and father – is buried on our land in a small cemetery that sits on the flattened crest of a hill where there is a particularly spectacular view of the Blue Ridge.

So the news I had a brother I knew nothing about floored me. But once I caught my breath, I realized we were talking about my father, Leland Montgomery, a devastatingly handsome and charming heartbreaker who had also been a serial womanizer. This time it had been a liaison between him and a woman named Olivia Vandenberg, who, a few years ago, became the first African-American Speaker of the U.S. House of Representatives. I found plenty of information about Speaker Vandenberg on the Internet, so it hadn't been hard to learn that, unlike Leland, she hadn't been married when she and my father got together. In fact she had just barely turned nineteen and, if the photos were anything to go by, she was stunning.

She gave up her baby boy, who had been adopted by the childless African-American Phelps family, and they had loved and adored David as if he'd been their own. But after his adoptive parents passed away a few years ago, he spat into a vial like I'd done because he wanted to find out who his biological parents were.

The day I got my DNA results I was given the choice of whether or not to agree to being contacted by other relatives: I clicked yes. I'd come this far, so, why not?

And, I swear to God, thirty seconds later David emailed me.

No pressure, but did I want to meet him?

After I got over *that* shock, I wrote back and told him that I did.

He told me to pick the place, date, and time so I chose the old Goose Creek Bridge, one of my favorite getaway places, because it was out-of-the way and, as a footnote historical site commemorating a minor battle in the Civil War, it was almost one hundred percent certain to be deserted. Besides, this didn't seem like the kind of family reunion I wanted to have at the Cuppa Giddyup in Middleburg.

He turned out to be funny and smart and charming and good-looking. And, to my utter astonishment after being raised under totally different circumstances, I discovered how completely alike we were – the way we thought, things we liked, values we cherished. That whole nature versus nurture debate about which is more important in making you into the person you become?

Here's what I learned: genetics is huge.

After that first meeting we were in touch constantly as though trying to make up for more than thirty lost years of memories as fast as we possibly could. He told me about his job as a professional photographer, which was when I realized I'd seen his photos before in *National Geographic*, *Smithsonian*, and the travel section of *The New York Times*. Before I knew who he was, I'd wondered about the person behind the lens who was clearly fascinated by vivid color and strong images, who took the kind of compelling pictures you'd look at twice, photos that made you think and remember them.

And his wedding gift to Quinn and me?

He would be our photographer.

Frankie picked up on my thoughts. 'What a wonderful wedding gift, having someone as talented as David take your photos.'

She reached for my other hand, oblivious to the original 'we'll just do one or two nails so you can see the color' plan. I didn't stop her.

'*Everything* about our wedding is going to be wonderful,' I said. 'Thanks to you. You've thought of everything. *Planned* everything, every detail.'

She gave me a rueful smile and said, 'With one exception. It might rain on Saturday.'

Quinn had nearly been right about her calling the National Weather Service to order up our wedding day weather.

'It's not going to rain.'

'Well, at least there's a backup plan. The tent in the garden for the ceremony. And we can always move the dinner inside to the Villa if we have to.'

'It's going to be gorgeous, just like today,' I told her. 'Although if you hadn't painted all my nails, I'd probably be crossing my fingers just to be on the safe side.'

'So I did. And don't you dare cross anything.'

'I won't.' I held out my hands and admired them. 'They look nice.'

She picked up a small foil packet that was sitting on the counter. 'This is a pad soaked with nail polish remover. You'll need it eventually and I sort of assumed you didn't have any on hand.'

'You sort of assumed right.'

'Let me stick it in your pocket for you. Otherwise you'll smear your nails.'

I jutted out my hip so she could slide the packet in my front jeans pocket just as my phone rang in my back pocket.

I started to reach for it but Frankie grabbed my arm. 'Don't even think about touching that phone. I'll get it for you.' She extracted it from my pocket. 'It's Quinn.'

She pressed the green button and the speaker button, laying the phone on the bar.

'Hey,' I said. 'I'm with Frankie at the nail polish summit.'

I'd expected a reaction, a laugh or a comment. He didn't say anything.

'Quinn? Are you there?'

'I just hung up with Eve. She's down the road at GSV talking to Vance and Sloane. She can be here in ten minutes. With Richard. I'm waiting on the crush pad.'

He sounded tense.

'I'll be right there.'

After Frankie disconnected for me she said, 'Is everything OK?'

'I don't know. You heard him. Eve and Richard are on their way over to look at the dying vines in the Cab Franc block.'

Frankie tightened the cap on the bottle of Gossamer nail polish as though she were strangling it. 'Those two,' she said. '*And* Jackson.'

'What?'

'You pour drinks for enough people, you hear things after a couple of glasses of wine.' She gave me an ominous look. 'Especially from folks who work at other vineyards.'

'Such as?' I really didn't need to ask what things she was hearing, not after what Josie had just told me.

I'm starting to watch my back.

Threats.

'Jackson is playing hardball, Lucie. From what I hear, so are Eve and Richard. Don't say anything, but I heard they're considering pre-emptively retaining a big-name D.C. law firm because they want to intimidate any vineyard that might be contemplating suing them for damages from dying vines. So you'd be dealing with a lawyer. A phalanx of lawyers. Not Jackson.'

A blood vessel started pulsing behind my left eye, always the first sign of stress coming on. 'How do you know this?'

I got her best poker face. 'Sources.'

She had plenty of them. They bellied up to our bar and, while she poured out wine for them, they poured out their hearts to her.

She zipped a finger across her lips. 'I was sworn to secrecy by someone who will lose their job if this gets out. So *please* don't mention it when you see Richard and Eve, OK?'

I zipped my own lips, making sure not to smear my nails. But this new development definitely was a game changer.

'OK,' I said. 'I'll let you know how it goes when I see you at the blending party tonight.'

She smacked her palm to her forehead. 'Damn. I told the florist I'd stop by after work to go over some last minute changes for the table centerpieces. Can you do without me?'

'Of course,' I said. 'We've got enough people coming. Don't worry.'

'Good. Thanks.'

'Frankie,' I said, 'it's going to be perfect. Thank you for everything you've done. Everything you *keep* doing.'

'You're welcome.'

I blew on my nails and waved my fingers. 'I'd better get going. I want to see Quinn before Eve and Richard arrive.'

'Good luck,' she said. 'Don't do anything with your hands until your nails are dry.'

'I won't.' I turned the handle to the front door with my elbow and pushed the door open with my hip.

Showtime.

FOUR

The crush pad is where we bring the grapes once we get them in from the field during harvest. There we weigh them, sort them, and then dump them into the hopper of a machine that feeds them into a large drum where a bar with paddles, known as beaters, spins around and separates the stems from the grapes. Next the grapes pass through a series of rollers that split them open to get at the sugary juice that will make wine. The machine is called a destemmer-crusher and while the process sounds brutal – all that beating, splitting, and crushing – actually it's not, because grapes are fragile and need to be treated with kid-glove care.

I met Quinn on our crush pad, arriving – as I'd hoped – before Eve and Richard did. He gave me a look that said we might be playing defense once they got here because our entire offense had packed up and gone home. My heart sank.

The call with Eve had been that bad?

Before I could ask, he headed me off. 'Nice nail polish. How did it go with Josie? What did she say?'

I held out my hands to show off Frankie's handiwork. 'It's called Gossamer and she thinks we might have black goo.'

He frowned as if he had to think for a split second about gossamer and black goo somehow being related to each other. Then he groaned.

'Goddamn. I hope she's wrong. That stuff is evil.'

'She's driving up from Charlottesville tomorrow, so she'll stop by at nine to confirm whether it's that or something else. Though she's about ninety-nine point nine percent sure she's dead-bang right.' I folded my arms across my chest, being careful of my nails, and said, 'How did it go with Eve?'

He didn't look me in the eye. 'It wasn't much of a conversation. She was pretty terse. And she sounded mad. Said she and Richard were at GSV talking to Vance and Sloane and that they'd be right over once they finished.'

Eve usually had all the bubbly rah-rah effervescence of a head cheerleader when the team was winning. Maybe Sloane and Vance were giving her grief about their dying vines.

'Did you tell her why you were calling?'

'No.'

So much for the California charm offensive. 'I told you she'd bring Richard. And Frankie just informed me in the absolute strictest confidence that Jackson is considering hiring a lawyer to smack down any pesky lawsuit a vineyard that bought rootstock from them might be thinking about filing.'

'Are you serious?'

'As a heart attack.'

Tires crunching on the gravel announced Richard and Eve's arrival. Richard Brightman was at the wheel of a red pickup with 'Landau's Trees & Vines' and their address, website, and phone number stenciled on the door in white. He looked like he was loaded for bear. Eve Kerr looked upset, just like Quinn said she'd sounded on the phone.

They got out of the truck and came over to us. If body language was anything to go by, Richard was running the show this time. Odd, because usually it was Eve, Miss Congeniality, who did most of the talking. Or sweet-talking. But something in Richard's attitude, his purposeful stride, and the hard set of his jaw said they'd switched roles.

He shook hands with Quinn, then me. Eve did the same.

'Nice to see you two,' he said. 'Getting ready for the big day? It's coming up.' His smile seemed forced, but it was the toothpaste commercial smile, part of the package of nerdy clean-cut boyish good looks that made him such a popular – not to mention adorable – professor among the female students at UNV who fell all over themselves trying to get a position as one of his lab assistants or TA's. Shaggy brown hair graying a bit at the temples, gold wire-rimmed glasses, serious brown eyes, collared pale blue Oxford shirt with the sleeves rolled up. Totally preppy. Smart as hell. Ready for anything.

'A week from tomorrow,' I said.

'I'm sure the wedding is going to be great. You must be so excited.' Eve pushed her sunglasses on top of her head to hold back her shoulder-length honey-blonde hair.

She looked spectacular as usual, in a pair of skinny jeans, work boots, and a sexy loose-fitting sleeveless cream-colored knit top with deep cut-out armholes that showed a teasing glimpse of the lacy bra underneath when she moved a certain way. Eve dressed to tantalize.

'We are,' I said and waited for Quinn to enthuse as well. Though I knew if he had his druthers, we'd elope and get married at sunset – just the two of us – on a beach in Tahiti. Or the Seychelles.

'We can't wait,' he said, 'to *be* married.'

Nicely side-stepped.

'That's so sweet,' Eve said. 'Lucky you, Lucie.'

'Yeah, it's great,' Richard said to both of us, and then he focused on me. 'What can we do for you two?'

So much for small talk. He was ready to move on to the main event. Especially because I was certain he knew why they were here. At least he'd started off with a nice, easy pitch across home plate.

We're here to help.

'We want you to see the Cab Franc block,' Quinn said in a neutral voice. 'The vines are dying.'

Richard exchanged glances with Eve and pushed his glasses up the bridge of his nose with a finger. 'Then let's go have a look, shall we?'

We took the four-seater Gator, Eve and Richard sitting in the back and not speaking, which was odd because usually the two of them traded an easy-going banter that went back and forth like a spirited ping-pong match. Now they seemed so tense and uptight I had a feeling they'd argued and whatever it had been about still festered. I caught Quinn's eye and got a raised eyebrow in return, like *how the hell should I know?*

Eve didn't have a boyfriend, which always struck me as odd since she was such a knockout. But she was also a workaholic and, as if her responsibilities at Landau's plus her volunteer time at the Ag Extension Service's public outreach program weren't enough for Superwoman, she was finishing up a PhD in viticulture from Cornell. She'd done most of the research remotely and had now reached the stage where she was supposed to be writing her dissertation. Not long ago she'd traveled to Ithaca to meet with her advisor in person.

Quinn half-glanced over his shoulder. 'So, how's the dissertation writing going, Eve?'

It seemed like a neutral enough conversation-starter to me, but it landed with a thud. Eve launched into a litany of complaints.

'Awful. Just awful,' she said. 'I've really got to park my butt in a chair and get some work done or I'll never finish. Last fall I rented a cabin in the Shenandoah, so I finally got a place where I can escape and just write. Unfortunately, so far it's only been a weekend here or there or holidays, but I'm going to take some real time off – soon – and get this thing done.'

'Her little hideaway has the added bonus of spotty Internet service since it's on a mountain,' Richard said. 'Meaning she's really off the grid.'

I couldn't tell if that was a dig. Or maybe he knew because he'd been there. Over the years I had wondered if there was something going on between Eve and Richard – an affair, maybe a little fling – then I figured it was probably just their Barbie-and-Ken wholesome attractiveness, along with the fact that professionally they were joined at the hip. Besides, Richard was married and his wife was a knockout in her own right. Dr Carly Brightman, vivacious, charming, and possibly even smarter than her husband, was the Deputy Director of the National Intelligence Council. She was constantly on the road to places she couldn't talk about, doing things she wouldn't talk about. But when she was back home in Middleburg, she volunteered a couple of weekend days a month at the food pantry run by St Michael the Archangel Church. She said doing that made her feel as if there was still some goodness and humanity and kindness left among us after being immersed in the savage, cruel world of terrorism, drugs, wars, and people who tortured others or trafficked in sex and arms and children. There was also another reason why Richard Brightman might not have strayed in his marriage: you didn't really cheat on someone whose professional title had the word *intelligence* in it, did you?

Quinn pulled up at the beginning of a huge swath of dying vines and stopped the Gator. Richard hopped out and trotted over to get a better look. Eve waited with Quinn until I got my cane and then the three of us joined Richard who was kneeling down to check the graft connecting the American rootstock with the French hybrid vine. Otherwise known as the Brightman Graft.

'The graft isn't callused over.' He got up and brushed the dirt off his hands.

'They're all like that. In various stages,' Quinn said. 'The whole damn acre and a half of Cab Franc.'

'Josie Wilde is coming by tomorrow to take a look since no one seems to be able to figure out what's causing this. She thinks it might be black goo,' I said.

'Josie is kind of on the warpath about black goo.' For the first time there was an edge to Eve's voice.

'She's been blaming the growers – us, the nurseries – instead of the vineyard owners because you guys are her clients,' Richard added. 'Of course it's not going to be your fault. Or hers for not advising you correctly about what to do to prevent these vines from failing. She knows where her bread is buttered.'

As foretold. *They're trying to discredit my reputation.*

'That's unfair,' I said.

'She's going around saying things she can't substantiate, Lucie, making accusations she has no evidence to support.' Richard wasn't giving an inch. 'It's damaging our reputation, that kind of slander. Costing us clients and revenue. Hurting business. *Our* business.'

I'm starting to get threats.

From Richard? Was he the source of Josie's threats? Plus he'd just said *our* business. How much was he in bed with Jackson Landau anyway? I'd thought most of his bread was buttered at the University of Northern Virginia.

'Black goo . . .' I said.

'Is one of many possibilities.' Eve finished my sentence.

'We prefer to call it Vine Decline,' Richard added.

'Oh, come *on*. You say tomato,' I said. 'What we've *got* are dying vines and whatever name you give what's happened, there's no cure. We're probably going to have to rip them all out.'

'Richard has been breeding some new hybrids at the nursery that we're having good success with. I think – *we* think – they'd do really well at Montgomery Estate Vineyard. And don't worry, Lucie. We'll help you out.' Eve made a hard, purposeful shift in the conversation. Handing us an olive branch. Attached to an anvil. We had to eat our losses.

I caught the surprised look Richard gave her, but he stayed mum. Apparently she'd gone off-script.

'We were supposed to have success with *these* vines,' I said, my temper flaring. 'Cab Franc is an easy grape to grow in Virginia. It does well here, which is why it's so popular. You *know* that. I seem to remember *talking* about it when you sold the vines to us three years ago, not long after you started working at Landau's.'

Eve gave me a tight little smile. Like: *I'm not going to say anything self-incriminating right now.*

'Look, Lucie. Look, Quinn,' Richard said and whenever anyone starts a sentence with 'look' and in that tone of voice, I know I'm not going to like what comes next. 'There are a whole heap of reasons why these vines are failing, especially after three years. They were doing fine until they weren't. I'm sure you guys knocked yourselves out for them, but we don't need to tell you that it's not a level playing field anymore because of everything from climate change to extreme weather to new pests moving into the region. We can't guarantee the health of these vines forever and ever. They were healthy when you bought them from us. I'm really sorry, but our hands are tied. The vines didn't come with a forever insurance policy.'

He held out his hands in a supplicant what-can-I-tell-you gesture and I wondered if he was aware of the irony that they didn't look tied at all.

Quinn laid a hand on my arm and I realized that my fists were clenched. We weren't going to get anything from him, that was clear. Not only that, but as Josie warned, they were trying to discredit us, insisting that what happened was our fault.

'Other vineyards are having the same problem,' I said, my tone still belligerent. 'Bacchus, for example. La Vigne, next door to us. GSV, before Sloane Everett even bought the place. And what we all have in common is we bought our vines from you. We do talk among ourselves, you know?'

Richard gave me a look as if I'd just told him I'd been talking to the Easter Bunny and the Tooth Fairy for corroboration. 'So what? Landau's is the biggest commercial nursery on the East Coast. We sell vines to a lot of vineyards, not just you guys around here.' He shrugged. 'A couple of bad apples – or bunches of bad grapes, to use the right metaphor – especially in a few vineyards located close by each other, doesn't mean the barrel is rotten.'

Eve cut in quickly. 'We were just talking to Vance and Sloane before we came to see you. Unlike you guys, they're not blaming us. Including Vance, who's been the winemaker there for years. He, Richard, and I were educating Sloane about last winter – since he was still in California – telling him how unnaturally warm it was in Virginia, how we had no snow to speak of. And before that one of the worst hurricane seasons in memory. More rain in the month of September than we had for the previous eight. You remember it was "pick or perish" back then, right? Nothing was ripening but if you didn't pick grapes that weren't ready, they'd be completely waterlogged because of all the rain.'

'Conditions like those resulting from the extreme *climate change* we've been witnessing these last years will cause the kind of Vine Decline you've got here,' Richard said, the heavy emphasis on *climate change* his way of making sure we got the point.

Blame Mother Nature.

'We're recommending to everyone – including you two – that you plant hardier grapes that will do better in what is becoming the new normal climate-wise,' Eve added. 'That's what Vance and Sloane are planning to do. Get out in front of this.'

'Of course you want us to plant hardier grapes,' I said. 'All we need to do is buy more vines. From you. Problem solved. *For you.* What about us? You think it's easy to write off a

nearly two-hundred-thousand-dollar investment as a total loss
and start over again?'

'Believe me, we sympathize.' Eve turned to Quinn and
placed her hand on his arm. '*We get it.*'

The weight of her words, the solicitous way she touched
Quinn's arm. Like, *you and I, we have an understanding, right?*

Which only made me angrier.

'When did you start suspecting that maybe the vines you
sold us were diseased and not pest-free like you thought they
were?' I asked her. 'If you didn't know *then*, you must know
now.'

'They weren't . . .' Richard said.

I cut him off. 'How many vineyards started reporting dying
vines before you began to consider – to realize – the problem
might be on your end? And what have you done about it?'

Before Richard could come out with a retort that was going
to escalate our conversation into something more combative,
Eve turned to Quinn again.

'What about you?' she asked, looking into his eyes. 'Do
you believe we would knowingly sell you vines that we even
remotely suspected might be diseased? That *I* would do
that? To friends and neighbors? *Seriously*, Quinn?'

She was still intent on making it personal. The California
charm offensive, but the other way around. She wanted *him*
on *her* side.

'I wouldn't like to believe it,' he said. 'And I sure as hell
hope you didn't.'

'As to Lucie's accusations.' Richard finally had the floor.
'The vines weren't diseased when you bought them from
Landau's. Look, it's not like a refrigerator or a piece of equipment where you can point to a defective part. What we're
finding is with the changing climate, new problems are cropping
up that we didn't anticipate. You don't know how devastated
we are to see something like this.' He swept his hand in a wide
swath encompassing a couple thousand dying vines.

'Let us help you put in grapes that can handle the climate
and fluctuating seasons and the pests we're dealing with
now,' Eve said. 'Plus we'll give you a break on the price. And
some time before you have to pay for them.'

'Eve,' I said, 'I don't think you get it. You either, Richard. We *trusted* you. And your solution to our problem is to keep trusting you and buy more vines from Landau's? You're not the only grower around, you know. Maybe the biggest, but not the only one.'

Eve opened her mouth to say something, but closed it. Richard held up his hand.

'How about we dial this down a bit and leave it here for today? You guys are upset and maybe we all need to calm down. Let's not do or say anything anyone's going to regret later.'

He meant *I* needed to calm down. For the second time, Quinn placed a restraining hand on my arm.

'I agree,' Eve said. 'Let's finish this conversation another time, shall we?'

Richard glanced at his watch and I knew what was coming next. Cue the graceful exit.

'Evie, we probably ought to get going,' he said, 'or we'll be late for our next appointment.'

Like I didn't see *that* coming. What I didn't expect, though, was that when Richard put an arm around Eve's waist as if to escort her back to the Gator, she turned away – actually she *jerked* away – and he dropped his arm as if he'd been scalded.

Without another word, he turned and strode toward the Gator while she stayed right where she was, glaring at him, hands on her hips. I tried to catch up to Richard.

He was standing next to the Gator when I did.

'What's going on?' I asked. 'What was that all about?'

'Nothing,' he said. 'Just . . . nothing.'

But he wasn't looking at me. Instead he was looking over my shoulder, his eyes narrowing. I turned around to see Eve and Quinn, right where we'd left them, deep in conversation. She was holding his arm, speaking quietly, earnestly in his ear. His head was bent close to hers to catch her words. When she was finished, he nodded.

'Eve.' Richard's voice rang out. 'We've got to go.'

She and Quinn looked up, faces impassive as they walked over to join us. No one spoke on the drive back to the crush pad where Richard had parked the truck.

After they were gone I said to Quinn, 'What was that all about?'

'What was what all about?'

'*Quinn.*'

'What?'

'You know damn well what.'

'It was nothing.'

'She kept you back to talk to you about *something*.'

'Come on, honey.' He shrugged. 'The same thing we've been talking about all along. She really wants us to consider planting something else instead of Cab Franc. Try a cross-breed.'

As lies go, that one was pretty lame. 'Is that so?'

'No.' His voice went quiet. 'Not entirely.'

I waited.

'She was trying to make peace, is all,' he said.

'With *you*, Quinn. She knows I'm angry and that I feel betrayed. She also knows they're not going to lift a finger to help us or admit responsibility. We've used Landau's since my mother started the vineyard and bought her vines from Jackson's father. His dad was always honest and by the book and I figured Jackson would be the same. Instead he's trying to cover up what they did, cashing in on his father's reputation and the decades of goodwill and trust he earned.'

'Eve knows how you feel, and she knows you're not the only one who's mad. But she hopes we can work this out without any of the divisiveness and bitterness that went on in California.'

'And she wants you to carry her water because you're both from California.'

He shrugged again, but when his eyes found mine I knew I was right.

'I'll bet she didn't tell you about the lawyer they're planning to retain, did she?' I asked. 'To keep us all at bay.'

'Lucie—'

'Did she bring up Le Coq Rouge?' I asked.

Because it would be her trump card. Quinn had enough painful memories of California and although Eve was too young to have been in the picture when the owner of Le Coq Rouge, one of Napa's most popular vineyards, had gone to jail for his role in a huge scam selling adulterated wine as the real thing in Eastern Europe, she would know that was Quinn's Achilles heel. He had been the winemaker there. She would also know that what happened to the owner had destroyed Quinn's professional reputation because no one believed that he really, truly had no idea what was going on *right under his nose*. Until he did find out and called foul. A whistleblower. His career as a winemaker was pretty much washed up in California, which was how he ended up coming to Virginia. Working for Leland, who offered him a job, got him to take a cut-rate salary, and didn't ask a lot of questions about Quinn's background because Quinn agreed to be a cheap date. Leland was a rascal himself; he could overlook little transgressions.

And now I had picked at that scab. The one that covered a wound that would never heal. He gave me a searing look as if I'd been the one to bring up his painful past, not Eve.

'She didn't say anything directly. But she knows I don't want a scandal – *another* scandal – here and my name comes up.'

'So she wants to cover up what they did?'

'She wants to make things right.'

Still defending her.

'Is there a difference?' I asked.

'She thinks there is.'

'Do you?'

'I don't know,' he said.

'Look, we're the victims here, not a bunch of spoilers.'

'I know that.'

'So how could you even consider taking her side?'

'I'm not. I'm on your side. *Our* side.'

He still wasn't telling me everything. Holding something back.

'This isn't going to end well. You know *that*, don't you?'

'I still hope it doesn't end badly.' He kissed me and said, 'I'd better go check on the filtering. Antonio should be just about done. Then I want to see if all the trellises have been repaired, so I'll be out in the vineyard for a while.'

Which was code for him wanting to take off and have some time by himself.

'Sure,' I said. 'I've got to call David. Frankie is about to skin me alive because I forgot to remind him about coming out here on Sunday to go over our list of wedding photos.'

'I don't have to be around when he does that, do I?' He gave me a look I recognized from the times I'd asked if he wanted to go clothes shopping with me. Like he'd rather have a root canal.

'No, you do not. You just have to show up on our wedding day and marry me.'

He gave me a weak grin. 'Very funny.'

Although this time when he left he wasn't whistling. And because I know him so well, I knew he hadn't told me the whole truth about what he and Eve had been discussing before they joined Richard and me.

What I didn't know was why.

FIVE

I f I could bottle today's weather the way we bottled wine – capturing the bright, clear sunshine and sweet breeze that carried the scent of freshly mowed grass without a trace of D.C.'s notorious damp dishrag humidity – I'd do it in a heartbeat. Then I'd open it on our wedding day next Saturday.

Since that was out of the question, Antonio Ramirez, our vineyard manager, and I did the next best thing: we moved tables and chairs outside to the crush pad so we could hold our Chardonnay blending party there. It was simply too gorgeous to be indoors.

By four thirty we were nearly set up and ready to go, except for the wine samples. And no Quinn. He hadn't answered Antonio's phone call nor my text.

'Where is he, Lucita?' Antonio asked. 'Do you want me to get the samples ready if he doesn't show up soon? Everyone's gonna be here in a little less than half an hour.'

'Yes, please,' I said. 'I suppose you'd better. Quinn told me he wanted to clear his head after our meeting with Richard and Eve this morning, so he was going to check to see if all the trellis repair work was finished.'

'There are still a few left,' Antonio said. 'And if he's repairing them, he walked there and carried all the equipment himself. Both Gators are here. And his truck is gone.'

'Oh.'

So he'd taken off and hadn't said a word to either me or Antonio.

Maybe it was his turn to have pre-wedding jitters. Maybe Eve Kerr had stirred up memories he preferred to forget. His first marriage had fallen apart after his wife had had an affair with his boss. That was just before the scandal at Le Coq Rouge had erupted and he'd left California for good under a cloud of suspicion. Now maybe it was happening again: another potential scandal that could blow up relationships and hard-won goodwill on the other side of the country, here in Virginia, just as it had done in California.

And our wedding was in just over a week. His second time saying 'I do.' Promising he meant it forever.

I pulled out my phone and texted him again.

Hey, where are you? Blending party in half an hour.

'Maybe he went for a drive,' Antonio said. 'He told me about that meeting and that we're going to have to rip out the whole block of Cab Franc. He was pretty . . . *enojado*. Upset.'

'I know he was. Richard and Eve told us the vines failed either because of the awful summer we had last year with so much rain or because we screwed up somehow.'

Antonio's face looked like thunder. 'We didn't screw up. The other vines are fine. How do they explain *that*?'

'They don't. They're just pushing back. After three years they say they have no control over what happens to the vines. That's on us.'

'Yeah, but three years ago they sold us sick vines and that's on *them*. So we push back too, right?' Antonio was dark, handsome, well-built, muscled. A good man. He'd walked into the U.S. from Mexico as a kid, worked hard, learned English, eventually became a citizen. He knew how to take care of himself and he was fierce in defending those he loved. You didn't want him pushing back if you could avoid it.

'Right. We push back, too,' I said. Although I still needed to get Quinn completely on board.

As if he read my mind, Antonio said, 'Don't worry about Quinn too much, Lucita. He'll be OK.'

Antonio was going to be the best man at our wedding. Quinn didn't have any family to ask, and he and Antonio had grown close over the years. Quinn had been best man at his wedding last year; we'd held it at the vineyard as a gift to him and Valeria. Now I wasn't sure whether Antonio was talking about our wedding or the situation with Richard and Eve.

'I know he'll be OK,' I said, but Quinn still hadn't replied to my text. My watch showed twenty to five. 'What about the samples?'

'Twenty-one. All numbered, all moved outside on the table. Do you want the master list?'

'Yes, please.'

My phone beeped. Quinn.

At Seely's. On my way home.

Seely's was the other local nursery in our region, but unlike Landau's, which was strictly a place that grew vines and trees for vineyards and orchards, it was the big commercial gardening center where you went to buy your bedding flowers, shrubs, bushes, seeds, mulch, and, of course, your honest-to-God real Christmas tree if you didn't have one you hauled out of the attic every year. Seely's was, however, on the other side of Middleburg.

Before I could write him to ask what he was doing all the way over there, he told me.

Buying new secateurs. Mine broke suckering in Merlot block. B back by 5. Maybe a few minutes late.

We had plenty of secateurs – the ubiquitous pruning shears no vineyard could do without – in the equipment barn. He needed to buy another pair *now*? And what happened to repairing trellises?

Whatever this was about, I'd find out after the blending party. Probably tonight when we were in bed, when I'd lie in his arms and we'd talk about everything else except the vineyard. No work talk allowed in the bedroom. We'd made that decision after Ali and Otto James told us about their sweet little beagle and how he barked every time they discussed anything vineyard-related at home, apparently sensing a change in their tone of voice and attitude – maybe some tension – that he didn't like. So they made the no-work-talk-at-home rule and, sure enough, no more barking. We'd adopted the same rule, modified for the bedroom, even without a dog.

I texted Quinn that I'd see him soon, closed my phone, and told Antonio we might have to get started without Quinn once everyone got here. It would take some time to go through all the samples of Chardonnay and then figure out the blend. Everyone who was coming here today was doing us a favor, taking a break from their busy lives. I didn't want to waste their time by asking them to wait.

Blending wine is a high-wire act – it's all about balance – but it's also fun. A bit of alchemy, a bit of chemistry, and a dash of what-the-hellism. As in: *We like this wine and hopefully our clients will, too.*

When it comes to making a blend, Chardonnay is one of the simplest but also most challenging white wines. Winemakers love Chard for a bunch of reasons, not the least of which is that it's the most popular white wine in America by a country mile. First off, it's dead easy to grow. Also Chardonnay doesn't have the distinct easy-to-identify flavors of other whites like Riesling or Sauvignon Blanc. So what you have is a blank canvas where you can be a little creative, show off what you can do. Winemakers like that, too.

As for the blend, you had a whole heap of options to choose from. Did you age the wine in oak barrels or stainless-steel tanks? A combination of the two? Quinn and I were purists – oak all the way. Old barrels or new? American or French? We liked to mix it up. Not quite eeny-meeny-miny-moe, but we changed things around from year to year, depending on what grapes we got from the harvest.

You tasted more of the flavor if a new barrel was used: spices like clove, vanilla, and nutmeg. Older barrels had less flavor and were more porous – think of a tea bag that's been used a couple of times – so their contribution changes from providing flavor to the wine to enhancing the aging process, making the wine softer, more complex, and less acid. Then there's the taste of the char from the fire used to toast the barrel: when it's done right, you think of mocha and coffee; when it's not, it tastes like a campfire.

The final component – and this is getting sort of technical – was fermentation, which is the process of grape juice changing to alcoholic wine. Chardonnay is unique for a white wine because it goes through two fermentation processes. All reds do it, but Chard is the only white. The second fermentation, or malolactic fermentation, makes the wine taste buttery or creamy. You can let malo, as it's called, go all the way until it's finished or you can pull the plug at various stages and stop before it's done, which Quinn and I had begun doing.

As a result, with so many permutations and combinations, so many interesting variables, making the blend was like looking through a kaleidoscope at the mosaic that appeared with each twist and turn before deciding which you liked best. Quinn and I knew winemakers who made the same exact wine year after year, because why keep reinventing the wheel when you've got a winner? We, on the other hand, didn't mind taking chances or believe we always had to play it safe.

I had gone into the wine cellar to get bread baskets for the baguettes Dominique was bringing from the inn, so we'd have something to nibble on between tasting samples, when Antonio stuck his head through the doorway and hollered that my cousin had arrived with my grandfather. By the time I joined them outside everyone else was there: Toby Levine and Fabrice Gilbert, his new French winemaker, from La Vigne Winery, Vance Hall from GSV, and Otto James from Bacchus. Except for Quinn, the gang was all here.

A gathering like this was exactly the kind of collaboration we wanted, needed, *dreamed of* – winemakers and vineyard owners helping each other make better wine. Sure, we competed with each other, but it wasn't as if we were Coca-Cola and we'd just asked Pepsi to help figure out a new blend of cola that would benefit our brand at the expense of theirs.

Instead we knew it was better when we worked together and that a rising tide floats all boats. And the only way to make that happen was years of building relationships, of creating trust and goodwill. Except maybe now those relationships were going to be tested among those of us who had bought dying vines from Jackson Landau. Some of us were going to be able to bounce back; others were not.

Sloane Everett, for example, could afford to replant since he had a bottomless piggy bank. He could rip out his acres of dead vines, chalking them up as his predecessor's decisions and problems, and make his own fresh start. For that matter, Toby Levine could afford to replant as well. As a former Secretary of State, Ambassador to the UN, and US Ambassador to France, he'd recently sold his memoir for a deal that tipped seven figures. Plus his speaking fees made my eyes water, they were so steep. At the opposite end of the spectrum were Otto and Ali James who were going to lose it all and would be lucky if they had bus fare to D.C. once they sold their equipment, their land and the house, and paid off their debts.

Then there were folks like Quinn and me. We didn't have a money tree in the backyard, which limited our options. Were we going to take out another loan, or mortgage Highland House? There was also a different, untested route: take on investors who would then have a voice, an opinion, in how we ran the place. I already knew neither Quinn nor I were ready to give up our independence.

But when there is a gun to your head, what do you do?

I'd been hoping that when we were all sitting around our table talking about Chardonnay on this sun-spattered late afternoon that we might start discussing what we could do together, because we certainly didn't have a prayer unless we were united. Bacchus and La Vigne were on our team, I knew that: the outlier was GSV. Based on what Eve had said this morning, not only did Sloane appear to be unwilling to blame Landau's for the diseased vines, Vance seemed to have drunk Jackson's Kool-Aid as well. Which seemed odd.

Although maybe I wasn't accounting for Eve's charm and powers of persuasion. Just now I caught Vance glancing at his watch as he chatted with my cousin. I didn't want to test his patience. We needed to get this show on the road.

'Would everyone like to have a seat, please, and we can begin? I know you're all busy and we really appreciate your time and help with this,' I said. 'I apologize that Quinn's not here, but he'll be along in a few minutes. A last-minute errand.'

'Any preferences for where you want us to sit?' Toby asked.

'Nope. Just leave the seats nearest to the samples for Antonio, Quinn, and me so we can pour wine for you.'

Toby, I knew, would sit next to my grandfather since the two of them got on like a house on fire. They would speak French, reminiscing about the old days in Paris when Toby had been Ambassador to France and my grandfather, a highly respected diplomat who held posts at some of France's most politically important embassies, had been on a rare rotation at the Quai d'Orsay, the nickname for the French foreign ministry.

As predicted, Toby said, 'I'm sitting next to Luc.' Then he added, 'Since he's the ringer in the group.'

Pépé laughed, Fabrice and Dominique grinned, Vance looked puzzled, and Otto said, 'You'd better explain, Toby.'

Toby smiled. 'Have you ever heard of the *Confrérie des Chevaliers du Tastevin*?'

Otto shook his head.

'The Brotherhood of the Knights of the . . . Wine Tasters?' Vance said. 'A group of sommeliers?'

'Not exactly,' Toby said. 'The Knights were originally a business group that started in the 1930s after World War I to promote the wines of Burgundy when the region was in a real economic tailspin. Now they have chapters all over the world. Their dinners and wine tastings are epic. Luc, here, has been a member for decades. They wear red and yellow robes and hats that make them look like they've been around since the Templars and meet in a castle that used to be run by monks.' He winked at my grandfather. 'So there's a lot of mystique around them and what they get up to at their meetings.'

'True,' Pépé said, 'although since the Harry Potter books came out we've also been told we look like we belong in Gryffindor.'

Everyone laughed and Otto said, 'And Chardonnay comes from Burgundy. Which is why Luc's a ringer.'

'All right, Luc,' Vance said, 'you make the blend, since you know everything there is to know about Chardonnay. The rest of us can leave.'

'Not so fast,' I said. 'We need you all.'

More laughter and Vance said, 'OK, I'll stay. Hopefully I'll learn a thing or two from Luc. Any instructions about the blend, Lucie?'

'Just one. We've got twenty-one samples of Chardonnay,' I said. 'Not all of them have to go in the blend, OK? If it's out, it's out.'

There were vineyards where the winemaker's philosophy was *if you've made it, it goes in the blend.* You've toiled for hours in the field and in the wine cellar to make that wine? You're damn well going to use it. *All* of it.

Not us. We wanted to make the very best wine we could. Plus there are other options for a less than stellar batch of juice.

'You want this to be all Chard?' Vance asked. 'One hundred percent?'

Vance asked all the right and on-target questions. He was a good, smart winemaker.

I nodded. 'We think we've got good enough samples to make a really good vintage. Quinn, Antonio, and I have already done some preliminary sampling. What we would like today is your collective opinion to help narrow it down to a final blend.'

One of the arcane rules of winemaking is that a bottle of wine only needs to have seventy-five percent of a particular grape to call it, say, Cabernet Sauvignon or Pinot Grigio, at least in America. Up to another twenty-five percent can be something else and we'll still call it Cabernet Sauvignon or Pinot Grigio.

We're allowed. Fair play.

Everyone nodded and I added, 'I'm sure Quinn will be here any moment, but I know how busy you all are, so we probably ought to get started.'

Toby glanced at Fabrice and said, 'We can wait a few minutes. It would be good to have Quinn here when we do this.'

Fabrice nodded. 'Fine with me.'

'I've got nowhere to go,' Otto said with such finality that my heart tightened.

'I'm good,' Vance said.

'Me, too,' Dominique said. 'Though I'd like to be back at the inn no later than seven o'clock. We have VIP guests coming for dinner and I need to make sure there are no wrinkles in the ointment before they arrive.'

If Dominique had been around when God created the world, she would have been whispering in his ear to make sure He didn't screw up. And though she'd moved here from France more than a dozen years ago to take care of Mia after our mother died, if you get her worked up or excited about something the English goes out the window. Especially the idioms.

Her VIP guests could be anyone from the President of the United States and First Lady on a date night to an off-the-record diplomatic dinner that would never be acknowledged or a romantic tryst when at least one of the extremely well-known parties was married. To someone else. I knew better than to ask who was coming: Dominique kept more secrets than the CIA.

'In that case,' I said, 'perhaps this gives us a few minutes to talk about a situation we all have in common.'

Vance seemed intent on arranging his wine and water glasses so they were in perfect alignment and didn't look at me or the others after I said that, but Otto spoke up.

'The dying vines we bought from Jackson Landau,' he said.

He was sitting next to Dominique – I'd noticed he'd made a point of it – and their heads had been bent close together in a quiet conversation as we were waiting to get started. She'd nodded, giving him a sympathetic look and laying her hand on his arm. I figured that they were talking about the other night and his drunken rant in the bar at the Goose Creek Inn. I also figured Otto had been apologizing for his behavior and it looked as if he'd been forgiven and it would be forgotten, at least by her. But his threat to commit murder if he didn't get financial remuneration from Landau's had been heard by a whole roomful of folks. Not everyone would forget *that* statement, how he'd snapped that night, just lost it.

'I saw your Cab Franc, Lucie, as we drove in this afternoon,'

Toby was saying. 'Forgive me, but those vines look like hell. Are you going to be able to save them?'

'Probably not. Josie Wilde will be here tomorrow morning. She suspects black goo. We'll have to rip them out.'

Otto cursed under his breath. Toby shot me an unhappy look, but Vance looked skeptical.

'If that's true,' Fabrice said in his heavily accented English, 'black goo – or Phaeomoniella – is not as common in France as it is here, but just like phylloxera, it won't be long before French vineyards also have it since no one knows how it spreads. It's fatal. And it has the potential to be just as devastating as phylloxera.'

Phylloxera was a tiny louse that hopped on a shipment of American vines that went to Europe in the 1800s. Within a matter of years, the damage it caused was worse than a plague of locusts, succeeding in wiping out some of the great vineyards of Europe, not to mention destroying thousands of acres of vines in America and Australia. As these things happen, the only solution to restoring those vineyards was taking a phylloxera-resistant rootstock – in other words, American rootstock, *the same rootstock that infected the vineyards to begin with* – and grafting it to the more desirable *vitis vinifera*, or European grapevines. The supreme irony was that in curing phylloxera we ended up with Phaeomoniella, or black goo, which insinuated itself into a grapevine at the seam – or graft – that joined the two different species of vines.

'What are you going to do about your failing vines?' I asked Toby.

He glanced at Fabrice and shrugged. 'We don't have any choice, either. Rip 'em out. Replant. But I want a pound of flesh out of Jackson's hide just like Otto does. He's responsible for this.' He turned to Vance. 'How about you and Mr Everett? What is Sloane going to do?'

Get Sloane on board with his name recognition and star power and boom . . . now you were cooking with gas. Except Eve had told us this morning that Vance sided with her, Jackson, and Richard. And Vance's word probably held a lot of sway with Sloane.

'Sloane hasn't decided,' Vance said. 'Eve's been over at

GSV talking to him a lot lately. And to me. Educating Sloane on the problems that have come with climate change here in Virginia and the perils of continuing to plant the same grapes.'

'What about you?' I asked. 'Where do you stand?'

I wanted to hear it from his mouth.

'Look, those vines didn't come with a forever warranty,' Vance said. 'I've done a lot of reading, attended my share of conferences and symposiums. Climate change is a big deal. We can't turn our backs on it.'

Yup, he was on Landau's side, all right. He was quoting Richard. Dammit.

'No one is suggesting we do that,' Toby said. 'We're all realists here.'

'Climate change doesn't exonerate Jackson et al from selling us diseased vines. One doesn't eliminate the other.' Otto had picked up his pencil and was drumming a rat-a-tat beat on his notepad with the eraser.

At the far end of the table Fabrice had leaned over and was speaking quietly in rapid-fire French in my grandfather's ear. Pépé nodded. The two of them seemed to realize that they had become the center of attention and looked up at the rest of us.

'My apologies,' Fabrice said. 'But what Luc and I were discussing is that before this goes any further, it would be a good idea to test everyone's vines and make sure they are suffering from the same, identical disease.'

'Sounds logical,' Toby said.

'I'll bet you we'll spend our money – money some of us don't readily have – on testing only to find out what we already know.' Otto stopped drumming and stabbed his pencil at Fabrice. 'It *is* the same, identical disease.'

'It would be good to be one hundred percent certain.' Fabrice ignored Otto's confrontational pencil. 'I know about these diseases. I've studied them. I got my Master of Science in grape virology from the Université de Bordeaux. There are variants of Phaeoacremonium, plus there are diseases like botryosphaeria, which is cordon decline, or cylindrocarpon, which is black foot. All of these Grapevine Trunk Diseases, as they're now being called, can mimic the same kind of Vine Decline.'

'We should listen to him,' Dominique murmured. 'The Ecole Supérieure d'Agricultures is France's top school if you are going to study grape growing and making wine.'

Then there was the fact that Fabrice was the fifth generation in his family to go into the winemaking business and the grandson of Jacques Gilbert, who had been our first winemaker. Twenty-five years ago, my mother had cajoled and pleaded with Jacques to leave France and come to Virginia to help her start a new vineyard. My mother being my mother, as well as being French, of course he said yes after she romanticized Virginia, baiting the hook in a way she knew would intrigue Jacques. It's the home of Thomas Jefferson, she'd said, one of the most Francophile of all Americans, a lover of French wine who toured France's legendary vineyards for several months when he was American ambassador to France in the late 1700s. *Come help me write the next chapter of Jefferson's story here in Virginia, the only place he loved besides France.*

And voilà, Jacques had come to Virginia. A few months ago, Fabrice had followed his grandfather at my recommendation after Toby and his partner Robyn Callahan had put out the word they were looking for a new winemaker. A French winemaker.

Now Toby was saying to Otto, 'As for getting everyone's vines tested, I'm sure we can work something out. Don't worry too much about that, OK?'

Otto nodded, but in a way that made me wonder how near the financial precipice he was. Just how broke were they? If Sloane bought Otto and Ali's vineyard sooner rather than later, did that mean Bacchus's vines wouldn't be tested, either?

'Surely you and Sloane would be on board to find out what's wrong with your vines,' I said to Vance. 'They really ought to be tested.'

'I can't speak for Sloane,' Vance said. 'And he runs the show.'

I smiled and nodded. True enough. But Sloane would listen to his smart winemaker. And Vance was plenty smart.

'I'll talk to Sloane,' Toby said. 'Tomorrow's Art in the 'Burg. Robyn told me that one of Sloane's daughters has a booth selling her equestrian photographs. Talented kid. I'm sure

Sloane and Isabella will be there to support her. I can pull him aside for a minute, have a quick word.'

Art in the 'Burg was an annual fundraiser – a vibrant, lively street fair – held in Middleburg every May to support local artists. Everyone in Middleburg and Atoka would turn out for it. There would be food, music, art, and plenty of homespun small-town charm – all of which would bring in hundreds of tourists from D.C., Maryland, and Virginia. Robyn Callahan, an artist who had been Toby's partner for many years, was one of the organizers. Eventually many of those folks would find their way to our vineyard, as well as to Bacchus, La Vigne, and GSV, and we'd all be slammed with guests who wanted to kick back with a glass or two of wine after a lovely day in town.

'If you can get the Iraqis to sit down with the Israelis,' Pépé was saying to Toby, 'I'm sure you can persuade Sloane to have his vines tested.'

Everyone laughed, but Vance's smile was noncommittal. Why in the world wasn't he one of our most ardent supporters? There was a lot more we needed to discuss – other vineyards that might be impacted and would be willing to join us, finding an impartial lab where we could keep our results under wraps until we knew where we stood, and what we were going to do if or when we ran into the brick wall of Jackson's hotshot D.C. law firm.

But with Vance here and apparently playing for the other team, it seemed wisest to end this conversation right now. Besides, maybe Toby could persuade Sloane to get his vines tested and it wouldn't matter what Vance believed because, as he said, Sloane ran the show. It was his vineyard.

Vance's eyes met mine and he gave me a look as if he had just seen all the gears whirring inside my brain and knew exactly what I had been thinking. And he didn't agree one bit. Which made me more than a little uneasy.

Because I didn't know *why* he wasn't on our side. Which was where he belonged.

Something didn't add up. And there was no way he was going to tell any of us what it was.

SIX

Quinn arrived just as we were wrapping up our awkward discussion – with Vance as the lone dissenter – about the need to get our vines tested and find out if Jackson Landau, Eve Kerr, and Richard Brightman were lying through their teeth to a bunch of friends and neighbors. Though Quinn was late, his timing was perfect for making an easy segue to the real reason everyone was here: deciding on the Chardonnay blend. He apologized profusely for his tardiness, but Toby waved a dismissive hand.

'It gave us time to have a little war council meeting on what we're going to do about all of us having diseased vines. Lucie'll fill you in,' he said, giving me a sly wink.

Quinn looked at me as if I'd stabbed him through the heart, talking about the Landau's vine situation without him. I returned his look with: *Don't blame me, you're the one who decided to drive to Seely's to buy secateurs.*

I smiled for the benefit of our guests and said, 'I'll tell you later, honey. Right now we really ought to start tasting wines.'

'Wish I'd been here when you were having that conversation,' he muttered to me one time when we were alone at the sample table.

'*Later,*' I said again, resisting the urge to glance in Vance's direction.

Because Vance had figured it out – I knew he had – that Quinn and I weren't exactly in sync on what do to about our dying vines. Plus he knew the reason.

The California connection. Eve.

Quinn and I had our talk in bed, as I expected we would, his arms wrapped around me, my bare skin soaking in the heat from his naked body. He was propped up against the pillows. I lay with my head on his chest listening to his heart beat slow and strong. He kissed my hair and said, 'OK, what war council?'

I told him. He grew tense as I spoke.

'You're not in favor of this, are you,' I said when I was finished. It wasn't even a question. He wasn't. I added, 'Why not?'

His answer was the last thing I expected.

'Because I think Eve might be coming around to our side.'

I sat up and half-turned so I faced him.

'You think or you know?'

'I don't know.'

Clear as mud. He didn't know what he thought or what he knew? He *thought* he knew, but he wasn't sure?

'I'm confused.' When he didn't answer right away I said, 'Were you really at Seely's this afternoon? Don't tell me they were out of secateurs, because you didn't come home with any.'

'No,' he said, and I felt the breath go out of me. 'I wasn't at Seely's.'

'You were with Eve.'

'It's not what you think.'

'How do you know what I think?' My voice rose.

'Lucie.'

'*What?* Our wedding is in eight days . . . wait. After midnight, it'll be seven days. Is there something you want to tell me?'

'No. I mean, yes.' His eyes were dark and troubled. 'I *wasn't* with Eve. I was supposed to be. She asked me to come by her place this afternoon. Asked me not to say anything about it to anyone. Including you.'

'That's what you were talking about when she kept you back at the vineyard.'

'Yes.'

I folded my arms across my bare breasts and gave him a stony look. 'Go on.'

'I don't know what she wanted to talk about. But there was something and I think it had to do with the problems all of us are having with Landau's vines,' he said.

I bit my lip. If I opened my mouth I was going to say something I couldn't take back and I knew I'd regret it. How dumb could he be? How naive did he think I was?

Finally I said, 'Why do you think that?'

'I don't know.'

'That's an awful lot of stuff you don't know, Quinn.'

'The reason I don't know,' he said, 'is because when I got to her place she was gone.'

'Gone?'

'Yup. Vamoosed, vanished, adiós, *gone.*'

'Did you call her? Text her?'

'My call went to voicemail. She never answered my text.'

'Maybe she forgot she asked you to meet her.'

He raised an eyebrow. 'Seriously?'

'I don't know. What other explanation is there? Maybe she decided to take off for her cabin in the Shenandoah to work on her dissertation,' I said. 'Have you checked your phone for messages lately?'

'No.' He reached over to the bedside table on his side of the bed and picked up his phone. After a moment of scrolling he said, 'Nothing.'

He set the phone back down. 'It just seems weird, don't you think? Why would she jerk my chain to get me out there and then take off and stand me up?'

Um, maybe to prove she could *do it?* Though, to be honest, I didn't think Eve was that kind of tease.

'You could always ask Jackson or Richard where she is.'

'She was pretty adamant about me not telling anyone she wanted to meet me.'

'Then I don't know what to say. She probably took off for her place in the mountains – that's the best explanation. Richard made a point of explaining that the Internet service is spotty out there, but you might have an apology from her in the morning.'

'Maybe.' He seemed relieved. 'It might be just that.'

'Either that or she has a thing for you and she's trying to find out if it's mutual.'

He reddened. 'No, she doesn't, and no, it's not.'

'She's gorgeous, a fellow Californian . . .'

'Lucie.' He bent and kissed me. 'There's nothing between Eve and me. I'm marrying you in . . .' He looked over at the alarm clock. 'Now it *is* seven days. Remember?'

'I remember.'

He lay me back down on the bed. 'Don't doubt me,' he said as he moved on top of me, leaning down for another long, lingering kiss.

When I could finally breathe again, I said, 'I don't.'

'Good,' he said. 'Because I plan to spend tonight proving to you how much I love you.'

I closed my eyes, letting his hands move over me. 'I love you, too,' I said as we found our rhythm and I swirled to the bottom of the ocean with him. 'You don't have to prove anything.'

But he did anyway.

By the time Josie arrived promptly at nine o'clock on Saturday morning, Quinn had checked his email at least five times. Not counting how often he'd cast surreptitious glances at his phone, waiting for it to ding with a text while we were getting dressed and eating breakfast.

Nothing from Eve. Crickets.

'You'll hear from her when she gets back,' I said finally. 'Maybe you should just give up and wait until she contacts you.'

He nodded. 'You're probably right. Look, you and I aren't going to say anything about her to Josie, OK? Eve was adamant. *Tell no one.*'

'I *know*. You've made that abundantly clear. I hear a car. She's here.'

Josie pulled up to the crush pad and climbed out of her red-and-white Mini Cooper with its VAYNDOC license plate. The first time we saw it Quinn guessed it stood for *Vein Doc* – or as he said, half-jokingly, *Vain Doc* – until I told him he'd missed the point totally and it was *VA Wine Doc*.

She looked beautiful, as usual, in her standard uniform of jeans, work boots, and white T-shirt under a quilted jewel-green sleeveless jacket that made her eyes look like the darkest emeralds. She was carrying a flask of coffee – black, strong, piping hot – and an attitude. From the back of the Mini she got a pair of lopping shears and a leather rucksack that she slung over one shoulder.

She eyed Quinn and me and said, 'Is everything all right with you two?'

'You mean other than a lot of dying Cab Franc vines?' Quinn asked.

'I asked for that,' she said. 'Besides the dying vines, I mean.'

'A wedding here in one week,' I said. 'And those vines look like hell.'

She held up her hand. 'OK. I give up. Don't tell me. I can help you with the sick vines. The wedding, you're on your own. But I do need a shovel.'

Quinn got the shovel, which he set next to the lopping shears in the back of the Gator and we drove out to the Cab Franc block with Josie, as we'd done the day before with Eve and Richard.

The first thing Josie did when we got there – just like Richard – was kneel down to check the graft.

'It's not callused over.'

Quinn and I crouched next to her, me leaning on my cane for support.

'Richard said that yesterday,' I said. 'None of the grafts are.'

'Because that's where the infection is,' she said. 'Whatever causes a graft to look like this – whether someone accidentally nicked the vine with the blade of a pair of secateurs or the vine is diseased – you get the same end result: a wound. Sometimes it's fatal, especially if you don't notice it right away. But *this*' – she tapped the bruised graft with her index finger and said with some anger – '*this* is disease, I guarantee it. Especially when it's a whole block of vines from the same grafting lot.'

'Now what?' Quinn asked.

'Now we prove it and see if we can figure out the cause.'

Quinn cleared off the dirt from around the sickly looking vine, scraping it away with the shovel. When he was done Josie took the lopping shears and made a clean cut through the trunk. Where we should have seen clear, clean sap, the veins were clogged with a thick black gummy substance.

I heard Quinn's sharp intake of breath. Josie had warned us, but seeing the in-living-color proof and knowing there was nothing we could do felt like the worst kind of defeat.

'Phaeomoniella,' Josie said. 'Black goo.'

'We talked about this yesterday at our Chardonnay blending party,' I said. 'Fabrice says we ought to send a sample to a lab to get it tested. Toby's in favor of doing that. Otto is, too, but he's pretty cash-strapped. Unfortunately Vance isn't on board at all. He agrees with Jackson, Eve, and Richard that our problems are related to climate change.'

Josie snorted. 'Why am I not surprised? Eve's got him wrapped around her little finger. Or maybe she's not the one Vance is in bed with.'

That was a surprisingly catty remark from Josie, but her eyes flashed with anger. She meant it. And then there had been her take-no-prisoners attitude when she showed up earlier.

'Wait a minute – Eve and Vance?' I said. 'Seriously? Or Vance and . . . who?'

'Don't you think it's *odd* that Vance would defend Jackson?' Josie asked. 'You ask me, there's something going on between those two.'

'What the hell . . .' Quinn said. 'You don't mean *literally* in bed, do you?'

'Eve and Vance, it wouldn't surprise me. Jackson, I think he's got Vance over a barrel and Vance *has* to take his side.'

I held on to Quinn's arm as if I could physically stop him from telling Josie none-too-politely what she could do with her barrel and her dead-bang-wrong opinion of Vance. Because I knew that's exactly what he wanted to do.

'What kind of barrel?' I asked, giving Quinn a warning look.

She shrugged. 'The only kind that matters. Money.'

'Jackson is paying Vance for his silence? Or his support?' Quinn sounded incredulous. He totally wasn't buying it. 'That's nuts.'

'Maybe yes, maybe no. But I think something's going on.'

Vance was usually the first person Quinn called if we ran into a problem in the vineyard or the winery and needed a good second opinion, some sound advice. Sometimes the two of them would discuss whatever it was over beers at the bar at the Goose Creek Inn or the Red Horse Tavern. They liked each other and Vance was coming to our wedding. I hadn't been comfortable about his position yesterday, but he'd always been independent-minded, not one to follow the crowd, and I'd never doubted his integrity.

'Vance is a straight arrow,' I said, backing Quinn. 'We've known him for years, ever since Harry hired him as his winemaker.'

'An arrow can bend without breaking,' Josie said. 'And everyone has a price. Everyone can be bought.'

'Including you?' Quinn asked.

'Mr California—' Josie sounded heated.

I laid my hands on each of their arms. Josie's anger. Quinn's testosterone. We couldn't go on like this. We'd end up tearing each other apart, just like they'd done in California, but *before* we even got started.

'Truce. Please. Stop.'

'Sorry,' Quinn said. 'That last comment was out of line.'

'It was.'

He bristled and I squeezed his arm tighter. *It's over. Enough.*

'OK,' I said. 'Now that we've moved on, what do we do next?'

'Fabrice is right. You should get these vines tested so you've got proof that it's Phaeomoniella and not just that you're taking my word for it. I can help you find a lab. You and Toby and Otto. But keep it away from the Three Amigos. Vance, too, for that matter,' she said. 'Jackson has already retained a lawyer. He's not going to take this lying down. I can tell you that for an absolute fact.'

'What are you talking about?' Quinn asked.

'I've already heard from Messrs. Dewey, Cheatum, and Howe, Esquire,' she said. 'They told me to back off badmouthing Landau's with unsubstantiated claims or they'd see me in court. And that it was a two-way street about badmouthing someone and ruining their reputation. That was my favorite part of their love letter, bless their hearts.'

I hadn't told Quinn about Josie getting threats and needing to watch her back. He shot a glance at me that said he realized he was playing catch-up. Again.

'What are you going to do?' I asked.

'I hate bullies and I hate ultimatums. All they did was make me even angrier, more convinced they're covering up what they did, and more determined to prove it,' she said. 'Getting your vines tested is the first step. Like I said, I'll help you. Plus you, La Vigne, and Bacchus aren't the only ones. I'm contacting other vineyards, too – folks who bought rootstock from Landau's. They may not realize what their problem is or why their vines are dying.' She gave us a grim look. '*Yet.*'

'Eve wants us to plant hardier vines. We need to talk with you about that once we rip these out,' I said, gesturing at the withering landscape surrounding us. 'We're not buying vines again from Landau's. I *can't*. We *won't.*'

'I don't blame you. They'll get it when more folks do what you're planning to do. Money talks. No money screams bloody murder. Have you told them?'

'Hell, yes,' Quinn said. 'Lucie practically double-dog-dared Richard to admit he knew their vines were contaminated. Things got a little heated after he said what happened was our fault.'

'When I told them we weren't going to use them as a supplier any more, Richard suggested we dial it down before all-out war broke out,' I said.

Yesterday's volatile cocktail of blame and recrimination. With more piling on just now with what Josie had told us.

'That must have gone over well,' she said.

'It was a quiet ride back to the crush pad,' I said.

'I can help you find other nurseries, too,' Josie said. 'Plus you could always hire a plant pathologist.'

'A plant pathologist?' I asked.

'Yup. I know someone.'

Of course she did.

'And what would he or she do?' Quinn asked.

'Check your shipment before it gets to you,' she said. 'Make damn sure the vines weren't contaminated.'

'How much would that set us back?' I asked.

'A buck a vine. Roughly.'

Quinn whistled. 'That's kind of stiff.'

'It is,' she said. 'Your other choice is to have this identical conversation again in three years, talking about ripping out more young vines. Phaeomoniella spores infect vines in multiple ways – starting in the hydration tanks at nurseries – but they can also travel in the air and infect new pruning wounds. In other words, it's a crapshoot. So up to you what you do.'

Her words fell into the cathedral-like silence of the vineyard, except for the soft breeze that rustled the tiny white blossoms on the vines and the distant chattering of birds as Quinn and I considered our options. Or lack of options.

'I guess we'll have to pick a few more dollars off that money tree,' I said finally.

'I'd like to clone your money tree, if you don't mind,' Josie said.

'Help yourself.'

It was a Hobbesian choice all right. Don't get someone to vet the vines and refuse to pay the premium for white-glove service and you could be back to square one in three years. One more instance of how to make a small fortune running a vineyard.

Start with a large one.

On the drive back to the crush pad, Josie told us that a reporter from the *Washington Tribune* was working on a story about vineyards in Loudoun County that were suddenly dealing with problems with dying vines.

I sat up straighter, instantly on alert, and said, 'Who's writing it?'

Though I knew what her answer would be.

'Katherine Noland. Do you know her?'

'Since we were five years old. She's my best friend and she's going to be my matron of honor at our wedding. I'm sort of surprised she didn't interview me already. Or at least tell me about it,' I said.

'Kit's the *Trib*'s Loudoun Bureau Chief,' Quinn said. 'She writes about local politics, local issues. She doesn't usually cover agriculture or wine. They already have a wine columnist and a reporter who covers ag for the whole metro D.C. area.'

'I know that,' Josie said.

Something in her tone made me add two and two together

and get four. 'She didn't come to you with this. You called her and said, "Have I got something for you?" Am I right?'

Josie's smile was pure cat-that-ate-the-canary. 'Maybe I did go to her. Precisely because she *is* the *Trib*'s Loudoun Bureau Chief. I read that paper every morning first thing with my coffee. She's a terrific writer and she backs up her stories with impeccable sources. I can't afford to put a foot wrong on this one.'

'Let me guess. You're her "impeccable source?"' Quinn asked.

'More like I'm pointing her in the right direction. You know, sort of a "grapevine whisperer."'

'Sounds like you're doing more than whispering,' I said.

'Maybe.' Another grin. 'I trust you two to keep it under your hat that I'm helping her.'

'Don't you worry,' I said. 'Plus the *Trib*'s lawyers will go over that story word for word to make sure there's nothing in it that's going to get them sued. It will be airtight.'

'Good. It has to be.'

We had pulled up next to the Mini. Before Josie got out of the Gator she said to Quinn, 'You don't seem as if you're all-in on this, so I'm willing to bet you don't want a repeat of what happened in California to happen in Virginia. Under the circumstances, Eve wouldn't be trying to lean on you, would she? I wouldn't put it past her to play that card if it helped her win you as an ally.'

It came out of left field. I looked at my fiancé and waited. Josie hadn't pulled any punches. She wasn't just talking about the acrimony over the California supplier who sold diseased vines: she was indirectly asking about what had happened at Le Coq Rouge and just how vulnerable Quinn still was. To his credit, Quinn didn't hesitate.

'I'd be an idiot if I didn't think you hadn't checked out Lucie and me thoroughly before you agreed to take us on,' he said. 'So we won't belabor my past history in California. As for Eve pressuring me, I can assure you, I can handle her. You don't have anything to worry about, Josie.'

'Fine, but you still didn't say where you come down on this.' Not letting up.

I knew Quinn wasn't going to tell her that Eve wanted to

see him or his theory that she had crossed over to the other side. Plus he respected Vance, who wasn't buying it that Landau's sold us vines that they couldn't guarantee weren't diseased and then lied about it.

'The fact that Jackson retained a lawyer bothers me,' he said. 'He wouldn't have done that unless he thought he needed one. And Richard seemed pretty feisty and defensive yesterday, as well.'

'What about Eve? Are you giving her a pass?' Josie asked with a shrewd look. 'Because you shouldn't. She's as much a part of this as the other two. The only difference is that she has no intention of going down with the ship. She's smart and ambitious, with her whole career ahead of her, so she's going to bail out as soon as possible, put as much distance between Landau's and herself as she can. No stink of scandal on her. Wait and see.'

'Is her name going to come up in Kit's *Trib* story?' Quinn asked.

'It might.'

Which meant yes.

'Did Kit get any vineyard owner to go on the record yet about Landau's?' I asked, hoping to shift the trajectory of the conversation away from Quinn and Eve. 'She won't run a story without presenting all sides. It has to be balanced – she's adamant about that.'

Josie nodded. 'You bet your boots she did. Bacchus.'

Otto. Of course. Everyone around here knew how angry he was with Landau's. He'd be the logical person to ask.

'Plus, to be honest,' Josie said, 'I'm sure Jackson is going to see my footprints all over this as well.'

'Be careful,' I said.

'He can kiss my go-to-hell, as far as I'm concerned. Eve and Richard, too. What they're doing is wrong. Wait until we get proof.'

We were still sitting in the Gator. Josie reached for her satchel and the lopping shears.

'There's something I didn't tell you,' she said. 'Do you know what I found in my driveway this morning before I left to come up here? Fortunately *before* I got in my car.'

She wasn't talking about her copy of *The Charlottesville Daily Progress*.

'What?' Quinn asked.

'Nails. Someone threw finishing nails in front of my car, and if I hadn't walked out to stick a letter in my mailbox for the mailman to pick up and *stepped* on a couple of them, the odds are pretty damn good I'd have run over them. Probably blown a couple of tires. You'd be sitting here waiting for me while I was at some fix-your-tire-right-now place.'

I let out a long breath. 'Jesus, Josie.'

'You believe it was deliberate?' Quinn asked.

'I don't believe it was an accident,' she said. 'There's no construction happening on my street.'

'You don't think Jackson or Richard or Eve drove down there and did that, do you?' I said.

'The law firm they hired has a satellite office in Charlottesville,' Josie said. 'Maybe it was their way of sending me a friendly warning.'

Quinn and I exchanged glances. If Eve had taken off yesterday afternoon for her cottage in the mountains, could she have made a quick detour via Charlottesville and scattered the nails in Josie's driveway? *Would* she do that?

I rather doubted it – *wanted* to doubt it – but you never knew about people, did you? Especially someone who had their back to the wall.

Quinn and I had gone home to change after Josie left so we could drive into town to support Art in the 'Burg.

'Do you think Josie was right when she said Eve wants to distance herself from this situation with Landau's and the diseased vines?' I asked as I slipped out of my jeans.

Quinn pulled off a gray T-shirt with our logo on it and tossed it in the laundry basket in the closet with a neat no-net swish.

'Could be,' he said.

'So she'd throw the two of them under the bus and try to come out squeaky clean?' The moment I asked the question I wanted to bite my tongue, take it back.

He could only have one answer: Yes. Because that's what people thought he'd done at Le Coq Rouge.

'You mean would Eve lie to save her soul – do whatever it took – and she wanted my advice how to pull it off?' Quinn's eyes were the color of a depthless ocean.

I should never have brought this up. 'That wasn't what I meant. I'm sorry.'

'For what?'

'You know what.'

'Forget it.' He took a Kelley green polo shirt out of a pile of clean laundry on the settee that neither of us had had time to put away and tugged it over his head.

I gave him a miserable look and said, 'OK.'

Nothing made sense. Could Eve really have had a Saul on the road to Damascus conversion, as Quinn seemed to believe, and suddenly she was on *our* side? If that were true then, one, she *was* throwing Jackson and Richard under the bus, and two, Josie might be right that Eve had figured out a way to shimmy out of any responsibility she might have for the diseased vines. Or as Josie said, 'No stink on her.'

Then there was this: if Eve turned on Jackson all of a sudden, his high-powered D.C. law firm would get *her* in their crosshairs and make sure her reputation was shredded when they were finished with her. Just like they were planning to do with Josie. Probably do a lot more than throw nails in her driveway.

'I think Josie's wrong about Eve,' Quinn said suddenly. 'She's not a bad person. Whatever she's up to, she has a good reason for it.'

'What about Vance?' I said.

'She's wrong about him, too. He's a standup guy. Honest.' He gave me a long, deliberate look. 'And I think I'd know if he was sleeping with Eve.'

'You would?'

'I would.'

Quinn *did* have blinders on where Eve was concerned, more than the California connection. He *trusted* her. He *believed* her.

I didn't.

Which, as I saw it, meant one of us was right and the other one was wrong.

SEVEN

According to the latest census, the town of Middleburg has a population of 830 souls – though that's give or take because it's been a few years since everyone was officially counted. The number of people in town – folks who come to visit – swells exponentially during our many seasonal celebrations and events: Christmas in Middleburg, the Middleburg Film Festival in the fall, the spring and fall steeplechase races, the Gold Cup, the stable tour, the garden tour, and most definitely Art in the 'Burg and its ancillary, slightly eccentric art-and-hunt-country fundraiser known as Foxes on the Fence.

On those occasions we are inundated by people – mostly from D.C. – who need a fix of sweet small-town charm and a dose of nostalgia that rewinds to a time when life was slower, gentler, and friendlier. The days when folks moseyed instead of multi-tasking and it was OK to linger, lollygag, dawdle, or tarry awhile because that was the pace at which life moved. Even our welcome sign as you entered town heading west on Mosby's Highway showed a picture of a sly, reclining fox under which was written: *Relax! You're In The Village.*

Middleburg has one main street as all small towns do. Ours is Washington – named for George – and we have a lone traffic light at the intersection of Washington and Madison (yes, named for James), which is where the town is divided into quadrants. Not that it's big and sprawling, mind you; it takes about a minute, maybe a minute and a half to drive from one end of Washington to the other unless you have to stop for the light. Outside Middleburg, Washington Street once again becomes Mosby's Highway, or Route 50, which meanders on an east–west trajectory for more than 3,000 miles through dozens of small towns across America, beginning in Ocean City, Maryland and ending in Sacramento, California.

Our little portion of Route 50 gets its name from Confederate

Colonel John Singleton Mosby, also known as the Gray Ghost. The Ghost was famous – or infamous – for making life miserable for the Union Army with the lightning-fast surprise raids he and his troop of Rangers sprang on Union trains, supplies, and camps. Fifty was their territory. Plenty of folks around here will tell you they still see Mosby on moonlit nights riding his horse across deserted fields looking for Union soldiers.

Though Middleburg was founded during America's colonial days, we also lived with the fighting – and the suffering – of the Civil War and its aftermath which lingered for a long time. In fact you can hardly walk more than a few paces around here without coming across a building, monument, marker, or hallowed patch of ground that isn't tied to something in our rich historical past.

Quinn and I managed to park the Jeep in one of the last remaining spots on the large field behind the Red Fox Inn, which was where everyone parked for all of our big events until it filled up and you were forced to retreat to other fields outside of town and take a shuttle bus. We followed a happy, chattering crowd of families, couples, and friends heading toward South Madison Street, which had been blocked off from traffic and was now lined with small white tents where local artists displayed paintings, photos, jewelry, and sculpture for sale. The weather was glorious, one of God's best days when you feel lucky to be alive, and for the millionth time I prayed for weather exactly like this next Saturday.

'What do you want to do?' Quinn said.

'Go see Monty. I hope we won him. We could put him in the garden for the wedding. He'd look terrific.'

Quinn grinned and slid an arm around my shoulders. I slipped my arm around his waist.

'OK, let's go,' he said.

Monty was our fox, or more precisely the four-foot prancing cut-out fox that Montgomery Estate Vineyard had sponsored and my sister Mia had painted and decorated. He had briefly graced our tasting room before we had to give him up so he could be hung on the wrought-iron fence around the Middleburg United Methodist Church last month – part of a fundraiser whose proceeds would go to the Arts Council, regional beautification projects, nature camp scholarships for kids, and the food pantry. Monty had been in good company on that fence: thirty-one other cut-out foxes – Middleburg's unofficial logo – were his still-life merry-go-round companions, each sponsored by other businesses and decorated by one of the region's many talented artists. The idea for Foxes on the Fence had been a collaboration between the Garden Club and the Arts Council and had attracted visitors to Middleburg in droves, who could – and hopefully *would* – go online to bid on their favorite. Last year, the foxes (and a few hounds) had raised over twenty thousand dollars before going to new homes.

This year's theme had been *Hunt Country Home*, so Mia had chosen the grapevine mosaic my mother had designed for the bar in the Villa as her inspiration, covering Monty, as we called him, with metallic paint, translucent multi-colored beads, and layers of different-colored glazes. When she was done he had a winking ruby eye and sparkled and gleamed as if he were draped in fabulous jewels. We'd heard he had been one of the most popular foxes this year and that bidding had been intense. We'd bid on him, of course, and I was hoping we'd won. My last bid had been way above my this-high-and-no-higher promise to myself, because I *really* wanted Monty.

Quinn and I crossed the street near the visitors' center, a doll-house-sized building painted cotton-candy pink and known, unsurprisingly, as the Pink Box. The front door opened and Jackson Landau stepped outside, a broad smile on his face as though he'd just heard good news. His gaze landed on Quinn and me and he sobered up, striding toward us and looking like he had something to get off his mind.

'Damn,' Quinn said in a low voice.

'We knew we'd probably run into him,' I said, 'because of Grace.'

Grace Landau was the president of the Arts Council and this year's chairperson of Foxes on the Fence.

Jackson met us on the pedestrian island in the middle of North Madison Street. The music of a fiddle, banjo, and guitar and someone singing – bluegrass, the toe-tapping kind

– floated up the street from somewhere among the tents on South Madison.

'Lucie, Quinn.' Jackson extended a hand and shook each of ours. He was a big man, tall, white-haired, barrel-chested. 'Nice to see you both. You're always so faithful about supporting the arts in Middleburg.'

'Grace did a terrific job of organizing Foxes on the Fence,' I said. 'We were hoping we managed to have the winning bid on the one my sister painted, the one we sponsored.'

'Monty? The one that looks like jewelry?' Jackson shook his head. 'Good luck. Gracie said folks have been bidding on that one like there's no tomorrow.'

'Well, I guess we'll find out soon since they announce the winners today,' I said. 'At least he raised a lot of money for the Garden Club and the other charities.'

'Sure did.' Jackson cleared his throat. 'Look, folks, I understand you had some words with Richard and Eve when they came out to see you yesterday. Richard said things got a little . . . contentious.'

'They did,' Quinn said. 'We have a lot of dying vines, Jackson.'

'Vines that have black goo,' I said. 'Josie Wilde confirmed it earlier this morning when she stopped by and cut one of them open. The xylem vessel was full of black, tarry ooze.'

'And no doubt she told you those vines were diseased from the get-go,' he said. 'In other words, when you bought them from us three years ago.'

Statements, not questions. Neither Quinn nor I said anything.

'I'll take your silence as a yes.' Jackson stabbed his index finger at us, his face turning red. '*That woman* is going around spreading false information about something she knows nothing about. She's got a goddamned agenda, trying to burnish her reputation by destroying ours. Peddling a lot of crap she can't prove. The Brightman Graft is an excellent graft and I can assure you that Richard dotted his i's and crossed his t's to make damn sure that our vines were disease-free. I give him a small gratuity for every one of the thousands and thousands of vines we sell with his graft, not because I *have* to, but because he's the one who came up with the brilliant solution of how to fuse two different vines without any risk of contamination or disease.'

Jackson had leaned in so close I could feel the heat coming off him.

'Jackson,' I said in a quiet voice, 'we're not the only vineyard with this problem.'

'No, you're not.' His voice grew louder and a few passers-by turned to see what the commotion was all about. 'But *all of you* are located practically in each other's back pockets. In other words, the same climate, the same soil, the same growing conditions. I'm sure Richard went over with you the problems everyone had to contend with last harvest after an unprece-dented season of rain and hurricanes. That's not on us. Or on you. It just is what it is. Climate change. Mother Nature.'

'Richard made that point abundantly clear to us yesterday.' I folded my arms across my chest and gave him a '*We don't need another lecture*' look.

'We still have to rip out an acre and a half of vines and eat a loss of a hundred and eighty thousand dollars.' Quinn sounded equally testy. 'Not to mention waiting another three seasons for new vines to begin to yield fruit. So even *more* time with no money coming in.'

'I get that, but we're *all* dealing with climate change. Either we're going to adapt or we're going to perish. Richard said he and Eve explained that to you – that you're gonna need to start thinking about varietals that are hardier and will survive with the climate we've got now,' he said, still angry. 'And you know what? Landau's is on the leading edge of that curve, developing those new hardier grapes. We're working with Richard, who knows and understands the science, so we're being smart about this and doing things right.'

'Good for you that you're trying to develop hardier varietals,' I said. 'But Cab Franc is one of the friendliest grapes to grow in Virginia. It's not like we were trying to grow something we knew was risky.'

'What are you saying?' Jackson didn't like us pushing back.

'That Quinn and I understand the future you're talking about. But what we're dealing with is what's happening right *now*. Come *on*, Jackson,' I said.

'You must have realized at some point that the vines you sold all of us were diseased. You can't stand here and tell us you're on the cutting edge of what's to come but you had no clue about the problems we're all facing now,' Quinn said.

'Of course we did.' He gave Quinn an annoyed look. 'That's why we moved so quickly to develop new varietals that could withstand what we're dealing with *now*.'

'No,' I said. 'No, no, *no*. You *knew* the vines you sold us couldn't be guaranteed to be disease-free. Then when you discovered so many of us were having problems, you blamed climate change.'

'I'm not *blaming* climate change, because it *is* climate change. Don't tell me you think it's all made up, that it's phony science? Do you?' He looked as if I'd just told him I believed in little green men and alien abductions.

'Of course not,' I said.

'One doesn't negate the other,' Quinn said. '*You* know that.'

'Lucie, Quinn,' he said with fraying patience, 'I hope you're not going to push this and jump on Josie's bandwagon. After three years in your care, what happened to those vines *is not our fault*. Do I make myself clear?'

'Crystal. But what if it is? It might not have been intentional, but you still sold us diseased vines,' I said.

'We. Did. Not.' He smacked his fist in the palm of his hand. 'Look, our families go way back. We have history, you and me. Your mother did business with my father. There is no way I would do something like that and then lie about it.'

'Jackson, you knew something was wrong—'

He put his hands on his hips and looked at me like a parent who has been badly let down by a child. 'Your mother would never pull something like this,' he said, his tone scathing. 'She would have taken responsibility for what went wrong. Maybe you just don't have the right temperament, the right disposition for running a vineyard, Lucie, like she did. It's tough work.' His eyes strayed to my cane, lingered there. 'You've got to adapt, you've got to deal with changes. Maybe you're just not cut out for it.'

'That's *enough*, Jackson.' Quinn had balled his hands into fists.

I grabbed his wrist and squeezed it. *Don't. Don't escalate this.*

Jackson looked at both of us, Quinn barely holding on to his temper, and me utterly furious that he could be so cruel and cutting. His eyes hardened.

'Yes, I believe it is,' he said. 'We're done here.'

He walked off before Quinn or I could respond, though I wanted to shout after him, and didn't care if everyone on Washington Street or even all of Middleburg heard, that he was *wrong – dead wrong.* Quinn pulled me close and put his mouth next to my ear, roles reversed as he tried to calm *me* down. 'Don't, baby. Just don't. We both need to let it go. He's not worth it. He's mad and he didn't mean what he said.'

'*He did.*' My voice shook. *I* shook.

Jackson had found the chink in my armor and used it against me like the most brutal weapon. My disability. I never wanted it to define me, never *let* it define me, and I became prickly, if not rude, when someone wanted to treat me as if I were made of spun sugar. Or assumed – as had happened from time to time – that I was somehow less than a whole person because part of me was broken. I also didn't want – or need – people to make allowances for me, believing I couldn't do an intensely physical job just because I had to use a cane.

But what hurt the most was Jackson telling me I couldn't handle something my mother would have taken care of without whining or complaining or blaming someone else, like he thought I was doing. She was tough. I wasn't.

Except he was wrong. *He* was the one trying to shift the blame elsewhere. On Quinn and me. On the other vineyard owners who'd bought vines from Landau's. And my mother – if she'd been alive – would have fought just as fiercely as I was doing to make sure Jackson took responsibility for what he'd done. And now it had come to this, the shouting and recriminations. Him hiring a lawyer. Trying to get out in front of what was shaping up to be an ugly, bruising battle.

Mud sticks, as they say. And right now Jackson was throwing it at us with a kind of reckless fury as if he hoped it would not only stick, but cover up any wrongdoing on his part.

'Come on,' Quinn said. 'Let's go see if we can take Monty home, OK? We need to get out of here.'

I had calmed down a little, but I said, 'We'll have to see Grace Landau. I'm still so angry . . .'

'Look, Grace has always been her own person. Just because Jackson's being an ass doesn't mean Grace feels the same way he does.'

'Guess we'll find out,' I said.

The Middleburg United Methodist Church is a pretty little red-brick building with a white spire and a historic past. Built in the 1800s, the church had been converted into a hospital treating both Confederate and Union soldiers during the Civil War. Today it looked especially festive and cheerful with the colorful collection of hand-painted foxes that hung on the low wrought-iron fence surrounding it on three sides.

Grace Landau was sitting by herself at a folding table in the tree- and flower-filled courtyard, engrossed in the screen on her laptop. She looked up when she heard the gate creak as Quinn and I walked in. Plump and petite with short iron-gray hair and bright-red glasses that usually sat half-way down her nose, she was also a much beloved high school art teacher respected for her no-nonsense, don't-give-me-any-crap-just-because-it's-*only*-art-class attitude.

The Foxes on the Fence banner – a bright-red silhouette in the modular shape of a sleeping fox – hung on the front of the table and fluttered in the breeze.

Grace's smile when she recognized us was warm, friendly, and guileless. 'Hello, you two. How nice to see you both. Are you coming to check up on Monty the Fox?'

I relaxed and smiled back. 'We are. We were really hoping we had the winning bid.'

Her smile dimmed. *Damn*. We hadn't.

'I was just finalizing all the bids. Do you know this year we raised nearly twenty-five thousand dollars? Monty brought in quite a lot of money, by the way. We can't thank you enough for sponsoring him.'

'You're welcome,' I said and hoped I didn't sound too deflated. 'So who did win him?'

'I'm so sorry, dear. At the last moment we had a final bidder that upped your offer by a thousand dollars.'

'A *thousand* dollars?' Someone *really* wanted him. I wouldn't have been able to match that ante for love or money.

'Who bid that kind of money?' Quinn asked.

'Carly and Richard,' Grace said. 'Monty is going home with them.'

The gate creaked again and we turned around. Speak of the devil.

Carly Brightman, in a bright-yellow halter dress, yellow sling-back kitten-heel sandals, dark hair pulled into a high ponytail, and Jackie Onassis sunglasses, had walked in behind us. She looked sensational, as usual – just the right amount of jewelry and perfect makeup on flawless, tanned skin.

'Hello, Lucie, Quinn,' she said. She turned her sunny smile on Grace. 'Did I hear you right? I won Monty?'

'You did,' Grace said. 'Congratulations. That last bid was very generous of you and Richard. Brought in the most money of any of the entries.'

Carly's smile broadened and her face lit up like Christmas morning. 'Our pleasure. And that's terrific news. I'm so happy – I *loved* that fox. Richard and I will take good care of him, Lucie, I promise. Please tell Mia he's going to a loving home with lots of animals, so he'll have good company.'

Though Carly and Richard didn't have any children – her choice; she was married to her job and kids didn't fit into her career trajectory – they had a menagerie of foster dogs and cats, along with the many animals they'd adopted.

'I'll tell her and I'm sure you'll take good care of him,' I said. It was hard not to be happy for her; she looked so delighted.

'We will,' she said. 'I've been taking a mixed-media class through the Arts Council's outreach program –sort of experimenting, amateur stuff – so I *know* just how much work she put into creating him.'

'*Amateur* stuff?' Grace raised an eyebrow and gave Carly an affectionate look. 'I saw your collage on display at the library, Carly. You're really talented. You should keep pursuing your art.'

'Thanks, Gracie,' she said. 'You're too kind. Though I've been thinking about taking more classes because I liked mixed media so much. After some of the stuff I see every day at work, I figure I can either go into primal scream therapy or get it out of my system by creating something. Which is why I just started a sculpture class. It's amazing how mellow and zen I feel after an hour of chiseling and carving a block of clay.'

We all laughed, and Grace said, 'So have you come to claim your bejeweled friend? I hope Richard is coming by to help you take him home. Monty is not going to fit in that little two-seater convertible of yours.'

'I brought Richard's car, so I'll be fine.' Carly's eyes slid to Quinn and me and there was a noticeable shift in her demeanor. 'He's busy at the lab this morning. Been working hard all hours on some new grape varietals he's been trying to cultivate.'

Her words landed with a thud and Grace's mouth twitched. Which meant they both knew what happened yesterday at our vineyard. Their husbands had told them.

'Yes, Richard was telling us about his new project when he and Eve stopped by yesterday,' I said, keeping my voice neutral.

At the mention of Eve a look of irritation flickered across Grace's face but Carly – diplomat, intelligence chief, stoic – remained expressionless.

'I heard that you two had a rather heated . . . discussion . . . with Eve and Richard.' Grace seemed to be choosing her words carefully.

Well, OK, it looked as if we were going to have this conversation for a second time. Hopefully not as hostile or with shouting as it had been with Jackson, but Grace definitely had something she wanted to get off her mind.

'Richard mentioned that to me, too,' Carly added. 'In fact, he said your meeting didn't go well at all.' Backing Grace. Chiding Quinn and me.

Quinn answered her back. 'We have a lot of sick and dying vines. So do several other vineyards that bought vines from Landau's.'

'The meeting did get a bit contentious,' I said, and then

changed the subject. 'But there was also something going on between Eve and Richard. Any idea what that was about?'

Carly and Grace exchanged fleeting glances, telegraphing some unspoken pact between them. They *knew.*

'What do you mean?' Carly asked.

'I got the feeling Eve was angry with Richard,' I said. 'Or maybe "upset" is a better word.'

Quinn stirred next to me. 'Have you had a chance to talk to Eve since yesterday?' he asked.

'No.' Carly shook her head. 'I haven't.'

'Me, neither. Why do you ask?' Grace said.

'Just wondering what's going on,' Quinn said. Non-committal. Casual.

Grace flashed another look at Carly, this one signaling she was *done* with the code of silence.

'*What's going on,*' she said with an edge to her voice, 'is that I don't think Eve has Landau's best interests at heart any more.'

Quinn tensed next to me. All of a sudden we were taking a little stroll through landmine territory.

I raised my eyebrows. 'Meaning?'

'*Meaning,* Eve's going to leave Landau's – and the East Coast if you ask me – once she gets her PhD. Even though Jackson spent the last three years *teaching* her, *grooming* her, *helping* her in every way possible,' Grace said.

She was angry. And she felt betrayed.

'Jackson and Eve had an understanding that she would play a bigger role in the business,' she went on. 'She would take on more responsibility, so Jackson could slowly start to step back now that he's getting close to retirement age. Instead, she's no longer interested. *That's* how she's going to repay him.'

'She did the same thing to Richard.' Carly sounded calm, but something told me that under that cool, collected surface simmered a low-boiling resentment toward Eve Kerr.

'What happened?' Quinn asked.

Carly pulled a strand of windblown hair off her face and shoved it into her ponytail. 'The usual. Brilliant professor takes talented young student under his wing. Richard's the one who convinced Eve to get her doctorate, told her she could do it, encouraged her. Told her that he'd help her. Of course he was expecting she'd stay at Northern Virginia and study under him. All of a sudden she ups and decides she wants to go to Cornell because UNV wasn't good enough and Cornell was an Ivy. Richard was disappointed – actually, devastated – because it was kind of a slap in the face. Still he was gracious enough to write a glowing recommendation for her, plus call one of his friends on the faculty at Cornell and put in a good word.'

She fiddled with her hair tie and then gave her ponytail a hard, angry yank to secure it.

'And now, of course, with you people blaming Jackson for problems you've got with your vines, Eve can't wait to put miles of distance between her and Landau's.' Grace sounded resentful.

You people. Quinn and me.

'Wait a minute—' I began, but Carly cut me off.

'What's really ironic is that Eve was the one who was so gung-ho about the potential for the graft Richard had invented,' she said. 'Practically from the day she started working there. Just cooing in Jackson's and Richard's ear, telling them: "Let's *really* get this out there. It could be a game changer." Plus pushing Jackson to let Richard cultivate his experimental varietals at Landau's instead of on the little plot of land UNV owns. In the beginning it was all roses and puppies and rainbows.'

I believed her. Eve appealing to Jackson's and Richard's egos – *C'mon let's be first* – along with the notion that they could make a lot of money: *No one else has this graft and we should really take advantage of it. Patent it so Richard owns exclusive rights.* And then there was her way of wrapping a man around her little finger, which she had clearly done with the two of them. As well as every other man she did business with.

I couldn't look at Quinn. He was still on Eve's team, I'd bet money on it. And now here was Carly assigning the blame for what was happening at Landau's squarely on Eve. Grace totally agreeing.

'I'm so sorry,' I said.

'Me too,' Quinn added, but I knew his sympathy belonged with Eve. He was sorry for *her.*

There was a long moment of silence where nobody looked at anyone.

Then Carly said, 'Well, y'all, I think we've kind of beat this dead horse enough for today, don't you? I've got to go into work later so I need to be getting home. Grace, I was hoping I could collect my fox now and take him with me?'

Grace stood up. 'Of course you can. Let me help you get him off the fence. And, Lucie and Quinn, thank you again for sponsoring Foxes on the Fence this year. We appreciated it. Good of you to stop by.'

Her way of saying 'class dismissed' because she and Carly wanted to talk in private.

'You're welcome,' Quinn said.

'Glad to do it,' I said.

When we were out of earshot, Quinn said to me, 'What the hell just happened?'

'What just happened,' I said, 'is that Grace and Carly blame Eve, everyone's sweetheart, for pushing Jackson and Richard to sell vines with the Brightman Graft before they'd been tested more thoroughly. And now that everything's starting to hit the fan, she's planning to bail on them.'

'Then why did she want to see me yesterday?'

'To tell you she's leaving?'

'No,' he said. 'It was something else. Something more than that. I'm sure of it.'

'Why are you so sure of it?'

'I just am.'

Nothing was going to change his mind about Eve. He didn't believe what Carly and Grace had just said about her being an opportunist who used people to get what she needed before casting them aside. Or that she was going to leave Landau's before the stink of an ugly scandal tainted her reputation.

Yet she had vanished after asking Quinn to come see her yesterday afternoon.

Which begged the question: had Eve Kerr already cut and run?

EIGHT

Quinn and I didn't say much during our quick tour of the tents on South Madison to see what everyone was selling. I bought an intricately beaded macrame plant hanger with an octagon-shaped pot to replace the weathered, fraying one out on the veranda.

Quinn took the hand-stenciled carrier bag the artist had used to pack my purchase and we said thanks.

'Let's go home,' he said. 'I've had enough.'

He wasn't talking about the art exhibits.

'I don't think we can do that just yet.'

'Why not?'

'Because Toby Levine caught sight of us and he's with Sloane Everett. Now he's waving at us to join them.'

Quinn groaned. 'No.'

'Come on. We can't pretend we didn't see them. It would be rude.'

He gave me a martyred look that I hoped Toby didn't notice as we made our way over to where Toby and Sloane were standing at the edge of the row of tents.

I got a kiss on both cheeks from Toby – in French we say *faire le bise* – and a hug from Sloane that felt as if I was being burrito-wrapped in pure solid muscle. The men shook hands. Toby caught my eye and I knew he'd been having the 'Get-on-board-with-us' talk with Sloane that we'd discussed last night. And that despite his decades of diplomatic experience successfully getting the most stubborn and balky parties from countries that hated each other's guts to sit down together and talk, apparently he was striking out with Sloane Everett.

Sloane confirmed it. 'Toby here has been working me over for the last twenty minutes, talking about sick vines all of us have and getting some kind of compensation or assistance from Jackson Landau. I gotta tell you, I'm not sure I want to jump into the middle of this. It happened before my time.'

He smiled to take the sting out of his words but losing him as an ally was a big letdown.

'I heard Eve Kerr has been talking to you,' I said. 'Trying to persuade you that the dying vines are a result of poor management on our part or else due to climate change. Or both.'

'She's been trying to educate me about how the climate's been changing in Virginia, how it's different from California, and why we need to start planting hardier grapes that will do better with this new kind of weather she says is here for good.'

Sloane did a neat job of rearranging my words: Eve was educating, not lobbying, him. Plus he was too smart and smooth to give away anything about her private tutorials with him other than to say that they were strictly business.

'What did you tell her?' Toby asked. 'If you don't mind me asking.'

Sloane shrugged. 'I told her what she said makes sense.'

'We don't disagree.' Toby was still trying to convince Sloane that he belonged in our camp. 'But that doesn't negate the fact that the vines Jackson and Eve sold us three years ago – with Richard's imprimatur that they were disease-free – are dying.'

'Vance brought me up to speed on what happened in California in the late nineties,' Sloane said. 'I made a few calls of my own to friends in Napa, Sonoma, getting their take on what went down.'

'And?' I said.

'There was a big nursery out there that had to shut its doors because of all the lawsuits brought against it for diseased vines. From what sounds like the same stuff – Phaeomoniella, Vine Decline, black goo – whatever you want to call it. And talk that it was hushed up to avoid people panicking and causing the price of land to fall,' he said.

'Look, we don't want what happened in California to happen in Virginia, either,' Quinn said, giving Sloane a meaningful look. Like: *We're both Californians, so we know how bad it can be.*

Toby threw a quizzical glance my way. I knew he was still

wondering about Quinn and where his loyalties lay. I returned his look with my blandest expression because, truth was, I wasn't entirely sure myself how committed he was.

Sloane stroked his goatee with a thumb and forefinger and studied Quinn. 'I'm with you on that, man. There was a lot of bad blood.'

'Nobody wants that kind of falling-out here, but everyone still ought to get their vines tested.' Toby wasn't giving up. 'It's common sense that we should know if we've all got the same disease.'

'All right, say we do that, then where do we go from there?' Sloane asked. 'Anyone who thinks only one move ahead in basketball is just asking to get outplayed.'

'Nobody knows how Phaeomoniella spreads,' I said. 'So if that's what we've all got, we need to stop it. The sooner the better. So we don't end up with the next phylloxera.'

'What about Jackson?' Sloane said. 'And Eve and Richard? You gonna get them involved in this?'

'Jackson hired a lawyer,' Toby said in a flat voice. 'I suggest we not wave a red flag in front of a bull.'

'Besides, Eve and Richard don't seem to be getting along at the moment,' I said. 'It's as if they're on different sides of the issue about what to do about the diseased vines and how Landau's is going to handle it.'

Sloane took a pair of mirrored sunglasses that he'd hooked around the back of his neck and slipped them on. I could no longer see his eyes, only my reflection.

'What's going on with the two of them doesn't have anything to do with business or dying vines.' His voice was cool, assured.

There was an awkward silence while the rest of us digested that piece of information.

'You sure about that?' Quinn asked.

'Aw, come on, man.'

The three men exchanged knowing looks. I wondered if Sloane knew about Eve and Richard, because maybe he and Eve . . .?

Toby cleared his throat. 'Well,' he said, 'how about it, Sloane? Are you in?'

Sloane took his time considering his reply. 'OK,' he said. 'I'm in. For getting my vines tested to find out why they're sick.'

'You'll tell Vance?' I asked. 'Get him to come round, too?'

'I got Vance.'

'Let's keep this discussion between the vineyard owners for now until we get some answers,' Toby said. 'I don't want to rile Jackson. So nothing said to Eve, either.'

I really wished I could see Sloane's dark eyes behind those opaque sunglasses. He gave Toby a cool nod, then looked up over the tops of our heads – which wasn't hard to do at six foot nine – at something behind us. It turned out to be some*one*.

'I'm being summoned,' he said. 'The boss wants me. Gotta go.'

The boss. Isabella. She really was keeping an eye on her husband. He started to leave, moving with the easy grace of an athlete in absolutely superb elite condition. Was the reason there was friction between Eve and Richard because perhaps there was some chemistry between her and Sloane? It wouldn't be hard to imagine. Drop-dead gorgeous golden girl and handsome, magnetic African-American NBA superstar, both from sunny California.

'Keep Vance in the loop, OK?' Sloane called to Toby. 'I'm heading out to LA for a business trip, meeting a couple of sponsors who want me to do some promotional stuff, so Vance is going to be running the show here.'

Toby nodded. 'Will do.'

After Sloane left, Toby turned to us. 'Well,' he said, 'at least he's with us and not against us. But getting him to agree to get his vines tested sure as hell wasn't a slam dunk.'

Quinn was quiet on the way home. He seemed pensive, lost in his thoughts. I let him be.

It was Eve. Probably what Grace and Carly had said about her being an opportunist, using Jackson and Richard and then planning to bail out and ditch them before things went south. I don't think he believed it. Or wanted to believe it.

My phone rang as we turned on to Sycamore Lane, the private road that led to the vineyard. I checked the display: Kit Noland.

When I answered she said, 'Any chance you have time to meet this afternoon? Say, four o'clock?'

After everything that had happened today – Josie's verdict about our vines, the revelations and accusations from all the folks we'd bumped into at Art in the 'Burg – a drink at the end of the day with Kit, my alter-ego, my conscience, my nonjudgmental best friend to whom I could say anything, sounded great.

'I'd *love* to. Come on by and we'll find a quiet place to have a glass of wine. Just the two of us.'

'Uh, how about if I bring the drinks and instead of meeting at the Villa we meet at our favorite place?'

Our favorite place was the old Goose Creek Bridge. The two of us had been going there since we were teenagers to share our angst-filled problems about school, boyfriends, parents – basically anything and everything over which teenage girls have angst. It was off the beaten track so we always had it to ourselves, and in those days I'd filch an unlabeled bottle of wine from the barrel room that we'd take turns passing back and forth as we sat on the bridge above the creek with our feet dangling over the parapet. Jacques was our winemaker then and, of course, he was wise to my sneaky ways and tricks so he played one of his own: watering down a bottle of wine that he left for me to 'find.'

'The Goose Creek Bridge?' I said. 'Um . . . sure. Is everything all right?'

'Yup, fine. Why wouldn't it be?' She sounded unusually cheerful, a little too quick to brush off my query.

Which meant something was up.

'I don't know,' I said. 'It's been that kind of day.'

Maybe she wanted to talk about the story she was writing – with Josie's help – about the problems we were having with our vines. Maybe she wanted to keep it off the radar that she was talking to me, though that didn't sound right.

Quinn looked over at me and I gave him a one-shoulder shrug.

'You'll have to tell me about it,' Kit said. 'Gotta go. See you later.'

'What was that all about?' he asked after I disconnected.

'No idea. She wants to talk today at four. Maybe it's something to do with the wedding, but it could also be that story she's writing on diseased vines and she wants to pick my brain.'

Somehow, though, I didn't think it was either of the above.

'Goose Creek Bridge,' he said. 'The place the two of you go to play hooky. Something's up.'

'I don't know,' I said. 'I guess I'm going to find out.'

The winery was packed with folks who had been in Middleburg earlier this morning and now after patronizing the region's artists, photographers, and sculptors they wanted to chill out with a glass or two of wine. Either in the tasting room or at one of the tables on our deck with its peaceful view of the vineyard and the Blue Ridge or seated at bistro tables and chairs under bright-red umbrellas in the courtyard. To handle the larger than usual weekend crowd, Frankie had hired extra staff to help pour wine.

I hadn't realized Hailey Adams, a UNV grad student who was one of Richard Brightman's lab assistants, would be in today, but when I saw her as I walked into the Villa I was glad she was here. When Frankie first took over running our retail business, she had quickly figured out that a great place to get competent, knowledgeable help who could come in on a dime when we were swamped were the grad students in the oenology and viticulture department at the University of Northern Virginia. Because poverty-stricken grad students could *always* use extra cash, not to mention the bottle of wine they took home with gratitude and appreciation at the end of the day, which was a huge step up from the Château de Plonk they could afford on their budgets. Frankie always went to Richard – also with bottles of wine in hand – to ask him for recommendations about whom to hire. He always delivered.

Hailey was, by far, my favorite of his students. She was smart, a quick study, and had the right kind of personality and temperament for dealing with all kinds of people. She was dark-haired, cute, and perky, and our customers loved her. Though she was probably still getting carded since she looked like she was about twelve, she had learned everything she needed to know and then some about our wines. Plus she knew just how to approach each customer and sweet-talk them – in the nicest possible way – to try something whether they were twenty-one or seventy-one. Not only did she pour wine in the tasting room, she sold a lot of bottles – and a few cases – that folks took home with them. Frankie adored her.

Hailey waved at me when she saw me, then went back to explaining the nuances of a flight of reds to a group of senior citizens who were paying rapt attention at one of the satellite bars we set up on days like this.

Frankie joined me and I said, 'I see you brought in the A Team.'

She laughed. 'Hailey? I'm lucky I got her to come in today. Apparently she's been working nonstop on a research paper about vineyard diseases – she tried to explain it to me but it was way over my head. She's the co-author with Richard and she's absolutely over the moon because it's going to be published in something called *Vitis*.'

'That's a big deal,' I said. 'Good for her. *Vitis* is probably the top journal for anything on the subject of grapevine research, canopy management, that kind of stuff.'

'I think she pulled a couple of all-nighters to finish on time, including last night, so she's exhausted. Though she swears she's on adrenaline right now and she'll crash later.'

'Sounds like there's a lot of that going around at UNV,' I said. 'Carly said Richard was hard at work at the lab so he couldn't stop by Art in the 'Burg.'

'I'm sorry I couldn't get by and support them, either, but I did win the origami fox that looks like the logo of the Red Fox Inn.'

'I loved that fox. Congratulations. They had some really great ones this year.'

'Who won Mia's?'

'Carly and Richard. She outbid us by a thousand dollars.'

Frankie's eyebrows went up. 'A thousand dollars? Are you serious?'

I nodded and she said, 'How was the rest of the festival?'

'Fine . . . great. Crowded.'

'It's always crowded.' She frowned at me over the top of her glasses, which meant I was about to be grilled. 'I know that look on your face and your fake smile. What happened? I mean, what *really* happened?'

I gave in.

'Quinn and I had an unpleasant exchange with Jackson. And Carly and Grace told us Eve is an opportunist who used their husbands to help her career and now she's planning to leave Landau's once she gets her degree. Especially since they're getting a lot of flak from customers about diseased grapevines.'

'Trouble in paradise?' Frankie asked in a tart voice.

'I guess.' I gave her a sideways look. My turn to ask a question. 'Everyone talks to you. What do you know?'

'I can't violate the seal of the confessional.'

'I won't tell.'

'It doesn't work like that.'

'How about if I guess? You can say warm or cold.'

She gave a half-laugh. 'Such as?'

'The subject is romance. Warm?'

Frankie's eyebrows went up. 'No comment. Go on.'

'Eve and Richard.'

'What about them?'

'There was something going on between them and it ended. Probably because she found somebody new.'

'Very astute.'

'Warm?'

'Hot.'

'Sloane Everett,' I said.

'*What?*'

'*Not* Sloane?'

'If there's something happening between the two of them, it's news to me.'

'OK. Vance.'

She shook her head. 'He's gaga over her, though.'

'That came across at the blending party,' I said. 'So who's left?'

She shrugged. 'You tell me. Name another man she might go for. And he'd go for her, too.'

I thought for a moment. *'Fabrice?'*

She grinned, enjoying my amazement. 'He's been helping her with her dissertation since he knows the subject she's writing about and can talk about it in his sleep. I think it's sweet and I think they make a cute couple. And he has the added benefit of not being married.'

'How did you find out? He didn't drop a single hint yesterday. I would never have suspected.'

'One hears things if one keeps one's ears open,' she said with an inscrutable smile. 'And speaking of marriage – which brings me to your wedding – do you want to go over the list of photographs you want David to take before he shows up tomorrow? I was thinking you might review it this afternoon so I can email it to him.'

Everything brought Frankie to our wedding.

'Didn't we already do this?'

'Well, this would just be a final look-see.'

'It's fine, Frankie, don't fret. I also promised Kit I'd meet her for a drink later on.'

Frankie brightened. 'What time is she coming by?'

'She knows her matron of honor duties. Honest. And she wants to meet at the Goose Creek Bridge.'

She looked puzzled. 'The Goose Creek Bridge, huh? Is everything all right?'

'Yes, everything's fine. Don't worry.'

'I'm not worrying,' she said.

'Good,' I said.

Because what I didn't want to tell her was that I had a feeling everything *wasn't* all right. And *I* was worried.

The Goose Creek Bridge is tucked away off Mosby's Highway at the end of Lemmons Bottom Road on the outskirts of Middleburg as you're heading toward the sweet little village of Upperville. The four-arched bridge, the longest stone turnpike bridge in Virginia, was built in 1810 at the end of Thomas Jefferson's presidency and was once a busy thorough-fare until Route 50 was built to replace it. These days almost no one goes there; the road is now filled in and overgrown with bushes and trees.

The bridge was the site of a Civil War skirmish in 1863 when Confederate Major General J.E.B. Stuart sought to keep Union General Alfred Pleasanton from discovering that most of Robert E. Lee's army was bivouacked nearby in the Shenandoah Valley just outside Upperville. With help from Mosby's Rangers, who scouted the location of Union soldiers, Stuart managed to delay Pleasanton from entering the Shenandoah Valley – but only for a few days. Still, it helped Lee, though ten days later the two armies would meet at Gettysburg.

To see the bridge today you'd never know a battle had been fought there because it was so peaceful and quiet. Tour guides showed up occasionally, giving talks to history buffs and those who assiduously followed the Civil War battles, even the smaller clashes. The local garden club cared for the place.

Kit's SUV was already parked at the end of Lemmons Bottom Road when I arrived promptly at four. She was nowhere to be seen so I figured she had already hiked down to the bridge, which was out of site at the end of a gravel path. Honeysuckle just recently in bloom lined the way, the overly sweet smell of hundreds of little white and yellow flowers so intense and cloying you could almost get drunk on it.

I had hardly gotten out of the Jeep when Kit emerged from the opening in the gate that had been installed to keep all but pedestrians from visiting the bridge.

'I just got here,' she said, 'and heard your car so I came back.'

She was carrying a small cooler and wearing jeans, a loose-fitting pink V-neck top, and sandals. Her peroxided Marilyn Monroe blonde hair was pulled up into a messy bun. I was used to seeing her in colors so strong they vibrated or else they downright clashed – her signature look that she said ensured she'd always get called on at press conferences.

'You can't miss me,' she always said and I could believe it.

We exchanged our usual air kisses. Kit and I know each other so well we can finish each other's sentences. Start each other's sentences. Breathe for each other. She had something she wanted to tell me and she needed to do it here in our sacred place.

'Are you all right?' I asked. 'I'm dying of curiosity to know what this is all about.'

She grinned and slipped her arm through my free arm, matching her pace to my slower one. Even with the cane, I can't walk fast on uneven surfaces.

'All will be revealed. Don't worry.'

'Good – hey!' I stopped walking and pulled her to an abrupt stop beside me.

'What?'

'The birds are quiet,' I said. 'They usually don't go quiet unless it's about to rain. Or something has scared them and they're hiding.'

Kit did a three-sixty turn, surveying our surroundings and we both listened hard.

'There have been sightings of bears and coyotes in the area lately,' she said. 'I really wouldn't like to run into either one of them when we're here on our own.'

'Me neither.' After a moment I said, 'If it's an animal, it might be as scared of us as we are of it. I don't hear anything.'

Kit shrugged. 'Maybe it's nothing.'

We started walking again. 'I hope so.'

When we got to the parapet, Kit bent over to set down her cooler and said, 'It's *not* nothing. Oh my God. Lucie, come here.'

She was pointing at the creek below us. I looked and felt as if I were about to gag.

Lying face-down in the water, blonde hair splayed around her like *Hamlet*'s Ophelia, was Eve Kerr still dressed in the clothes she'd been wearing yesterday morning when she and Richard had come to the vineyard to look at our failing vines.

She hadn't driven to her cabin in the Shenandoah to work on her dissertation. Instead she had taken a dive off the parapet of the Goose Creek Bridge – probably from precisely the spot where Kit and I were standing now – and either drowned or sustained injuries that were life-ending when she landed on the rocks in the stream bed.

'What *happened*?' Kit draped a hand protectively across her belly. 'Did she slip and fall? What was she doing here?'

'I don't think she slipped,' I said. 'Either she jumped, meaning she committed suicide. Or she was pushed. Which means she was murdered.'

NINE

K it was already on her phone calling Bobby. When you're married to the senior detective at the Loudoun County Sheriff's Office, you skip the 911 call and go directly to the head of the line.

We had both stepped away from the parapet so we could no longer see the creek below and Eve's crumpled body face down with that beautiful hair fanned out around her like the golden halo of a saint.

'Bobby's on his way. He's in Middleburg – he stopped by MPD to talk to the Chief about something – so he'll be here in a couple of minutes.' Kit's voice was tense, tight. 'I told him not to bother with lights and sirens. It's too late. She's gone.'

'How did she end up in the creek? Her car's not here. She didn't walk. I mean, from *where*? There's nothing else around here.'

'I can't believe she came here on her own, either,' Kit said. 'She must have come with someone.'

'And whoever it was pushed her off the bridge and *left*? Jesus, Kit. Who would *do* something like that?' I said. 'And if they did, it means she *was* murdered.'

If someone brought Eve here – a man, which seemed the most likely possibility, considering it was Eve – it had to be a person she knew, someone she trusted. Maybe they'd argued. Maybe she slipped or stumbled, and he panicked and fled. Which would make it an accident, rather than murder. But still . . . *leaving her*?

And why the old bridge? Because it was private? The same reason Kit and I came here – we knew we'd be alone?

Kit fumbled in her purse, pulling out a reporter's notebook

and a pen. She flipped open the notebook until she found a clean page and scribbled something.

'You're going to write a story about this,' I said. 'Rhetorical question.'

She sighed. 'I have to. It's my job. This is news. Plus I've been working on a story about Landau's and the problems they've been having with some of the local vineyards. Eve's name came up. I didn't want to say anything to you until I had more information, but I was definitely going to talk to you about it.'

'Josie told Quinn and me about your story this morning. Also that she was your grapevine whisperer.'

Kit gave me a weak smile. 'She did a lot more than whisper.'

'Is that why you asked me to come here today?' I said. 'Background information for your piece? Or something off the record? It's stirred up a lot of people already, you know.'

'I know it has. But I asked you here for another reason.'

Her eyes held mine. My oldest and dearest friend since childhood. We knew each other like we'd been stitched together at the seams into one person. It had always been like that.

Her hand over her belly when she first saw Eve. Protective.

'You're pregnant,' I said, and she nodded and burst into tears.

I put my arms around her and let her sob on my shoulder.

'My hormones are a mess,' she said, finally lifting her head and sniffling. 'I have to tell you that I'm expecting a baby while we're standing here, possibly at the scene of a murder.'

'So I'm guessing that's not a bottle of wine in your cooler,' I said and she smiled and hiccupped. 'But you look kind of pale, sweetie. Have you got something to drink in there? I don't want you to pass out on me.'

Kit fished in her purse again and brought out a tissue. She wiped her eyes and said, 'Coconut water.'

The Kit I knew slurped down Diet Cokes like there was no tomorrow. If it wasn't a Coke, it was a Starbucks caramel macchiato. The occasional energy drink when she was working, up against a tight deadline. Evenings were for a glass or two of wine.

'Eating and drinking healthy for the baby, I see?'

She nodded and wiped her eyes again. 'Working on it.'

I opened the cooler and pulled out a bottle of coconut water. After I unscrewed the cap I handed it to her. 'Sit down and drink this.'

She sat on the parapet, her back to the creek. I stayed far enough away that I didn't have to look down to where Eve lay.

An approaching car crunched on the gravel on Lemmons Bottom Road. Someone driving fast.

'I think Bobby just got here,' I said.

A moment later, he came into view, sprinting down the path toward us, his eyes searching for his wife. She stood up and turned toward him. He went straight to her and took her in his arms.

He murmured something and she said, 'No, no. I'm OK . . . don't worry. It was just such a shock. So brutal.'

Bobby let go of Kit and turned to me. 'You OK, Lucie?'

'I don't know,' I said, and I really didn't. 'By the way, this is a horrible time to say it, but congratulations, Bobby. Kit just told me.'

He looked puzzled but then his eyes cleared, and he said, 'You found out here? Now? Aw, *jeez*. And, yeah, thanks. We're thrilled.'

Then he went to the edge of the parapet, looked down, and said, 'Goddammit.'

There was more commotion on Lemmons Bottom Road. A couple of Sheriff's Office deputies showed up and Bobby instructed them to start searching the area around the bridge. The road. The woods. The stream bed. Kit and I stood on the sidelines, my arm around her waist, the two of us trying to stay out of the way.

'This isn't good for the baby,' I murmured.

'This baby's father is a cop,' she said. 'She is going to be strong and tough. Just like her dad.'

'You already know it's a girl?'

'No. But I think so.'

'This woman didn't float down there,' Bobby was saying to the deputies. 'And her car's not here. We need to get someone to check her house. Find out why she took a header off an out-of-the-way bridge where no one was likely to find her for quite a while.'

'Bobby,' I said, 'her car wasn't at her house last night.'

He turned around and said, 'And how do you know that?' Cop's voice, cop's demeanor.

This was going to sound worse than it really was, but I had to tell him. Besides, he would find out sooner or later anyway. Better to get out ahead of the story.

'Because she asked Quinn to meet her at her place yesterday afternoon when she and Richard stopped by the vineyard in the morning. Eve told Quinn she wanted to talk to him about something. When he got to her house, her car was gone and so was she,' I said. 'He told me about it later that evening because he couldn't figure out why she stood him up.'

Bobby's eyes narrowed and he said, 'What exactly did she want to talk to Quinn about?'

I folded my arms across my chest as though I could shield myself from what came next: More questions, no answers. Or else answers that sounded incriminating. All of it weaving a web of suspicion around Quinn.

'I don't know and neither does he. She asked him not to tell anyone – including me – that she wanted to see him.'

'What time was this, about?'

'I don't know. He was about twenty minutes late for a blending party that started at five. So before that.'

I could tell he was doing the math, figuring out the timetable.

'Then what happened?'

'Last night he tried calling her and texting her, but she never responded. Finally I told him that she might have decided to take off for a cabin she rented in the Shenandoah where she's been going to work on her dissertation,' I said. 'Richard made a point of saying that the Internet service is lousy there because it's in the mountains in the middle of nowhere. Quinn and I figured it was that. She'd call Monday when she got back here and apologize.'

'Neither of you mentioned this to anyone else?' he said.

'Jackson, maybe? Or Richard? Asked if they knew where she might be?'

'Not them, but Eve's name came up this morning at Art in the 'Burg when we were talking to Grace Landau and Carly Brightman,' I said. 'Both of them said Eve was planning to quit Landau's and leave as soon as she got her doctorate. They were pretty upset about it because they thought she was bailing out after Jackson and Richard did so much to help her career and her education. Since we were talking about Eve, Quinn asked if either of them had seen her recently and both of them said they hadn't.'

'I'll need to talk to Quinn to confirm this.'

'I know.'

Bobby looked up and over my shoulder. 'Win's here.'

Winston Churchill Turnbull was Loudoun County's newest medical examiner, an octogenarian who had retired from his practice of nearly fifty years and then decided he needed to do his 'Peace Corps service,' as he called it, so he volunteered to go to Iraq during the US military involvement there and work in an army field hospital.

What he saw in Iraq – limbless children who had lost their parents, American soldiers and kids going home with injuries so severe their lives would be changed irretrievably, the worst things that man can do to his fellow man over land and power and grudges so ancient no one remembered their genesis – made him decide that returning to Virginia as a medical examiner where he had to piece together reasons people killed each other was infinitely preferable to the hellhole he'd left behind. He was down-to-earth, calm, and the person you wanted right here, right now, to examine the body of a beautiful young woman who lay dead in the middle of a creek for reasons no one could ascertain. Win being Win, he'd have an explanation before long about what had happened – though he probably wouldn't know *why*.

Win stopped to talk to Bobby and acknowledged Kit and me. Then he pulled on a pair of waders and, with surprising nimbleness, climbed down the embankment to the creek. Before he knelt down to examine Eve, he looked up at us and said, 'I don't think you're going to want to see this unless you have a very strong stomach. Decomposition slows down in water because of cooler temperatures than in the air, but if the current has dragged her at all there could be a lot of abrasion and sloughing of the skin. It's not going to be pretty. She may also have been the victim of whatever insects or animals fed on her while she's been here.'

Kit gagged and I pulled her away. 'Come on,' I said. 'We don't need to give your baby nightmares this early in life.'

Truth be told, I didn't want nightmares, either. By the time Win emerged from behind the parapet, we had learned a few meager things that Bobby was willing to share. Eve's car was still not at her house and the house was locked up tighter than a drum. The Loudoun County Sheriff's Office was now actively looking for her car. The grid search of the area so far had turned up nothing. Any tire marks on Lemmons Bottom Road were now probably obscured or obliterated by Kit's SUV and my Jeep because we'd parked where whoever came here with Eve would have parked.

Win, on the other hand, had fresh news. He pulled off a pair of blue nitrile gloves inside out and tucked them in his medical bag. Then he joined Bobby, Kit, and me.

'Poor girl,' he said. 'So beautiful, with everything in life ahead of her. I can tell you this: she died here. She wasn't killed somewhere else and then dumped in the creek. I'm fairly sure I'll find water in her lungs. There's a wound to the back of her head, almost like the claw end of a hammer.' He looked at Bobby. 'Did you find anything?'

Bobby looked grim. 'Not yet.'

Win nodded as if that was the answer he was expecting but he'd had to ask anyway. 'Any blood from that wound was washed away by the water, as you might imagine. But I'm fairly certain the blow was strong enough to knock her off the bridge. I suspect she was unconscious when she hit the water. She landed face first, as you saw, and there are more facial wounds that were the result of the impact. She probably wasn't dead because ultimately, I believe she drowned. So it was a brutal death.'

Kit's face had turned ash-colored and she sucked in a small breath when Win uttered that last part. Bobby put his arm

around her again. 'Are you OK? Let's sit you down. You don't
need to hear the rest of this.'

'Sorry. I think it's the baby. Giving me a queasy stomach.
I'm not usually like this.'

She let Bobby take her over to the parapet where she sat
down again. The bottle of coconut water was still there so he
handed it to her. Bobby gave me an inquisitive look, as if I
should join Kit, but I wasn't budging. I wanted – *needed* – to
hear the rest of what Win had to say. Bobby was going
to question Quinn. The more I knew the better.

When Bobby returned, Win went on.

'The good news, if you can call it that, was that she landed
so her body became wedged between a couple of stones and
an old log that acted like a dam. The creek's swift moving
enough at this time of year that the current might have carried
her a ways – though I doubt she'd have ended up in the
Potomac. There are too many obstacles.'

'How long has she been in the creek?' Bobby asked. 'Give
or take.'

Win exhaled, long and slow, thinking. 'Well, that's tricky.
The water slowed down the decomp. I'd say anywhere from
eighteen to twenty-four hours.'

Bobby did more math. 'Eighteen hours ago would have
been ten o'clock at night and it would have been pitch black.
No one comes here then. If she wasn't dumped in the creek
then she walked here on her own two feet. So it's gotta be
when there was still some daylight and these days the sun
sets around eight fifteen.'

Win nodded. 'Makes sense. I'll have a better answer for
you after I do the autopsy.'

As he spoke, two sturdy-looking EMTs who had arrived
earlier carried a stretcher with a body bag up the embankment and headed toward the gate where a van was probably
parked waiting to take Eve's body to Win's lab.

We watched them depart in silence. As they disappeared
from view into the tangle of honeysuckle, Bobby said, 'You'll
let me know when you're done with the autopsy, right?'

'Of course,' Win said.

Bobby looked from Win to me. 'Well, it looks like this has

turned into a murder investigation.' His gaze remained on me. 'I need to talk to Quinn, Lucie.'

I looked right back at him and said, 'I know. I told you what happened, Bobby.'

'Yeah, but I need his statement. You know that.'

I did.

'I wonder who would want to kill her,' I said. 'Who could do something so . . . violent?'

'I don't know,' he said, and I could sense his simmering anger. 'But I'm gonna find out. And then I'm going to put away the sonofabitch who threw Eve Kerr off this bridge and walked away to let her bleed out and drown in Goose Creek. Make sure he or she never sees the light of day again.'

TEN

B obby wasn't going to let any grass grow under his feet before he talked to Quinn now that, thanks to me, he knew Quinn had driven over to see Eve at roughly the same time she had disappeared. Maybe Quinn had seen someone or some*thing* like a car passing him on the road heading in the opposite direction. Maybe, just maybe, Quinn had glimpsed Eve's killer without realizing it.

Just before Bobby took off he said, 'Lucie, don't warn Quinn I'm coming, OK? I want to know what comes straight out of his mouth unfiltered, which won't be the same thing if you tip him off.'

I knew Bobby – had *known* Bobby since he was seven and I was five, because he had been one of my brother Eli's closest friends until they drifted apart in high school after Bobby started hanging out with the wrong crowd and getting into trouble. Fortunately after distinguishing himself during two tours in Afghanistan, he'd come home deciding he'd rather *be* the law than on the wrong side of it doing time for some half-assed crime he sort of fell into.

'Did you really have to tell me that?' I asked him.

'No, but I did anyway.'

Belt and suspenders. Dot the i's and cross the t's. The devil is in the details. All the cliches about not making a careless mistake – that was Bobby.

'Quinn's not a suspect,' I said. A statement, not a question.

Bobby didn't bite. Like Kit always said, he gave away nothing. 'I'll see you later,' he said.

After he was gone and the deputies were putting yellow crime scene tape at the gate, Kit said to me, 'Don't worry about Bobby talking to Quinn, Luce. He just wants to know if Quinn noticed anything, maybe something that didn't register as being important.'

'I know.'

'Come on,' she said. 'Let's get out of here. I need to go home and take a power nap. Baby makes me sleepy. And you look like you could use a drink. Or two.'

More air kisses at our cars and she said, 'Before all this happened I was going to ask if you'd be the baby's godmother.'

My eyes filled with tears. 'Of course. I'd be honored.'

'There's something else,' she said and now her voice cracked. 'This might be lousy timing, or exactly the right moment to ask.'

'Ask me anything,' I said.

'OK. Here goes. If something happened to Bobby and me, would you and Quinn be willing to raise our child, become the baby's adopted parents? Since neither of us has any siblings there's no family to take on that kind of responsibility – or at least no one we'd *want* to take on that kind of responsibility. It would mean a lot to us to know Baby Noland would be raised in a loving family if we weren't around.'

Kit knew I couldn't have children as a consequence of my accident. She also knew how hard it had been for me to come to terms with that realization, the invisible but deepest wound, the one that hurt the most and left the most scar tissue – at least, emotionally.

Our arms went around each other, and I whispered in her ear, 'Yes. Of course, we will. I need to talk to Quinn, but yes.'

'Thank you,' she said and wiped her eyes. 'When this pregnancy is over, I hope I get my old hormones back. Now

I weep over sad television commercials. The other day I bawled for half an hour when the SPCA showed a couple of dogs and cats that were up for adoption. You know, the ones with those long faces and mournful eyes that make you go "Awww." How pathetic am I?'

We both laughed half-heartedly and got into our cars. I left first because we were parked one behind the other on the narrow road so it was last-in, first-out. I navigated a couple of tight three-point turns so I didn't have to back the Jeep out on to Mosby's Highway. Kit was right behind me. At the end of Lemmons Bottom Road, we honked our horns and turned in opposite directions.

On the drive home I couldn't stop thinking about Eve. Whoever killed her was enraged beyond reason when he or she pushed her off the bridge. Maybe it was premeditated, maybe not. But there was no denying it was a crime of passion.

Over the years Bobby and I had talked about the motives that would provoke a person to commit murder. Again and again he said the reasons almost always boiled down to one of four things: love, revenge, money, and ideology. Then there were the secondary, or ancillary, motives: greed, obsession, jealousy, or a secret that must be kept at all costs.

What had provoked Eve's killer? If I were a man in love with a woman who was a total stunner like she was?

Jealousy.

I turned off Atoka Road on to Sycamore Lane at the entrance to the vineyard. It hadn't taken Bobby long to question Quinn. He flashed his lights as he headed toward me on his way out. I slowed down and when his car was opposite mine he powered down his window.

'Are you OK?' he asked. 'I know that scene at the bridge was tough to take. Kit went home and threw up.'

'I'm going to have a very stiff drink and pray I don't have nightmares,' I said. 'Whoever killed her was someone she knew, Bobby. Meaning it was probably someone *we* know.'

'You got any idea who her enemies might be?'

'Talk to Kit. She was working on a story about a bunch of vineyard owners – including us – who were upset at her and Jackson and Richard for selling us vines we believe they

knew were diseased,' I said. 'We're all out a lot of money –
I'm talking about hundreds of thousands of dollars. That
means people were angry, but what would killing her
accomplish? It wouldn't get anyone's money back.'

'Anybody in particular who was especially angry with
her?'

I thought about Otto and his meltdown in the Goose Creek
Inn bar. 'Nothing that was directed specifically at Eve. Jackson
owns the nursery. So why her?'

'Good question. I intend to find out.' Bobby drummed his
fingers on the steering wheel. 'How upset with Eve were Carly
and Grace when you talked to them this morning?'

'Upset. But if they were angry that she was going to leave
after their husbands did so much for her career, pushing her
off a bridge wouldn't help them, either. They'd be better off
trying to talk her into staying. Besides . . .'

'Besides what?'

'Doesn't this seem to you like a crime a man would
commit?'

Grace was a little bit of a thing. And Carly, the Deputy
Director of the Bureau of National Intelligence? A powerful
woman in a powerful job. I couldn't imagine her doing
something like that. The remaining suspects were all men.

Bobby was watching me. 'I try never to make up my mind
before I have all the facts, kiddo. You can really screw up an
investigation if you do.'

'You always say that.'

'I rarely regret it.'

'What about Eve's car?'

'What about it?'

'Do you think there were two cars at Lemmons Bottom
Road – hers and someone else's? And then after she was dead
the killer had to hide Eve's? Or did she drive her killer to the
site of her own death?'

'Either way, her car's somewhere – because it's not in her
driveway, nor is it in the parking lot at Landau's. My guess
is it's not far from the bridge. Probably off the side of a
road, some place it wouldn't be obvious. Unless you were
specifically looking for it.'

'I hope you find who killed her,' I said. 'I just don't want it to be someone I know.'

Though somehow I didn't think I would get my wish.

'Oh, I'm going to find her killer,' Bobby said, his voice grim. 'You bet your life I am. Though I'm going with Occam's Razor.'

I knew what that was: the simplest, most logical explanation for what happened and why was usually the correct one. No stranger slithered into Middleburg and spirited Eve off to the Goose Creek Bridge – willingly – before shoving her off the parapet to her death.

'Well, at least you know Quinn didn't do it,' I said.

Bobby gave me an inscrutable smile. 'See you, Lucie.'

He powered up his window and drove off.

Which left me with the uneasy feeling that maybe he hadn't ruled out Quinn as a suspect after all.

Quinn had a head start on me alcohol-wise when I got to the house a few minutes later. The moment I walked through the door he handed me a Scotch on the rocks that was light on rocks. He also told me Pépé had gone over to Toby's for a guys-only dinner and a game of Go, a complicated Chinese board game vaguely resembling chess. Robyn was dining at the Red Fox Inn with the organizers of Foxes on the Fence and Art in the 'Burg for a combination post-mortem and celebration of another successful year.

So we had the house to ourselves. Persia Fleming, our housekeeper and cook, had left everything ready for dinner before she'd gone back to her apartment above Eli's office in the carriage house. I checked the fridge: chicken in a garlicky marinade ready to be grilled, a tossed salad with a bottle of her homemade buttermilk dressing, and because she had a sweet spot for Quinn, his favorite rice and peas – which was actually rice and red kidney beans – a traditional dish from her native Jamaica.

We ate dinner on the veranda and watched the sun set behind the Blue Ridge. Hamish had built Highland House precisely for this western view; two hundred and fifty years later, Quinn and I never tired of watching it, just as Hamish must have done. Especially on nights like this – full fireworks – as the long slender clouds strafing the sky turned red, then orange and gold, and finally a deep shade of iridescent indigo as the sun sank behind the mountains. When it was dark, I lit two chubby white pillar candles sitting in wrought-iron candle holders on the table. Quinn got up to get more wine for us and his evening cigar.

Finally he said what I knew had been on his mind all evening.

'I might have been able to save her if I had gotten there earlier.'

'You don't even know when she left. And you showed up when she asked you to come. So don't,' I said. 'Just don't.'

'I have a feeling Bobby thinks I'm holding something back.'

The admission caught me off guard. *Was he?*

'What makes you think that?'

'His questions were very pointed and probing.'

'Well, they would be. That's just Bobby being a detective. And it is a murder investigation.'

'It was something more than that.'

'You aren't, are you? Holding something back?'

He was still looking out at the mountains, his profile to me so I couldn't see his eyes in the flickering, golden candlelight.

'Of course not, why would I be?'

'You tell me.'

'I'm *not*. You do believe me.' He turned to me. 'Right?'

'Of course I do.'

'Good.'

'Kit told me Bobby just started reading all the Sherlock Holmes stories. Do you know what his favorite quote is?'

'"Watson, the game's afoot"?'

'Good guess, but no. It's this one: "When you have eliminated the impossible, whatever remains, however improbable, must be the truth,"' I said. 'So because of the timeline, you're automatically eliminated from anything to do with Eve's murder. It's impossible you could have been in two places at once. And as improbable as it seems, Eve must have known and trusted her killer well enough to go to the bridge with him. Which means that's the truth.'

'You're so sure it's a guy?'

I held out my wine glass and let him refill it with the Washington State Pinot Grigio we'd drunk with dinner. 'I don't see a woman committing a crime like that, do you? Eve was pretty fit. She could fight off someone who was her size, her weight. Besides, there was no indication she'd been dragged there, so it seems she went willingly to an out-of-the-way place. I think it has "assignation" or "tryst" stamped all over it.'

He sat back in his chair and puffed on his cigar. 'A clandestine meeting with a lover that went all wrong?'

'Quinn, it's *Eve*. Was Eve. Why do you think she was Jackson's secret weapon? She crooked her little finger and every male in two counties wanted to do business with her. With Landau's. Every man she dealt with was crazy about her.'

'Don't say present company included.'

'I don't need to.'

Even in the gray velvet darkness I could see his cheeks redden. 'You know I love you. Want to marry you. Want to spend the rest of my life with you.'

'I know that. It doesn't mean you're not human. She was beautiful.'

'I wish I knew why she wanted to talk to me. And why I had to keep our meeting a secret from Jackson and Richard and you.'

'I don't know and now you'll never know,' I said. 'You're going to have to let it go.'

He blew out a perfect smoke ring. 'I wonder if it had something to do with the reason she was murdered.'

I wondered that, too. Because if it did, that meant Eve wanted Quinn to be involved in whatever it was, wanted him to keep her secrets.

Which also meant that even though he wasn't a suspect in Eve's murder, Bobby might still come circling back to Quinn as he looked for her killer.

ELEVEN

Word went around Atoka and Middleburg faster than a scandal gone viral on social media that Kit and I had discovered Eve Kerr's body at Goose Creek Bridge. That is the way of small towns: everyone knows everything about anything that just happened in a matter of minutes. Phone calls, texts, emails, an encounter at the General Store or the post office – the information flows from one person to the next and the next, invariably embellished in the retelling.

Before long I was letting the calls on my mobile go straight to voicemail, as well as ignoring the text messages that kept popping up like bad weeds after rain. By the time I went to bed I wouldn't have been surprised if the next caller didn't get a 'voice mailbox full' message. I just wasn't ready to talk about what had happened or answer questions.

Quinn and I both slept badly, each for our own reasons. He talked in his sleep, mostly gibberish, but a frown creased his forehead and I knew he was arguing with someone, angry and upset. As for me, I was convinced I heard noises outside under our window – something rustling, *footsteps*. But each time I checked no dark form emerged from the insubstantial shadows of the bushes and our flower-filled garden. The third time it happened I wondered if I was going crazy, spooking myself, imagining that whoever was out there might be Eve's killer.

Kit and I had discovered Eve's body less than twenty-four hours after her death. I was fairly sure the killer hadn't bargained on that happening. Otherwise why pick such a desolate, deserted place to commit a murder? We must have upset someone's plans.

And, footsteps or no footsteps, that gave me the creeps.

When I woke up on Sunday morning, Quinn was gone and I smelled coffee downstairs. I hadn't even realized he'd gotten up. I found his note propped against the coffee maker: *Decided to get an early start on repairing the last few trellises, I love you.* Which was his way of telling me he needed some time and space alone.

I love Quinn to distraction with one glaring flaw: when he made the morning coffee it could be used to fill potholes. Or maybe serve as rocket fuel for the next mission taking supplies to the International Space Station. On the other hand, he thought my coffee was as thin as dirty dishwater and tasted as bad, so there you are. We've had a deal that has kept our relationship mostly harmonious ever since he moved in, which is that the first one up can make the coffee and the other one doesn't get to bitch about it. I solved that problem fairly neatly a few months ago by adding a second coffeemaker to our wedding registry. So after our wedding next week: his and her coffee makers. Of course we could have just *bought* a second coffee maker ages ago, but that's not the point.

I picked up the coffee pot and smelled boiled tar. Quinn wasn't around. I was about to break our sacred rule and dump out what was there to make a fresh pot when my mobile rang, the ring tone I have for Eli.

'Hey,' he said, 'did I wake you?'

'No, I was just about to make coffee.'

'Have you seen the *Trib* this morning?'

One of the few texts I'd looked at last night had been from Kit who told me she'd written Eve's story, which was going to land on the front page of the Metro section of the *Washington Tribune* Sunday print edition. Above the fold, she'd said, meaning it was a big deal. It was also splashed all over their website, along with a photo of Eve, alive and well and looking impossibly beautiful. Which meant the story was sure to make national headlines, maybe even the tabloids and those entertainment news shows that thrived on sensational or lurid stories like this one. *Murder and mystery in Virginia's tony horse and hunt country: Beautiful blonde pushed to her death off remote Civil War battle site bridge tragically drowns in historic Goose Creek.*

'I haven't had a chance to read the paper yet,' I said to Eli, but I knew he was talking about Kit's story.

'I didn't know you and Kit found Eve Kerr's body at Goose Creek,' he said. 'I had no idea she was dead.'

'Eli, what cave have you been living in since yesterday?' I asked. 'Everyone from here to Richmond knows about it.'

'I've been in my studio since four o'clock yesterday afternoon trying to finish a job for a client,' he said and yawned.

'You pulled an all-nighter? You never went home?'

'I took a few breaks to walk around outside trying to clear my head and get the kinks out, but otherwise I've been here all night.'

'Did you walk around the house, by any chance? Around back, that is?'

'Yup. Why? Don't tell me I woke you up. I'm wearing sneakers. I practically tiptoed.'

'You scared the wits out of me.'

'I didn't mean to. Jeez, Luce, you have ears like a bat. I don't know how you could have heard me.'

'I don't know either, but I did. If I make coffee, do you want to stop by for a cup before you go home?'

'I've got some that's already made and it's not that old. Why don't you come over here? Besides, I've got something I want to show you.'

Coffee that wouldn't taste like mud.

'I'll be right there.'

When Eli and my niece Hope had moved back in with me after his divorce from his first wife, he decided to start his own architectural design firm and we agreed that the carriage house would make the perfect studio. Since the quid pro quo for paying no rent had been that he would design and supervise a renovation of the winery, it also meant he was on site to oversee the construction work once it started. Then when I hired Persia as our full-time housekeeper – and later part-time babysitter for Hope when she wasn't at daycare – Eli turned the upper level into a cozy apartment, so Persia had her own place, which she loved.

My brother was still hunched over his drafting table when I let myself into his studio a few minutes later. Although he did most of his work on the computer, he was a gifted artist like our mother and Mia and still liked to do some of his drawings for his clients by hand. He stretched like a cat after a nap when he saw me and picked up his coffee cup. I'd given it to him for Christmas one year. *World's Okayest Architect.* He looked tired; dark disheveled hair, stubble that was a couple of days old, and hooded eyes. He got up and walked over to the coffee pot, filling his mug and one for me.

I got the one that said: *Because I'm the Architect, That's Why.*

'What did you want to show me?' I asked.

'This.' He walked back to his drafting table and fished something out from under a pile of drawings. A piece of paper with the stamp of the Loudoun County Court Clerk on it. 'Look what came yesterday. I drove over to Leesburg and did my thing in front of the judge. Got permission to marry you and Quinn after I posted my $500 bond.'

For better or worse, Virginia was one of those loosey-goosey states where just about anyone – friend, family member, neighbor, your mailman if you wanted him to – could marry any couple, as in perform the wedding ceremony, if he or she got a one-time temporary authorization after going in front of a judge to get permission. It was a law that had been on the books for a hundred years and was receiving more and more attention. I couldn't imagine getting married in a church since neither Quinn nor I were religious. Going before a justice of the peace who didn't know us also wasn't appealing. When we talked about who might marry us, Eli said, 'What about me?'

The only caveat with having my brother perform our ceremony was that he had exactly five days after the wedding to drop off the completed marriage certificate at the clerk's office. Otherwise, he'd forfeit his $500 bond. And Quinn and I wouldn't actually be married. He had sworn on a stack of Bibles that there was no way he'd forget, no matter how busy he was with work.

I took the paper he handed me and ran my thumb over the embossed stamp of the County Clerk. 'This is great. Thanks for doing this.'

'No problemo. Though do you think you could get Frankie to ease up on hyper-planning this wedding? I'm not going to screw up, I promise. Although just for the rehearsal I could do my Peter Cook *Princess Bride* wedding scene imitation. Hope *loves* that movie. I've seen it so often I can recite it in my sleep. Plus I'm pretty good at it, if I do say so myself.' He flashed a wicked grin. '"*Mawage is wot bwings us togevah today.*"'

I burst out laughing. 'That's hilarious, but Frankie would have a coronary if you said that.'

'And your point is?'

'Eli.'

'I'm just joking. I'll stick to the script.'

'Thank you.'

He pulled up a stool next to his drafting table, gesturing for me to sit, and plopped down on his own stool, suddenly serious. 'Tell me about yesterday. What happened?'

I told him, leaving out the more graphic details about the state of decomposition of Eve's body.

'Who would want to kill her?' he asked when I was finished. 'She was a knockout, a real stunner. Not to mention she was a nice person.'

'I don't know who would have done it,' I said. 'A lot of vineyard owners are mad at Landau's and we're blaming them for selling us diseased vines.'

'You think her death had to do with business? You don't think this was personal? Like a lover's quarrel gone really wrong? We *are* talking about Eve Kerr, Luce.'

I thought about what Frankie had said about Eve and Fabrice being a relatively recent couple. And wondered if that relationship had caused any jealousy among any of Eve's other admirers.

'Sounds like you have an opinion,' I said. 'Is it based on something you know?'

Eli set down his empty coffee cup on top of a sheet of bumwad, the nearly transparent paper architects laid over their drawings so they could sketch alterations or changes for the client to see the new design. He picked up a mechanical pencil and started doodling.

'Not really. But you know how people talk.'

'In other words, you've heard whatever gossip is emanating from the General Store.'

'You've got to admit the Romeos do get around.'

'And their consensus is?'

'There is no consensus. But there are a lot of possibilities. A lot of guys had the hots for Eve.'

My phone rang. I pulled it out of the pocket of my jeans. The little red numbers on the display reminded me of all the calls I hadn't returned, along with the unanswered text messages, all asking about Eve.

This call I was going to take.

'It's Kit,' I said to Eli.

Years ago my brother and Kit had dated and when they'd broken up it had been epic. To this day they'd never totally patched things up between them.

He shrugged. 'Answer it.'

I did. 'Hey, sweetie, what's up? How are you feeling today?'

'Luce. I have news.'

That wasn't going to be good.

'The baby . . .?'

'Is fine. Bobby just called. They found Eve's car.'

Eli's eyebrows went up when I mentioned the baby. He pointed to his stomach and mimed a protruding baby bump, mouthing *she's pregnant?* and I nodded.

'Where?' I asked.

'On Crenshaw Road.'

Crenshaw Road was directly across from Lemmons Bottom Road. It was paved for a bit and then turned to gravel. Because the creek ran alongside, when it rained hard the road washed out, a not-infrequent occurrence. It was also almost always deserted, though a couple of miles down the road was Slater Run, a pretty family-owned vineyard that sat on the crest of a hill.

'Where on Crenshaw?'

'In a bunch of bushes, so it wouldn't be easy to spot. Maybe about half a mile down the road from the turnoff at Mosby's Highway. You'll love this irony. It was right next to the creek, practically in it.'

Almost like Eve.

'Obviously Eve didn't leave it there,' I said. 'Her killer did. Any clues about him?'

'No. None at all.' She sounded worried. 'Bobby told me the car was wiped clean. Not a single print, not even Eve's. Even the back of the rearview mirror was clean, plus all the other usual careless places. Nothing, nada.'

'Someone was thorough.'

'Yeah,' she said. 'A pro. Someone who knew what they were doing.'

'Now what?'

'They're checking her house, her office at Landau's. Looking for . . . anything. Oh, and Win ought to finish the autopsy today.'

'That should be pretty straightforward, don't you think?'

'I do. Though Bobby always says you don't know until you know.'

That sounded like a Bobbyism. 'When you find out, will you let me know?'

'Sure,' she said and disconnected.

Eli was watching me. He ran both hands through his hair so it stuck straight up making him look like a wild man. 'That is sick,' he said. 'Someone shoved Eve off a bridge and then stashed her car on Crenshaw Road. Who would do something like that?'

'I don't know. Someone who was pretty calculating and thorough.'

Eli had finished the doodle on his bumwad while I'd been talking to Kit. A quick rough sketch of a beautiful woman. Unmistakably Eve.

Her mouth was open in a round 'O' of horror and her eyes were wide with terror.

'Tell me,' David Phelps said, holding up his phone and showing me Frankie's familiar-looking list of photos, 'is this wedding going to be a bigger deal than an opening ceremony for the Olympics? Because I happen to have photographed a couple of them.'

We were standing in the circular driveway in front of

Highland House and he was unloading gear from the back of his SUV. He pointed to the carving above the front door of a woman holding an anchor in one hand and a severed head in the other. The Montgomery family crest.

'I'm ready for it. Just like that warrior chick up there,' he said.

When Hamish Montgomery built the house in the late 1700s, he had a stonemason carve our family crest into the lintel. After two and a half centuries the woman's features were mottled with lichen and softened by age and the elements, but it wasn't hard to imagine that she had once looked fierce – especially holding that severed head. Above her were the words *Garde Bien*. Our family motto.

Watch well. Watch out for us. *We mean business.*

I sighed. 'You've obviously heard from Frankie. Again.'

'I have editors at *NatGeo* and *Smithsonian* who are less demanding.'

'I'm sorry. I'll talk to her. She just wants everything to be perfect.' I leaned in and he bent down so we could exchange kisses. 'You know how grateful Quinn and I are that you're our wedding photographer.'

'I'd be insulted if you asked someone else.'

He had shown up at four o'clock for a quick run through of Frankie's list of 'must-have' shots and anyone we specifically wanted to be photographed. He also wanted to do his homework, take his own test photos and discover where the light and shadows fell in the slanted golden sunshine of a late-May afternoon.

Photography, as I'd been learning from him, wasn't about luck or that you just happened to be standing in the right place at the right time when the perfect shot appeared in your viewfinder. It was about research and planning and patience and waiting and waiting and sometimes waiting some more.

He yawned and I said, 'You're tired. This won't take long. We've made some changes to the garden. I wanted you to see it before Saturday.'

He covered his mouth, stifling another yawn. 'Don't worry, I'm good. I just wrapped up a book project, so I've been blitzing up and down I-95 between D.C. and Richmond. That drive is a total misery.'

It was. Traffic. Construction. Accidents. Too many cars on the road.

'I've also pulled an all-nighter or two,' he added and I thought of Eli and his all-nighters and how odd it was to keep discovering similarities between a brother I hadn't known existed until a few months ago and me and my siblings.

'What book project?' I asked.

We walked over to a gate that led to the side yard. It was set into a brick wall where a climbing purple clematis was in full bloom. David lifted the wrought-iron latch and held the gate open so I could go through first.

'The Confederate monuments,' he said. 'I'd already been photographing them for a different project. Then when Black Lives Matter got so much momentum a couple of summers ago and protestors started spray painting graffiti and defacing those statues – especially the ones on Monument Avenue in Richmond – I went back so I could photograph them being toppled over and carted off.'

He said, sounding almost smug, 'I got the only photographs of the Silent Sentinel being taken down. That happened in the dead of night. No one was happy about me being there, but I said I wasn't trespassing or doing anything illegal and they had no right to stop me.'

The Silent Sentinel was a statue of a young Confederate soldier that had stood for years in front of the courthouse in Leesburg, where Eli had just gone to get his temporary marriage license for our wedding. From one day to the next, the statue vanished. All that was left was an empty plinth and no official explanation about why it had disappeared so precipitously or how it had been removed.

I wondered if David would have gotten less pushback if the color of his skin was more like my father's than his mother's. And then decided that was a dumb thing to wonder.

Of course he would.

'How'd you find out?' I asked.

'Some folks thought it shouldn't go undocumented.'

'Some folks you can't name?'

'Some folks I won't name.'

'I didn't know you were taking photos of the monuments,' I said as we walked down a flagstone path lined with beds of yellow, white, and purple irises.

The irises were lovely when they were in bloom, but they never lasted long; their beauty was fleeting. The subject we were talking about had been around for more than a century. It was old and complicated and ugly.

'I didn't bring it up because I didn't know how you'd feel about it.'

It was a loaded statement. I stopped walking and turned to face him.

'What do you mean?'

'Most of the Civil War monuments are in Virginia. *Were* in Virginia. It's a powder-keg issue, Lucie, you know that. Plenty of people have come to blows over it. Your family . . . *my* family . . . on Leland's side fought for the Confederacy,' he said. 'You told me our ancestors – the Montgomerys – owned slaves. My mother's ancestors *were* slaves.'

'I'm not my ancestors,' I said, though I felt the weight of all of them settling on me just now. 'I'm me. Did you really think we couldn't talk about this? David, you're my brother.'

'I brought you an advanced reader's copy of the book. And I'd *like* to talk to you about it,' he said.

'Good,' I said. 'I'm glad.'

'Before we do that, I need to see what you've done to your garden. And I need a model, so you get to be the bride.'

'All right, I'll be the bride.'

For the past few weeks I'd been working flat out with a crew from Seely's to transform the overgrown bushes and tired-looking garden beds in our backyard into a beautiful setting for our wedding ceremony. Parker Lord, a landscape designer who had been close friends with my mother, had planned it down to the last detail – his wedding gift to us – shortly before his recent death. Over the years he had renovated gardens and given advice to the White House, the Capitol, Mount Vernon, Hillwood, Dumbarton Oaks, the National Botanic Garden, Monticello . . . the list went on. I knew our garden was going to be amazing when we were done.

It was.

Besides, here in the Old Dominion where we abide by the Four Sacraments of the South – kinship, civility, tradition, and hospitality – our gardens are not just for show. They are places to entertain, extensions of our homes. Although truth be told, we do show them off during Historic Garden Week, an event that has taken place like clockwork every single April since 1927. We call it 'America's Largest Open House' and it's sponsored by garden clubs throughout the Commonwealth. As the name implies, it goes on for a week and the money goes for – what else? Renovating and caring for Virginia's historic gardens, some of which are among the oldest in the country.

David stopped walking when he saw ours. I had told him we were doing some sprucing up, but I hadn't elaborated.

'*Wow.* You didn't tell me it was going to look like *this*. This is *gorgeous*, Lucie. I mean it.'

His praise meant a lot. He'd photographed national parks and beautiful places all over the world. He knew what he was looking at.

'Thank you. It was a lot of work, but it was worth it. We're keeping it a surprise for the wedding. You're the first person to see it like this.'

'I can't believe Frankie, who leaves absolutely nothing to chance, who wants everything planned to the nanosecond, didn't order you to tell me about it.'

I laughed. 'It's still my wedding and I swore her to secrecy. I wanted you to see it when everything was blooming, when it looked perfect.'

'You got your wish. I wasn't ready for this. I'd been figuring I'd keep my shots tight or else use a fast lens with a wide aperture to get a lot of bokeh, you know, keep the background sort of out-of-focus. Looks like I won't need to do that now.' He set his equipment bag down and began taking pictures as he walked around the garden. 'I love the arbor. It's a perfect place for the ceremony.'

'I love it, too.'

It was new, my favorite addition to the garden. White lattice with a slatted arched roof and two benches that faced each other. We'd planted Our Lady of Guadalupe pink hybrid tea roses on either side because of their fragrance and because they were good climbers. The rest of the garden was just as beautiful. Parker had told me he wanted it to appear as if it had evolved naturally over the years rather than 'Look what we just did to the garden.'

We'd kept all of the established trees – an enormous saucer magnolia near the veranda, two tulip magnolias, a Yoshino cherry, and a crimson crepe myrtle my mother had planted near the summerhouse. There was also a hillside at the back of the property that was thick with blooming rhododendrons and azaleas in shades of red and white. We added new roses to my mother's beloved rose garden, filling it out, plus Parker designed a butterfly garden with a small pond at my request because my mother loved butterflies and had always said they symbolized the immortality of the soul.

For the next half-hour I stood where David asked me to stand, turned when he asked me to turn, and smiled when he asked me to smile. When he was done, he showed me the pictures on his camera's LCD screen.

'I'm not photogenic,' I said. 'What did you do to make me look so good?'

'Nothing,' he said. 'You did it. And you *are* photogenic.'

'You're a magician. It wasn't me.'

He grinned. 'Come on. Let's go see where you're having the reception. Have you got any surprises there I should know about?'

'It's still the Ruins. No changes. No surprises.'

We took his car. On the drive over he asked if the nursery that provided the plants for the garden was the same one where Eve Kerr had worked. His way of bringing up the subject of her murder. He'd obviously heard about it on the news. By this point, who hadn't?

'Landau's sells only to farms and vineyards. We worked with Seely's, the other nursery in town,' I said. 'Are you going to ask me about Eve or just dance around the subject?'

He smiled and looked rueful. 'Well, obviously I've been wondering. I wasn't sure how you felt talking about it. It must have been awful finding her like that.'

'It was.'

'You OK?'

'I don't know. It was such a shock. I still can't imagine who could have killed her in such a brutal way.'

'Any ideas?' he asked.

'None I like,' I said as he pulled up next to the Ruins and stopped the car. 'She very likely knew her killer since she died there and not somewhere else, which means it's probably someone from around here.'

'My God,' he said. 'I'm so sorry.'

'Bobby's looking for him. He'll find out who did it.'

'What else?'

'What do you mean?'

'Something's bothering you.'

I wanted to say nothing was bothering me, but he was giving me a look that said: *And don't try denying it, either.*

I tried, anyway. 'What makes you think that?'

'Oh, come on. I'm your brother.'

I told him that Eve had asked Quinn to come by the afternoon she disappeared and to keep quiet about it. Which he had done.

'She didn't give him any idea what she wanted to talk about?'

'Nope. I'm wondering now if maybe she wanted to tell him she was planning to leave.'

David's eyes narrowed. 'Were they . . . *good* friends?'

I knew what he meant. 'Not that way – I mean, I'm *marrying* him in a week. Apparently she was involved with the winemaker at La Vigne. Fabrice Gilbert, the grandson of our first winemaker.'

He nodded, digesting that information. 'But it still bothers you.'

'I guess it still does.'

'Quinn loves you, Lucie. Anybody can see it in the way he looks at you, how he lights up when you're around. You don't know what she wanted to talk to him about and now you'll never know. Don't let it eat at you, especially right now.'

'I know.'

'Come on,' he said, stirring. 'Let me take some more photos

of you while the light's still good. And forget the other stuff, OK? It's not worth it.'

I wanted to believe him. It really wasn't worth it.

Really.

He took photos as he'd done in the garden and I posed for him again. When he was finished, the two of us were standing on what had once been the main floor of the old house. Next week it would be a dance floor where we would celebrate our marriage with our families and closest friends. There would be music and laughter and wine and food catered by the Goose Creek Inn on a moonlit night and it would be magical.

'Do you know where the slaves who worked for your family – our family – lived?' David asked.

The question, abrupt and out of the blue, took my breath away. We had never discussed that subject before. First the Confederate monuments. Now the family slaves. I wondered if he had asked because he thought they might have lived right here in this house. Right here where we were standing. On our dance floor.

'I don't know where they lived, but I do know it wasn't this house. We have all the papers and documents about the people who did live here. Eli discovered a rundown cabin a few months ago that we know was used as a stop on the Underground Railroad. It's possible it was also the home of the family who worked here as our slaves.'

'I'd like to photograph it, if you don't mind.'

'Of course.'

'I'm also planning to photograph the Goose Creek Bridge.'

I gave him a sideways look.

'I thought maybe you could come with me,' he added.

'David—'

'You took me there the first time we met. You told me that place has always been your sanctuary, where you and Kit went – still go – to talk out stuff you need to get out of your system,' he said. 'You went there on Saturday, so it must have been for a special reason. You weren't expecting to find Eve.'

'No,' I said in a low voice. 'We weren't.'

'So?' He kept his voice gentle, not really pushing now, but he wanted an answer.

'Kit wanted to tell me she was pregnant.'

He looked as though his heart had just split open. 'Aw, Jesus. You found out about her baby *then*?'

'Yes.'

'You have to go back, Lucie. Go with me.'

'I don't know . . . I don't know if I could do that yet.'

'You can. The sooner the better, to get past it.'

'Can I think about it?'

'Sure. But you know I'm right.'

It was after five and in the fading light the view of the Blue Ridge Mountains softened as if it had been filtered through a gauze curtain.

David lifted his camera to his eye again and took more photos. 'I love photographing these mountains because of all the different shades of blue, all the layers,' he said. 'The Blue Ridge always seem to be kind of mystical to me because of that blue haze.'

'I love them, too,' I said. 'Although the reason they look blue is because the trees give off a hydrocarbon to protect themselves from really hot days and the heat of the sun.'

'Seriously?'

'It's called isoprene. When it's released into the air, it mixes with other molecules and that's what produces the blue haze.'

'I almost wish I didn't know that.'

'Sorry. I didn't mean to burst your romantic bubble. You can still think of them as mystical. I do.'

He grinned. 'I think I've got everything I need for today. Next time it's the real deal. Your wedding.'

I smiled. 'I know.'

'Come on, I'll drop you at the house,' he said.

'Can you stay for a drink? A glass of wine? Pépé would love to see you. So would Quinn.'

'I'd like that,' he said. 'But just a quick one. I've got to drive back to Georgetown and get some work done tonight.'

'Great,' I said. 'I'll text them.'

For someone six years away from a century old, my grandfather was pretty quick to reply to texts. Pépé said he'd have a bottle of wine opened and ready for us when we got there.

Quinn said he was wrapping up something in the barrel room with Antonio and would be along soon.

When we were sitting in David's car again, he turned to me. 'Don't worry about anything, OK? Everything's going to work out fine.'

I wasn't sure what he was talking about – Eve's murder, what she had wanted to talk to Quinn about that last day, or the wedding. But I said, 'I won't. I know it will.'

No one knew who had murdered Eve so savagely at the Goose Creek Bridge. Media interest in her death was already intense, hyped, and sensationalized because of where it had happened and the fact that the victim was a stunning young woman who should have had her life ahead of her. My fiancé might have been one of the last persons to see her alive. Maybe even the next-to-last.

In spite of what I'd just told David, I didn't think everything was going to work out fine.

What I really thought was there would be more to come.

TWELVE

As promised, my grandfather was waiting for us on the veranda, sitting in the wicker loveseat reading *Le Monde* on his iPad, his glasses perched low on his nose, and a bottle of wine chilling in a silver bucket next to him. Four pale-blue Biot glasses were placed next to the bucket.

Pépé started to get up when he saw David, but David was quicker and got to his side first. 'Don't get up, Luc, please. It's good to see you again.'

They exchanged kisses on the cheek – David was getting used to our French ways by now – and then he joined me on the glider across from my grandfather.

He unzipped a satchel he'd brought from his car and pulled out a slim, soft-covered book that he handed to me. His book on the Confederate monuments. The cover was simple and stark. White words on an all-black background: *The Monuments of the Lost Cause.*

The Lost Cause of the Confederacy. It was the southern explanation of what the Civil War had really been about: the issue of states' rights. *Not* about slavery. That the states could make their own decisions about contentious issues – such as slavery, for example – and not be bossed around by the federal government. Truth be told, it was a rather romanticized reimagining long after the war was over: although the South had lost, its cause had been noble and just, a valiant battle against Northern Aggression to preserve the chivalric values of the Antebellum South.

As for the monuments, most of them had been erected in the late 1890s and early 1900s, decades after the last battle had been fought, during a period marked by racial segregation that was known as the Jim Crow era. The statues were not so much about memorializing Confederate war heroes, but a reminder that the Lost Cause lived on. That it hadn't been forgotten. Virginia, the capital of the Confederacy, had erected more statues than any other state – hundreds of them – as well as naming roads, schools, and public places for Lee, Stonewall, Stuart, and the others. The northern states took a different view of what the war had been about – that it most *definitely* was about slavery.

The photographs in David's book took my breath away, they were so intense and angry. Close-ups of the graffiti, a lot of profanity, covering the statues of Southern generals and war heroes, most of whom had graced Monument Avenue in Richmond for over a century, now paint-splattered in gaudy cartoonish colors. David had taken multiple pictures of the same monuments over time, so it was possible to see the evolution of the first words, epithets, and images which then disappeared underneath layer upon layer of paint and more graffiti until the final result looked like an angry explosion of color. The red paint looked – as it was meant to – like blood.

Pépé silently uncorked the wine and filled three glasses. 'Are those your photographs, David?' he asked.

'They are.'

I passed him the book and my grandfather handed each of us a glass of wine. We said *santé* and drank and then Pépé set his glass down and slowly looked through David's book.

When he was finished, he said, 'These are extraordinarily moving. It's a powerful book.'

'Thank you.' He glanced at me. 'What about you, Lucie? What do you think?'

'I'm . . . stunned. Your photographs are very, very good, David. You're incredibly talented.'

He gave me a slight smile and nodded. I knew why. I'd only talked about the photos, not the reason he took them or what they represented.

'When will the book be out?' I asked.

'This summer. July third, actually. My editor wants the publication date to coincide with the anniversary – more or less – of the statues being pulled down. And, uh, Independence Day. He's big on irony.'

A release date that was timed to make an impact. A statement. On the back flap were David's bio as the photographer and the bio of the author, along with their photos. One white man, one black man.

'Are you and the author going to tour for this book?'

'We are.'

'Are either of you worried about . . . people . . . showing up at your book signings who might not be fans?'

'No.'

I wanted to shout: *You should be!* And: *Please be careful!* But he already knew the risks he was taking. He might not be scared, but I was scared for him. By the Fourth of July the searing summer heat could make a lethal cocktail with edgy reckless folks and a hot-button subject like the Confederate monuments. Put them together – shake, don't stir – and you could get something that could spin out of control before you knew what hit you. The Charlottesville riots had happened on a scorcher of a night in August.

'So what do you think?' David said, shifting the conversation away from my escalating concerns about his safety. 'Should those monuments have been pulled down? Or left as they were?'

I'd told him I wanted to have an honest conversation, so here it was. Fish or cut bait. Put up or shut up.

'I'm kind of all over the place,' I said. 'Which I know isn't an answer. But I'm not trying to dodge your question, either. First, it's a moot point whether they should have been pulled down or not, because they were. Some people say removing them was erasing history – for better or worse. Plus now you have the problem of what to do with them. You can't just throw a tarp over a thirteen-ton statue of Robert E. Lee and stick him on someone's back lot. And there's also the question of where do we stop – what other monuments need to be removed, *should* be removed? Do we want to take down the Washington Monument and the Jefferson Memorial because both George Washington and Thomas Jefferson owned slaves?'

I stopped talking and reached for my wine. David gave me a steady look. I couldn't tell if he was disappointed or not in what I'd said.

'Is your answer you don't know?'

'My answer is it's complicated. Especially growing up in Virginia, which makes it personal. I guess I'm still working through how I feel about it, mostly about what we do now.'

He turned to my grandfather. 'What about you, Luc? You're from France, so this isn't your battle. What do you think?'

Pépé leaned back against the sofa cushions. He'd just turned ninety-four. On this last trip to America, he'd looked wearier and more diminished than I'd ever seen him and it worried me.

'France has its own battles, David,' he said. 'America is not alone facing national moral issues. France's ugly scar is the collaborationists who helped the Vichy government, the people who helped Nazi Germany during World War II. Do we airbrush that awful stain from our history as if it didn't happen? It's never easy.'

'What you're saying is that history is written by the victors,' David said.

'Ah, yes. Winston Churchill. Napoleon said something similar but much more cynical: that history is a set of lies that are agreed upon. One of the many differences between the way the English and the French see life.'

'I never heard that statement by Napoleon,' I said. 'Do you think it's true?'

'Surprisingly, I am more Churchillian,' Pépé said as he picked up the wine bottle. David placed his hand over the bowl of his glass and shook his head, so Pépé refilled my glass and then his own.

'Have either of you ever heard of Fallen Monument Park?' he asked.

I said, 'No,' as David said, 'I've heard of it but never seen it. It's in Moscow.'

One of my grandfather's diplomatic posts had been as the Chief of Mission, the number-two position, with the French Embassy in Moscow during the waning years of the Soviet Union.

'The park began as a dumping ground for the gigantic statues of Communist leaders that were pulled down during those last months before the Soviet Union ceased to exist in 1991,' he said. 'It was a vacant plot of land along the Moskva River. The new Russian government designated it as a sculpture park – which was a brilliant idea – and called it Muzeon. Now it's part of Gorky Park and it's extremely popular. But everyone still knows it as Fallen Monument Park. These days it has hundreds of statues of fairy-tale characters, literary figures, even abstract art. The result has been that the old Soviet statues have lost their power to intimidate, lost their symbolism – there are over seven hundred statues there now.'

'Do you think that's what we should do?' I asked. 'Put all of our statues in a huge outdoor park?'

'I don't know, but it's certainly a possibility. Russia isn't the only country that has done this,' he said. 'But what America does with its statues should be up to Americans. It should be a national decision and it should teach history and heal wounds.'

'Heal whose wounds?' None of us had heard Quinn, who had let himself on to the veranda through the back door to the house. 'What are you three talking about? You look as if you've just been to a funeral.'

'I'll tell you about it later,' I said.

'Sit down and have a glass of wine,' Pépé said and Quinn threw himself into a wicker chair next to me.

His eyes fell on David's book.

'May I?' he asked.

'Of course.'

My phone rang as he took Pépé's glass of wine and started to look through the book of photographs. I checked the display.

'It's Kit. I think I should take this. Would you all excuse me?'

They nodded as I got up and hit answer. 'Hey, what's up?'

'Luce,' she said, 'there's some news.'

We knew each other too well. It wasn't good.

'Give me a minute, OK?'

I walked to the far end of the veranda.

'What is it?'

'It's Eve. Win's autopsy turned up something. She was pregnant, not that far along. Bobby just told me.'

A baby. 'Oh my God, that changes everything.'

'I know.'

'Do you think she knew?'

'I don't know,' Kit said. 'She would have missed her period. Twice. She would have at least suspected she might be. Maybe she got careless. Or he did. And, of course, if she was dealing with morning sickness like I am, she would most definitely have realized it.'

Hard to argue with her.

'I wonder who the father was.'

'That's another matter entirely. Involving DNA and whether the father's DNA is in a database that Win has access to.'

'How long is that going to take to find out?'

'A few days,' she said. 'Win is not the only one in line.'

'I wonder if the father knew,' I said. 'Or who he was?'

'Who are the possibilities?'

'I heard she was seeing Fabrice.'

'The dishy Frenchman? Yeah, I could see that.'

'Or maybe it was someone else.'

'You mean, she was sleeping with more than one guy?'

'I don't know. Maybe.' It was Eve. Who could say? 'Whoever it was, she was discreet.'

'So who else does that leave?' Kit asked.

'Well, Vance was crazy about her, if you ask me, but maybe it was one way. And then there's always Richard. Or Jackson.'

'Two married men. Do you think it could be one of *them*?'

'I don't know.'

'If you're right, neither of them would want word to get out about her being pregnant.'

'No.' This wasn't going down a good road.

'I'm wondering if maybe she met the father to deliver the news at the bridge,' she said. 'Whoever he was.'

'And then he shoved her off the bridge and she died?' My nails dug into the wooden railing. So much for Frankie's manicure. 'And he walked away and left her there.'

'I know. I don't want to think about it, it's so awful,' Kit said. 'If she *wasn't* monogamous, I wonder if *she* knew who the father was.'

'Jesus,' I said. 'This just gets worse and worse. What a mess.'

I didn't say anything to Quinn, David, or Pépé about Kit's bombshell news when I joined them after her call, even though all three of them guessed something was up. I appreciated none of them asking me, although I knew Quinn and I were going to talk about it later this evening when it was just the two of us and we had some privacy.

David left not long afterwards and Pépé, Quinn, and I had dinner outside on the veranda. Quinn grilled salmon that Persia had marinated in lime, soy sauce, and garlic. She'd also made tabouli and left a vinaigrette to go on top of cold poached asparagus. Pépé threatened he was going to try to steal Persia away from us and invite her to go to Paris with him when he returned home after our wedding.

'I will make her an offer she can't refuse,' he said. 'After all, it's Paris.'

'She might be tempted,' I said. 'But please don't ask her to leave. I don't know how we ever got along without her. And, as you say, it *is* Paris. The city of wonderful restaurants

and fabulous food. You couldn't eat a bad meal anywhere if
you tried.'

'That,' my grandfather said with a smile, 'is true. Still,
Persia is a gem.'

'That she is. But hands off.'

'Are you OK, Lucie?' Quinn asked as the three of us sat
down together for dinner. 'You seem awfully quiet tonight.'

I wasn't ready to tell him about Kit's latest news, not yet.
Because it begged another question: was Eve going to tell
Quinn she was pregnant that last day when she wanted to see
him privately? And if so, why?

'Just thinking about David's book and the conversation
we had about the monuments,' I said and hoped he wouldn't
push.

'I'm sorry I missed it,' he said. 'His photographs were
incredible.'

A sudden sharp gust of wind whipped through the veranda
and set off the two sets of wind chimes that hung from
the ceiling so they sounded like a dissonant symphony. The
macrame hanging basket I'd bought at Art in the 'Burg and
filled with a lacy pink geranium swung back and forth like a
clock pendulum gone crazy. Quinn reached up to steady it
as I blew out the pillar candles so no spark would land on a
cushion or the wood floor.

'Where did that wind come from?' I said. 'It's going to rain
later. My left eye just started to pulse.'

Eli affectionately refers to me as the human barometer
because my eye is never wrong. It always pulses when there
is a sudden drop in air pressure and sometimes I end up
with a splitting headache. Usually those symptoms are
followed by a wicked rainstorm.

'We're in for a storm.' Quinn confirmed my unscientific
prediction. 'They changed the weather forecast. We're supposed
to get a lot of rain tonight with some wind.'

They. We lived and died by the weather forecast. We were
completely dependent on it as farmers – which, as vineyard
owners, is what we really are – so when the forecast was
wrong or changed suddenly, as apparently it had done today,
it could leave us scrambling. Quinn liked to grumble that

weather forecasters had that rare job where you could be *really* wrong – even more than once – and not get fired. Three inches of partly cloudy. The hurricane that sent everyone prepping for the end of the world and then went out to sea.

'I hope this storm doesn't bring too much wind, but rain will be good for the new gardens,' I said. 'It's been dry since the beginning of May. I won't have to water everything tomorrow like I've been doing every single day for the last few weeks. Which I won't exactly miss.'

Those were the orders from Seely's once the gardens were installed: daily watering for four to six weeks – depending on whether we had rain – until the plants were established. I'd been diligent.

The subject of Kit's call didn't come up again until Quinn and I were finishing the dishes in the kitchen. Pépé had stayed outside on the veranda to smoke one of his allotted Gauloises for the day – he allowed himself two cigarettes and only in the evening – while he watched the remnants of the sunset as the sky turned blue-black and the almost-full moon rose. My hard and fast rule: no tobacco in the house or else.

Quinn slipped a clean dishtowel around the back of my neck and pulled me to him. He bent down and gave me a long, deep kiss.

When he lifted his mouth from mine, he said, 'What did Kit tell you? You were pretty upset after you took that call.'

I pulled away so I could look him in the eye. 'Eve was pregnant when she died. Did you know?'

He removed the dishtowel and tugged on it with both hands so it looked like a rope. 'Jesus, no, I didn't know. Why would I?'

He sounded defensive. Plus now the rope was becoming a series of knots. He knew damn well why I thought he'd know.

'I'm just asking, that's all,' I said in an even voice. 'Maybe it's what she wanted to talk to you about the other day. Maybe she dropped a hint or said something when you two stayed behind at the Cab Franc block.'

Now it was a very tight cord. 'If she did, I was too dense to pick it up. She just said she wanted to talk to me about

something and asked me not to say anything to anyone else.'
His eyes bored into mine. 'And I hope you don't need to ask
the obvious question. *Do* you?'

'No,' I said right away. I didn't. He *wouldn't*. 'Of course
not.'

'Good.' He unknotted the dishtowel and folded it, laying it
on the counter, smoothing out the wrinkles and caressing
it as if it had suddenly morphed into the Shroud of Turin.

'Kit said it's possible Eve didn't even realize she was
pregnant. Or that she did know, and she met the father at
Goose Creek Bridge to tell him about it.' I folded my arms
across my chest and waited for his response.

'And the father of her baby pushed her off the bridge?' He
looked as horrified as I'd been when I found out.

'It might not have been welcome news.'

'Jesus,' he said again. 'Who would do something like that?'

'Someone who was married? I don't know. Who do you
think are the possibilities?' I wondered if he had any ideas
that were different from the ones Kit and I had discussed
earlier.

'You mean Richard or Jackson,' he said right away.

So much for the obvious suspects.

'They're in the lineup,' I said. 'I heard she was seeing
Fabrice. Who else? What about Vance? Although you told me
you'd know if Eve was sleeping with him.'

He shrugged. 'I don't know. I suppose it's possible that
I'm wrong. Maybe they kept it really quiet. He was crazy
about her.'

I could have told him that. 'Well, then, that means Vance
is on the list, too.'

'He wouldn't kill Eve.'

'Quinn, neither of us would like to believe that anyone
we just mentioned killed her. But someone did.'

'I know.' He gave me a pointed look. 'What about Sloane?'

Sloane. Lord, I'd completely forgotten about him. He
was strong, powerful, an athlete. Plus his reputation would
never survive another scandal after what had happened
before, especially if this time he got her pregnant instead of
just a little casual sex.

'My God, I hope it's not him, either,' I said. 'Kit implied Eve was maybe eight weeks along. How long was Eve, uh, educating Sloane about the problem of climate change and Virginia vineyards?'

'Search me. No idea.'

'Who else is left since we don't like any of the possibilities?'

'I don't know. Honest, I really don't know.'

Or maybe he just didn't want to guess.

Same as me.

THIRTEEN

After the kitchen was cleaned up and Pépé had gone upstairs to read in bed, I asked Quinn if he wanted to go stargazing out at the summerhouse before the clouds really rolled in and the rain came.

One of the most surprising things I'd learned about my fiancé when I first met him was that he was an avid amateur astronomer. Years ago when he was still living in the wine-maker's cottage – which was surrounded by woods – my father had given him permission to set up his telescope next to our summerhouse with its commanding view of our land, the neighboring farms, and the wide open valley that stretched all the way to the Blue Ridge. Before long, I was joining him once it got dark, usually with the rest of the dinner wine or a brandy, as he slowly educated me about the night sky, teaching me to recognize the planets, the constellations, the Milky Way, assorted comets, annual meteor showers and what to look for at a particular time of year. Now I'd become as addicted as he was.

We both needed a break from the stress of the last few days, especially after that last tense conversation about Eve. But I had another reason for asking him if he wanted to look at the stars and planets tonight.

My wedding gift to him was a new telescope.

I'd done my homework, getting advice from a patient astronomer with the Analemma Society, a group that ran Turner Farm Park Observatory, a small observatory belonging to the Fairfax County Parks Department up the road a ways in Great Falls. The telescope – a Celestron – had arrived last week. I'd had it delivered to Eli and Sasha's house and a few days ago Eli and I brought it here and had hidden it in the coat closet in the foyer when I knew Quinn wouldn't be around.

Two nights before our wedding the full moon would be one of this year's three supermoons; it would also coincide with a total lunar eclipse. Each one by itself was definitely worth watching. The two events happening together were rare and unmissable.

A supermoon occurs when a full moon is closest to Earth – known as the perigee – one of those nights when the moon rises and appears so big and bright as it sits right there on the horizon that you swear you can reach out and touch it. It's *huge*. A total lunar eclipse happens when the sun, Earth and the moon align perfectly, and the moon turns a reddish color that's referred to as a Blood Moon.

Quinn had been talking about it for weeks. If I gave him the new telescope now, he could have it set up and ready for Thursday.

His answer surprised me. 'Not tonight, sweetheart, no stargazing. I'm worried about this storm. I think I'm going to take a quick drive over to the barrel room and make sure everything outside is secure.'

'I'll come with you.'

'No, stay here with Luc. I'll be right back.' He kissed me and looked into my eyes. 'Are we all right?'

'We are.'

'You sure?'

I wanted to be sure. But I wished I knew what had happened to Eve at Goose Creek, who had murdered her in cold blood, and why she wanted to talk to Quinn that afternoon just before she was killed.

'Yes,' I said. 'I'm sure.'

He left and we both knew there was still something

gnawing at each of us that wouldn't be settled until Eve's killer was found.

I went upstairs, undressed, and changed into my nightgown. Quinn would be here soon and we'd sort out what was troubling us as we always did, by tumbling into bed and making love.

I was reading when my phone started beeping, the squawking sound that always reminded me of an angry goose and meant there was a National Weather Service emergency alert. I picked up the phone from the bedside table and read the message as it flashed on the screen.

Severe thunderstorm alert until 11:30 p.m. with damaging winds that could reach Category 1 hurricane status, possibly gusting up to 90 mph. Take shelter immediately. Damaging winds expected imminently. TAKE SHELTER IMMEDIATELY.

The winds began buffeting the house before I could even get out of bed, a low moaning sound like an airplane coming straight at us. There had been zero time between the warning and when the wind had picked up. Weird, because tornado warnings always gave you a halfway decent chance of getting to your basement or some safe place before the funnel cloud landed. This storm, or whatever it was, came out of nowhere.

I yanked off my nightgown, pulled on a pair of leggings and a sweatshirt, and grabbed my cane, calling Pépé's name as I walked across the hall to his bedroom as quickly as I could. He was already up, wearing a silk bathrobe over his pajamas, calm and collected, looking for all the world like an aging matinée idol waiting to stroll onstage.

'What's happening?' he asked. 'That wind sounds like a *tempête* is coming at us.'

A tempest. Good description.

'I don't know. The National Weather Service says it's a very bad thunderstorm heading our way with a lot of wind. We should get to the basement,' I said. 'It will be safer there. We need to hurry.'

Two of us with canes. Hurrying.

As if.

There was a quiet explosion from the basement as the power went out and the lights flicked off. Damn. Our eyes weren't adjusted to the darkness so we'd need to be extra careful on the stairs. And the flashlights and lanterns, which we really could have used right now, were downstairs in the pantry. I should have thought to bring at least one of the lanterns upstairs so we had light.

I couldn't run or move quickly, and neither could Pépé. We were at the mercy of whatever was coming at us. We had two choices: the back staircase that led to the kitchen, or the sweeping spiral staircase from the second floor to the foyer. The door to the basement was closer if we took the spiral staircase.

My grandfather gave me his arm as we made our way down the big staircase. I thought about turning on my phone's flashlight and wondered if it was such a good idea because I hadn't had time to charge it up after using it all day today. How long would the power be out? Maybe it would be smarter to save the battery.

Lightning strobed through the windows like a lighthouse beacon and then suddenly we were plunged into blackness again. The thunder sounded like bombs exploding in the distance. How loud would it be when it was over the house? Thank God Pépé, who had been through so much over nearly a century of living, wasn't one for panicking and that calmed me down. But I hated feeling helpless, knowing that we couldn't move fast when we had to.

'Can you see well enough in the dark?' I asked him. 'My phone isn't charged up very much or I'd risk using the flashlight.'

'I'm fine,' he said. '*Ne t'en fait pas, chérie*. Don't worry.'

Outside it seemed as if all hell had broken loose. Objects pelted the house, branches and God knows what else, and I prayed nothing would come crashing through the ceiling or collapse on us before we could get to the basement where we'd be safe.

My phone beeped with a text. Quinn.

U ok?

Taking P to basement. Power out. U ok? Where r u?

I hoped he was still in the barrel room, where he'd be safe, and not in the old Superman blue pickup driving back here. Where he wouldn't be safe. As it was, that truck was held together by duct tape and chewing gum.

He didn't reply and Pépé stumbled on a stair as another clap of thunder – this one much closer – made us both jump. I grabbed his arm and shoved my phone into the waistband of my leggings. It still sounded as if the apocalypse was happening around us along with the relentless droning of an airplane coming our way. More banging and pounding followed by an ominous cracking sound as something slammed on to the roof of the veranda. The whole house shuddered.

'What was that?' Pépé asked.

'I think it might have been a tree. Maybe the magnolia. God, I hope not,' I said. We had reached the bottom of the staircase and were now in the ink-black foyer. I could just see the faint outlines of the windows and doorways to the other rooms. 'Wait here until I get a lantern from the pantry. We'll need it in the basement.'

There was another crash as something else hit the roof, followed by thunder that sounded as if the sky just split open. I stumbled and nearly tripped over a chair leg and even Pépé, who'd been cool as a cucumber, seemed unnerved.

'Do you think we have time, *chérie?*' Spoken calmly but urgently.

More thunder, this one almost directly overhead.

'Maybe not. All right, I'm turning on my phone flashlight because the basement stairs are really precarious. Better no battery than a bad fall in the dark.'

The furious sound of pelting rain, driving wind, and teeth-jarring claps of thunder were muted once we were down in the basement, but the storm seemed scarier than when we'd been upstairs. I sent Quinn another text. This time it didn't go through.

I bit my lip and tasted blood. My phone was dead. *Where was he?*

'Is this a tornado?' Pépé asked.

'I don't know what it is. The weather service alert said it was a bad thunderstorm with dangerous winds. But it sure seems like more than that.'

Then as swiftly as it had arrived, the storm was gone. The house stopped shuddering as the thunder receded, heading elsewhere to wreak more havoc. My guess: Washington, D.C. It was still raining hard, though, and the relentless drumming continued to pound the roof. I checked my phone again and again. Quinn would be as frantic about Pépé and me as I was about him.

'Let's go upstairs and see if everything's all right,' I said to Pépé. 'Then I'm driving over to the winery. I'm worried about Quinn. My phone is dead since there's no power. I can't even text.'

'I'll come with you,' he said.

'It would be better if you stay here in case he shows up while I'm out looking for him.'

'That was not a very original, or even convincing, explanation for why you don't want me to come with you. I'm not made of sugar, *chérie*. I won't melt in a rainstorm.'

I didn't want to have to arm-wrestle him over this. My ninety-four-year-old grandfather was safer at home now that the storm had moved on rather than driving with me through God-knows-what wreckage that had been left in its aftermath.

'I know you won't melt. But I'd feel better if you'd stay at the house. There's a wind-up radio in the pantry closet where we keep the lanterns. I'll get it for you. The all-news station will be covering this storm non-stop. Maybe you can find out more about what's going on, what's happening.'

'All right,' he said. 'You win. I'll hold the fort at home.'

'Thank you.'

I got Pépé settled at the oak trestle table in the kitchen, listening to the radio by lantern light, and went upstairs to change into jeans. Even from my bedroom on the second floor, I could hear the loud voices of the announcers and reporters, their urgency and barely tamped down alarm evident as they started to piece together what had just happened. After the storm left us here in Atoka and

Middleburg, it had barreled straight on to D.C. – I'd guessed right – which was now also plunged into darkness.

I came back into the kitchen to get the keys to the Jeep and the pair of lopping shears I'd left in the mudroom from when we installed the garden. My grandfather looked up when I walked in.

'It's called a *derecho*,' he said. 'That's what they're saying on the radio.'

'A what?'

'A derecho. A violent windstorm accompanied by a line of thunderstorms,' he said. 'The winds are horizontal, so they travel in a straight line like a bullet, and that's what makes them so damaging and deadly.'

Deadly. Meaning people might have died, probably *had* died if they were in the wrong place when this derecho – which I'd never heard of until today – slammed into us.

'Those winds came out of *nowhere*,' I said. 'They were incredibly fast. We weren't ready.'

'I know,' he said. 'But they didn't come out of nowhere, because for a storm to be a derecho it must travel at least two hundred and fifty miles. So that wind came from *somewhere*.'

Except it had seemed to materialize out of thin air. The National Weather Service alert had given us no time to prepare, warning us seconds before the keening noise that preceded the first violent wind gusts.

'I'd better get going,' I said. Pépé's comments about the deadly impact of a derecho and how powerful it could be had only ratcheted up my anxiety. 'I hope nothing has happened to Quinn.'

'Everything's going to be all right, *chérie*. Quinn's fine. I'm sure the storm has knocked out the power everywhere, just like it has here. He's probably trying to reach you as well.'

'I know. Of course he is. Still, I'd better go. I'll be back. *Both* of us will be back.'

'I'll be here,' he said. 'I'll wait up for you.'

I kissed his weathered cheek and said, 'I won't be long.'

He nodded. 'Be careful.'

* * *

It was still raining, a light, steady rain, when I stepped outside, but it took less than thirty seconds to realize I'd been an idiot to think lopping shears were going to help me cut through whatever branches and trees had come down in the storm. We were going to need a chain saw and the Bobcat 'dozer.

I wasn't going anywhere, at least not in the Jeep. A huge tulip poplar had split in two as if it had been cleaved down the middle and now barricaded the entrance from the driveway to Sycamore Lane. The jagged shards of exposed wood gleamed as white as old bone in the light of my lantern.

A flashlight beam shone through the darkness from the direction of the carriage house. I turned and saw Eli walking toward me wearing mud boots and his old Virginia Tech rain slicker. He was carrying an oversized umbrella with the logo of the Washington Football Team on it that could have protected the entire starting lineup under its shelter. It felt as if the cavalry had arrived. I was more grateful than he could have known to see him just now.

My voice caught in my throat. 'Eli, what are you doing here? Are you all OK? The kids? Sasha?'

'I came to find out about you. Everyone's fine, although Hope is the only one at home because Zach is still with his dad for the weekend. Sasha's trying to reach them but there's no power. As you no doubt know. I just stopped by to check on Persia. She's all right but pretty spooked. She thought her apartment was going to detach itself from the carriage house and take off like a flying saucer. She's burning incense to purify the air now that the storm's gone. And trying to calm herself down.' I couldn't see his face in the darkness, but I knew from his rough tone of voice when we let our guard down with each other that he'd been worried about Pépé, Quinn, and me.

As if he read my mind he said, 'Hey, Luce. Is Pépé OK? How'd he handle this? Are you and Quinn all right?'

'Pépé's fine. I'm fine. Quinn is over at the winery, though I haven't heard from him in a while, so I'm worried.'

'I'm sure he's OK. Quinn knows how to take care of himself. But it was a hell of a storm.'

'It wasn't just any storm. Pépé's in the kitchen listening to the wind-up radio. He told me they're saying that what just happened is called a derecho.'

'A what?'

'Derecho. A storm with flat-line horizontal winds and really bad thunderstorms. The winds are what cause the damage.'

'No fooling.'

'Is your house all right?'

He had lovingly designed it and just finished construction earlier this winter. In March, just before he and Sasha eloped, they had moved in with his daughter and her son. The party they threw had been a combination housewarming and wedding reception to which it seemed everyone in Atoka and Middleburg had been invited; a big, noisy, joyous celebration that folks were still talking about.

'I think we got off light as far as the house goes,' Eli said. 'What about the Big House?'

His nickname for Highland House.

'I heard a lot of branches and stuff hitting, but I just came outside so I haven't had a chance to see what was damaged. I think we'll have to wait until tomorrow since you can't see much in the dark. Although there's a chance the magnolia came down. I heard something crash on to the veranda. It was loud. And it was something big.'

'Damn. That tree's over a century old.'

'I know.'

'So what are you doing out here?'

'I thought I'd drive over to the winery to make sure Quinn's all right. I'm . . . kind of worried.'

'You're not driving anywhere until that gets cleared away.' Eli pointed to the tulip poplar and its screen of leafy branches and seed pods spilling onto the driveway. 'We're going to have to walk.'

We. I gave him a grateful look and said, 'Can't we take your car instead?'

'Ixnay to that,' he said. 'I can't get out of my driveway either. Sycamore Lane – what I could see of it – is a mess. And, Luce, leave the lopping shears here, OK? They're only going to be a pain in the ass to carry around. We're going to need to climb over trees and make our way through all the stuff that's come down. Too bad we don't have caving head-lamps, because we'd have both hands free.'

'It's that bad?'

'Yup. You going to be OK to do this?' Even in the dark I saw his eyes stray to my cane.

'I'm going to be just fine.'

'OK,' he said. 'Then let's go. Let's take a walk.'

FOURTEEN

I f Sycamore Lane was blocked by downed trees, that meant Quinn couldn't get back here either. With any luck he had turned around and driven to the winery once he realized the storm was about to hit, or else he hadn't left to begin with and had been safe the entire time.

As the crow flies, it was less than a quarter mile from the house to the barrel room. Driving was another story, a little more than half a mile. A few hundred yards after you come through the gates at the main entrance to the vineyard, Sycamore Lane splits in two directions in front of the ancient sycamore that gave the road its name, and becomes a big loop. If Highland House was at one o'clock from where the sycamore was located, the barrel room was at eight o'clock. That meant the shortest way from here to there was past the pond, the family cemetery, and the Ruins.

It was slow going making our way along the debris-strewn dirt and gravel road even after our eyes grew accustomed to the dark. Our boots made squishing, sucking sounds in the mud and every so often my bad ankle rolled as I stepped on an uneven patch of ground. Eli, who was leading the way and using his enormous closed umbrella like a scythe to push branches out of our way, held tight to my hand to keep me from falling, though he stumbled once or twice as well. I would have used my cane to help him clear our path, but on this terrain I really needed it for its intended purpose.

'I think the rain is tapering off,' I said. 'And the clouds seem to be breaking up. Maybe with an almost full moon we'll have some light.'

'That would be useful.' We ducked as he pushed away another low-hanging branch so it wouldn't hit us in the face. 'We've left the road, you know. It's impossible to keep to it with everything that's come down.'

'Where are we? I'm completely disoriented,' I said. 'I thought I saw moonlight gleaming on water on our right so we must be near the pond. At least I hope it was the pond.'

'It was the pond.'

'Can we get back on to the road?'

'No, I'd much rather slog through mud and trip over dead tree limbs and get scratched by thorns, so we'll just stick to the woods.'

'*Jeez*. OK, Indiana Jones. You don't have to be so testy.'

'I'm not testy. You want to lead the way? I'm doing the best I can.'

'I'm sorry. I know you are. You're doing just fine.'

'Thank you.' He stopped suddenly and I nearly collided with him. 'Hey.'

'What?'

'I think that's the blue pickup.'

The Superman-blue pickup truck wasn't quite as old as I was, but it was awfully close and probably had enough miles on it to have circumnavigated the earth a few times. I'm sure my heart stopped beating for a few seconds. My mouth went dry.

'Where?'

'Underneath that tree. Come *on*.'

'Oh my God. *No*. Please. No.'

If a tree had landed on the truck as Quinn was driving back to the house . . . People *died* when that happened, if they or their cars were struck when a tree came down unexpectedly and they happened to be in precisely the wrong place at precisely the wrong time.

It was impossible to tell where the tree had fallen on the pickup because the truck was completely covered with leafy branches. It was another tulip poplar, so common around here and with roots so shallow the trees toppled over at the drop of a hat.

Eli and I shouted Quinn's name as we clawed through branches trying to get to the driver's door. The engine wasn't running, nor were the headlights on, so either the tree had landed on the hood and shut it down or maybe Quinn had been able to turn the key in the ignition before he passed out. *If* he'd only passed out and it wasn't something worse.

'Can you see him yet?' I asked Eli. 'Can you tell if the tree hit the cab?'

'I think the back of the truck took the brunt of it. Looks like the tree – the main trunk – fell across it, not on it. The cab is covered by leaves and smaller branches.'

'Thank God.'

Quinn was unconscious but breathing when we finally got to him, crumpled over the steering wheel. Eli managed to wrench open the driver's door – how I don't know – and unfasten Quinn's seat belt. Quinn slumped sideways and nearly fell on top of my brother, who caught him in his arms. I could see a gash above his right eye and his forehead was smeared with blood. More blood ran down the right side of his face, but in the dark it was hard to tell if it was from the gash or another injury.

'Quinn,' I said, 'can you hear me? You need to wake up. *Please.*'

'Let's get him out of the truck before he falls out,' Eli said, struggling to hold him. 'We can work on him there. Help me, Luce.'

'I'm trying.'

Eli shifted so he was grasping Quinn under both arms. I tried to take his legs as Eli pulled him the rest of the way out of the truck. But Quinn was dead weight, there was too much momentum, and I wasn't steady on my feet. We managed to slide him from the truck and away from the protruding branches of the poplar before Eli tripped and landed on his back. Quinn fell on top of him. I hit the ground on my hands and knees next to the two of them. Eli let out a loud *oof* and swore; Quinn groaned.

At least we hadn't impaled ourselves on one of the broken

shard-like branches; our falls had apparently been cushioned by a bed of leaves. I moved closer to Quinn and Eli, feeling useless. Wondering if either of them had any broken bones and, if so, what were we going to do about it out here?

'I'm so sorry, Eli – I couldn't hang on to him . . . are you OK?'

'Fine, just fine. Help me, Luce.' Eli sounded as if he was in pain. He wasn't fine.

Somehow we managed to shift Quinn so Eli could slide out from under him. I cradled Quinn's head in my arms as my brother rolled off to the side and lay on his back. Quinn groaned again and stirred.

Eli had set the lantern on the ground when we pulled Quinn out of the cab, so our faces were now mostly in shadow, our bodies silhouetted against the tangle of the downed tree and its branches. I moved the light so I could see his face better. The gash on his forehead had stopped bleeding, but the cut looked deep. I had nothing to clean it with until we got back to the house.

'Quinn. *Please.* Wake up, my love.'

His eyelids fluttered and opened. He blinked and lifted a hand to shield his eyes against the brightness of the lantern light. 'What happened?'

I kissed him, more grateful than I could say, and told him about the derecho.

'Derecho,' he said, slurring his words a little. 'Never heard of it. Means "straight" in Spanish.'

'Probably because the winds came straight at us, horizontally,' I said. 'Come on, we need to get you back to the house. We're near the pond, so it's not too bad a hike. Do you think you could manage to walk if you lean on Eli and me?'

'Do I have a choice?' He was speaking more clearly and his eyes were fixed on mine. Plus he was joking. A good sign.

I kissed him again. 'Actually, no, you don't.'

'Well, then, your answer is yes.'

'Good. What about you, Eli? Are you OK?'

My brother didn't answer right away.

'*Eli?*'

'Yeah, I hope so. My back hurts like hell.'

'Can *you* stand?'

He managed to get up but he moved like the Tin Man in *The Wizard of Oz* before Dorothy found the oil can. Great, just great. Very likely I was the most able-bodied of the three of us. My phone still showed *No Service*. Nada. Nothing. We were on our own.

I have no idea how long it took us to make our way back to Highland House, but it seemed like an eternity. The wind had finally blown away the remnants of the storm clouds, leaving a blue-black sky and an almost-full moon that cast stripes of ghostly light on to the negative spaces between the trees and the road.

If Quinn had a concussion – which I couldn't say for sure – he needed to keep talking, to remain awake and alert. I plied him with questions about what had happened. He said the last thing he remembered was an enormous crack of thunder and a flash of lightning. Then the truck stopped as if it had slammed into a concrete wall and something landed so hard on the truck bed that the whole truck shuddered, and the wheels left the ground.

'My head hit the steering wheel and probably the gear shift. Hurt like hell. Next thing I know I'm half-awake lying on the ground on top of Eli.' He turned to my brother. 'Sorry, man, I hope you're OK.'

'I'll live. Good thing I'm married to a physical therapist.'

'I'm *really* sorry.'

'It's OK. Glad we found you.'

By now we had reached the downed tulip poplar that was blocking the driveway. Highland House was eerily dark and silent.

'Eli, do you want to come inside?' I asked. 'Take something for your back?'

'I really want to get home to Sasha and Hope. Sasha'll fix me up.'

'Text me when you . . . never mind. Be careful, OK?'

'Don't worry. If we have power in the morning I'll call or text. I know a couple of tree surgeons, but I can't reach them with no cell phone service. I'll bet they're gonna make more money in the next few days than they'd make in an entire year. We'd probably be at the bottom of the totem pole.'

'We'll get the chain saws out first thing tomorrow,' Quinn said to him. 'So at least we'll be able to get out of here. Maybe drive over to see your tree surgeons.'

'First place we drive is to a doctor who can check you out,' I said.

'I'm fine.'

'Sure you are. Good thing under that sweatshirt you're wearing your Superman outfit.'

'I'm a little banged up is all.'

'You're more than a little banged up.'

'Hey. I'm going to leave you two lovebirds to work this out without my help,' Eli broke in. 'I gotta get home.'

'Be careful,' I called after him again.

He raised his umbrella over his head as if he were brandishing a sword. 'Just call me Indy,' he said over his shoulder. 'And don't worry. I got this.'

Pépé was in the kitchen where I'd left him, still listening to the wind-up radio. A suspicious smell of Gauloises hung in the air, but tonight I figured *what the hell* and pretended not to notice.

'I found the brandy on the sideboard,' he said. 'And three glasses. I thought you two might need a drink when you got back.'

'You thought right,' Quinn said, pulling out a chair for me and one for himself.

'First I'm cleaning that cut,' I said. 'Give me a minute to get the gauze pads upstairs in the bathroom.'

Pépé poured our brandies while I cleaned Quinn's gash with gauze and a bottle of water I got from a case in the pantry.

He winced and I said, 'Are you sure you should be drinking if you have a concussion? Alcohol—'

'I'm *fine*,' he said. 'A brandy won't kill me. *Ouch.*'

'Sorry. That's the Neosporin, so it won't get infected. You can be so stubborn, you know that?' I put a new piece of gauze over the cut and then taped it to his forehead.

'It's one of my endearing qualities,' he said. 'And right now,

I could use a brandy. I have a feeling tomorrow the bruises are going to start showing up. I might've gotten a little banged around in that cab – bounced around like a pinball.'

'Tomorrow you take it easy, then.'

'Tomorrow we start cleaning up. No rest for the weary.'

'*Trinquons*,' my grandfather said. 'Let's drink. At least tonight we're alive and well. And lucky.'

We drank and I said, 'Speaking of being lucky, I hope everyone else was, too. I'm worried about Mia. She would have been all by herself in Quinn's old cottage.'

'Once we get that tulip poplar cut up so we can get out, we'll drive over and see her, check on everyone,' Quinn said.

'I bet the emergency responders are going crazy tonight,' I said. 'People must be calling nine-one-one nonstop.'

'If they do no one will answer the phone,' Pépé said. 'The entire emergency system is down. The derecho knocked it out.'

'It did *what*?' Quinn said.

'That's not possible,' I said. 'It's state-of-the-art. There's a backup to the backup. It's supposed to be completely failsafe.'

'That may well be, but the backup generator was taken out, too. It's dead. There's nothing. No nine-one-one.'

'You've got to be kidding,' Quinn said.

'I am not.'

We sat in stunned silence for a moment. A storm of this magnitude and no way for the police, fire department, or an ambulance to respond?

'So what is anyone with an emergency supposed to do?' I asked in a faint voice. 'Because there are probably a few of them tonight.'

My grandfather set his brandy snifter on the table. 'The reporter I heard spoke to a county spokesman who said – and I quote – "Your best option is to walk or drive to the nearest fire department or police department or hospital if you need help."'

Unless a downed tree in your driveway kept you from doing that.

'In other words, we're on our own,' Quinn said.

'Yes,' Pépé said, 'I suppose we are.'

*   *   *

Before we went upstairs I told Quinn I wanted to take a look outside and see how the wedding garden had fared in the storm.

'Do you really want to do that tonight?' he asked. 'It probably got as torn up as everything else. Why don't we try to get some sleep and then we'll look at the damage in the morning? Nothing's going to change between now and then.'

When I didn't answer he said, 'OK, we'll look tonight.'

'I want to get it over with.'

He unlocked the door to the veranda and we stepped outside. I hadn't expected it to be this bad.

'Oh, *no*. No, no, no, no.'

'I'm so sorry, sweetheart. It'll look better once we get it cleaned up.'

In the bright moonlight we could see the ruined garden, the arbor under which we planned to be married destroyed, the enormous saucer magnolia leaning crazily against the veranda roof, the yard wild and windblown and full of branches and flower petals and debris.

'Where's the summerhouse?' he asked.

His telescope was in there. He sucked in his breath.

'I can't see it.'

'Damn. Maybe the storm took it out.'

'Your telescope might still be OK,' I said.

'Yeah. Maybe.' He didn't sound convinced.

He'd been right. We should have gone to bed and checked out everything in the morning when it was light outside. To take in this much devastation and damage at one in the morning – especially when we couldn't see what it really looked like – hadn't been my best idea.

'I can't look at this any more,' I said.

'Me, neither. Let's go to bed.'

We took the back stairs to the second floor. A pale sliver of light shone under Pépé's closed bedroom door – the lantern we'd given him – so I knocked and asked him if he was all right or needed anything.

'I'm fine,' he said. 'How bad was the garden?'

'Bad.'

'I'm so sorry, *chérie*. Try to get some sleep.'

'You, too. *À demain.*'

Quinn was already in bed, naked under the sheets. I shed my clothes and joined him. He pulled me close and we lay in each other's arms, both of us staring at the ceiling. The house, airless and silent, felt like a tomb.

'I'm going to open the windows,' I said. 'I feel like I can't breathe.'

I got up and Quinn said, 'I wonder how long we'll be without power since it also means we don't have any water.'

We had a well, the same as everyone else around here. When the power went, the well pump went, too. There was enough water to flush the toilets. Once. Showers were now verboten. I could live without electricity, but no water got old real fast.

'We have those carboys we've stored in the basement,' I said. 'But we should use that water for cooking and drinking. And brushing our teeth.'

'I think we're in for the long haul,' Quinn said. 'It's going to take a while to clean up after that storm. We may be without power for a while.'

'I think you're right.'

My last thought before I finally fell asleep was that our wedding was supposed to take place in six days.

Maybe.

We both woke at first light. A cool breeze blew the curtains so they billowed into the bedroom. I got up, shivering, and padded over to close the window, getting my first good look at the damage to the wedding garden in daylight.

'How bad is it?' Quinn asked from the bed.

'So much worse than we thought. The arbor is a total loss. The butterfly pond is full of debris. It looks like we had a red and white blizzard because the petals from the azaleas and rhododendron are scattered all over the lawn. I think the roof on the summerhouse collapsed. Or it's gone. I can't see it from here. What a mess.'

'I hope it's not this bad in the vineyard.'

'I know. If we lose too many flowers we'll end up with necrosis.'

No winemaker wants or needs that. Lose the flowers during bloom and instead of grape clusters that are uniform size, you get floral necrosis, or large and small grapes – known as hens and chicks – instead. On the plus side, necrosis also meant you'd get clusters that would probably ripen better because more air would be able to circulate. You'd also be less likely to get mold.

'Losing flowers and necrosis might be the least of our problems. I hope we didn't lose too many vines. But whatever happened, happened,' Quinn said. 'We couldn't have prevented it if we'd wanted to. Even with plenty of warning. And we got *zero*.'

I walked back over to the bed. 'We'd better get dressed and get started,' I said. 'There's so much to do.'

He pulled me on to the bed and on top of him. 'I know,' he said, kissing me. 'It's going to be a hell of a day, so how about we take it slow? First things first. We can get dressed and do all those things later. They're not going anywhere.'

'Are you trying to seduce me?' I said.

'You catch on fast,' he said.

When we were down in the kitchen, I said, 'Was that what they call survivor sex?'

He grinned. 'Call it whatever you want. It was good.'

'It was. In a few days we can have dirty sex if you want, and it'll be literal not figurative if we still have no water.'

He laughed and I said, 'Speaking of which, there's no coffee until we get out the camping stove. Which is over at the Villa. What *can* we have?'

'There's bread but no toast.' Quinn opened the refrigerator door. 'There's orange juice. Your homemade strawberry jam from last summer. A big bowl of fruit that Persia made.'

'Well, that's breakfast then. We've only got a few days before we have to throw everything out so we may as well eat it.'

I fixed our fruit and bread and jam using paper plates and bowls decorated with holly leaves and berries left over from a party we'd thrown at Christmas while Quinn cranked the wind-up radio. It was still on the all-news station.

'Why do they always have to sound like they're trying not to shout when there's breaking news?' he said as we sat down at the kitchen table. 'We know it's bad.'

What we hadn't realized was just how bad it was everywhere. The storm, already being called one of the worst ever for our region, had traveled over seven hundred miles from Iowa to Maryland: we got the brunt of it. The governor had declared a state of emergency in Virginia. Washington, D.C. was completely shut down. Four million people were without power, the largest non-hurricane outage in history in our region. Dozens and dozens of trees – some quite ancient – were uprooted. Multiple areas had boil-water edicts. Grocery stores were dark because they had no power and shelves were already empty. Bottled water had vanished. With no electricity to run gas pumps, the only places to get gas were stations with backup generators and cars were already lining up. As for when the power would be restored: maybe a week, maybe longer.

'Damn,' Quinn said. 'It's really bad.'

I heard Pépé's footsteps on the back stairs. A moment later he was in the kitchen, somehow having managed to shave and wearing his usual uniform of a dress shirt and dark trousers. No tie meant he was going casual.

'Good morning,' he said. 'Or is it?'

Quinn filled him in on the news while I started to get his breakfast. Persia walked in as I was pouring him a glass of juice. Her dark eyes were hooded, and she looked as if she hadn't slept much, but her face lit up when she saw my grandfather.

'Antonio just showed up in the driveway with a mean-looking chain saw,' she informed us.

'Bless his heart,' I said as we heard the stuttering sound of a motor starting up and catching. I got another Christmassy paper plate and bowl from the cabinet and reached for the bowl of fruit. 'Let's go talk to him, Quinn. He'll have news about Mia. Plus he might already know whether there was any damage to the winery.'

'I'll finish fixing Luc's breakfast, Lucie,' Persia said, holding out her hand for the bowl of fruit. 'You and Quinn go along and do whatever you have to do. I'll take care of him.'

'Perhaps you'll join me for breakfast, Persia?' Pépé asked. 'I would enjoy the company.'

'I'd be delighted,' she said, and her cheeks turned pink.

'Well,' I said, 'since you two seem to have everything so well taken care of here, we'll see you later.'

Antonio had already stripped down to a T-shirt with the vineyard logo on it when we joined him, jacket cast on the ground next to a cooler and a dented gas can. He was wearing ear and eye protectors and wailing away at one of the big branches. It took him a moment to realize Quinn and I were standing there.

He cut the motor and set the saw down, pulling a bandanna out of his back pocket and wiping his face.

'How are you all?' I asked. 'Are Valeria and the baby all right?'

'Yup, fine. The baby yelled her head off the whole time the wind was blowing, though. She didn't like the storm one bit.'

'She wasn't the only one,' I said.

'How about the cottages?' Quinn asked.

'And Mia,' I added.

'Both cottages are OK. Built pretty sturdy. Our walls shook but we didn't have no damage,' he said. 'Mia's place looks fine, Lucita, though I haven't seen her in the last two days. Car's been gone.'

'She wasn't there when the storm hit?' I asked.

'Nope. The place has been dark. A tree came down at the turnoff from Sycamore Lane to the cottages so Benny and Jesús are there now cutting it up. It wasn't a big one, so it won't take long. Their places are OK, too, by the way.'

Benny and Jesús were our two full-time employees who lived with their families in a barn Eli had turned into a comfortable duplex. Everyone was fine. We'd been lucky.

So where was my sister? A free spirit who floated on the wind according to her whims, she could be anywhere. You never knew.

'Have you been out to the vineyard yet?' Quinn asked Antonio.

'No, I came here first because I knew you couldn't get

out. I saw the blue pickup and the tree that landed on it. You were lucky, *mi hermano*.' Antonio held up his thumb and forefinger so you could barely see daylight between them. 'That close.'

'I know.'

'Is that why you've got that bandage on your forehead?'

'Yup.'

'What happened?'

'I had an unfortunate encounter with the gear shift when that tree hit the truck. I passed out after that.'

'Lucky it wasn't your eye. If it's deep you might need stitches.'

I mouthed *thank you* at Antonio behind Quinn's back.

'Maybe,' Quinn said. 'I went over to the winery to make sure everything was inside before the storm hit. Didn't make it home in time.' He shrugged. 'And then I was in the wrong place when that tree came down.'

'There's stuff everywhere,' Antonio said. 'Trees, branches, debris. Lotta stuff to clean up. Luckily the barrel room looks like it's OK and so does the Villa. I drove over to Golden State a little while ago since I know those guys real good. We've got extra cans of gas. They got two more chain saws. They're gonna bring the chain saws here, help us first, then we're going over there to take care of their damage. Their *jefe*'s out of town so Vance is in charge.'

Sloane had said something about going to LA this week to shoot promotional commercials for his sponsors. So he'd missed the derecho. And he was out of the direct line of fire in the investigation into Eve Kerr's death. Unless that had been sidelined by the storm.

'How'd you get over here?' I asked Antonio.

'Got one of the Gators out of the equipment barn.'

'How much gas does it have?'

'Yesterday I made sure the Gators, the tractor, and all our equipment – like the chain saws – had full tanks,' he said, with a smug grin. 'I filled up the gas cans, too. We're good.'

'Antonio, you are a prince.'

'I know,' he said, still smiling. 'Valeria tells me that all the time.'

'We're going to take a look at the damage in the vineyard,' Quinn said. 'So we'll borrow the Gator for a bit unless you need help here?'

'We don't have another chain saw and the GSV guys will be here soon with theirs,' he said. 'It won't take long for three of us to get this taken care of. They'll drive me back to the winery, so keep the Gator as long as you need it.'

Quinn nodded and turned to me. 'Before we go, I want to see something.'

The summerhouse. He wanted to find out about his telescope.

The little building had collapsed on itself – pancaked would be the most apt description. The telescope was somewhere under the rubble.

'Damn,' he said when we saw it. 'Damn.'

He'd tried to keep the disappointment out of his voice, but I knew how upset he was. I slipped my arm around his waist. The summerhouse had been my playhouse when I was a child – a sanctuary, a castle, a library, a clubhouse where Kit and I made up rules that we'd change the next day and the day after that. His loss was real; my loss was intangible – my childhood memories. And some others that were more recent: the nights Quinn and I spent out there looking at the stars, which was when I began falling in love with him.

'You'll get a new telescope and we'll rebuild the summerhouse,' I said, and my voice caught. 'Eli will design it. Good as new.'

This evening once we got back to the house, I was absolutely giving him his wedding gift.

'Yup,' he said. 'If this is the worst casualty of the storm, we got off easy.'

'We did.'

He sighed. 'Come on,' he said. 'Let's go look at the vineyard.'

'OK,' I said.

And wondered what we'd find there.

FIFTEEN

'I want to stop by Mia's cottage,' I said to Quinn as we climbed into the Gator. 'Antonio said her car hasn't been there in two days. I hope she's OK.'

'She's pretty resourceful.'

'She can also be pretty flaky.'

'That's true, too.'

Benny and Jesús had cut up enough of the downed tree and moved it so we could get into the cul-de-sac where Antonio's and Mia's cottages were located. We stopped and chatted with them and that's when I saw my sister's car parked in front of her place.

She was home. She must have just gotten there.

'Give me a minute,' I said to Quinn as we pulled up next to her car. 'Unless you want to come with me?'

'I'll let you handle this. Sister to sister.'

Meaning he didn't want to get near our conversation with a barge pole. 'Right. Thanks.'

When Mia answered the door, she was barefoot in jeans with holes in them and a midriff-baring T-shirt with a guerrilla mask on it, the logo of the Guerrilla Girls, a group of female artists protesting the dearth of art by women in museums.

To my surprise she threw her arms around me and said, 'I was so *worried* about you. And Eli. And Quinn and Sasha and Hope and Zach.'

Mia wasn't usually the worrying kind.

'We're fine. Everyone's fine. Antonio says your car hasn't been here for two days. We were so worried about *you*.'

She stepped back. Indignant. 'Is Antonio *spying* on me? And reporting to you?'

'Oh, come on. Of course not. But he does drive by your place every day. You're his only neighbor. Why would you think he wouldn't notice if your car wasn't there? When we saw him this morning, we asked him if you were all right since we couldn't get to you or reach you once the power went out. He was worried about you, too.'

'Oh,' she said. 'Well . . . OK.'

'So?'

'So what?'

'You weren't here.'

'No.'

This could go on forever. 'Mia,' I said, 'can I ask where you were for the last two days?'

'No,' she said. 'You can't.'

'Were you OK during the storm?'

'I was fine,' she said. 'It was scary, but we were fine.'

We.

'Sweetie,' I said. 'We?'

Mia's most recent boyfriend had been on the run from the law in New York, the last in a long line of bad boys going all the way back to middle school. My sister's theory was that even though she knew they'd eventually break her heart, the ones who were trouble were more fun while the party lasted.

She gave me an exasperated look. 'Oh, what the hell. It will be all over town soon anyway since there are no secrets around here. I was with Fabrice. At his place at La Vigne.'

Fabrice. I'd thought he was involved with Eve. Mia saw the look on my face and said, 'Lucie. Don't *judge.*'

'I'm not judging. But the rumor going around is that Fabrice was . . . seeing Eve. Who is dead. And she was pregnant. I hope he's not . . .'

'Not *what*? Using me as an alibi?'

'For starters. Come on, Mia, he's almost a member of our family. He's Jacques' grandson. I'm the one who recommended that Toby hire him. I don't like what this looks like any better than you do. I'm fond of him but you're my sister. I care about *you.*'

Mia wrapped her arms around her thin waist. 'I care about you, too. It was over between Eve and Fabrice when we started . . . seeing each other.'

Which sounded like a euphemism for sleeping together.

How they had managed to keep it under the radar was beyond me.

'When?' I asked.

'About three weeks ago. He was helping Eve with her dissertation. That's it.'

'I thought there was something between the two of them.'

Mia blew a lock of hair off her face, like: *Oh, please.* 'Eve wished there was. Then, well, she found out she was pregnant. So obviously there's someone else in the picture, right? Fabrice wasn't getting in the middle of *that*.'

So Eve did know she was pregnant.

'Did she say who the baby's father was?'

She gave me the dumb question look. 'Duh. No. Why would she tell Fabrice who got her pregnant when she's interested in *him*?'

Which begged the question what happened to Eve's relationship with her child's father to go downhill so fast that a few weeks later she was interested in another man? A quarrel? An accidental pregnancy? The end of an affair?

'Why did she tell Fabrice she was pregnant?' I asked. When, that early in her pregnancy, she could have kept it a secret because what better way to put off a new love interest than to tell him you're having another man's baby? And that it obviously wasn't that long ago you were, uh, having sex with the other guy.

'She was sick as a dog one day. Morning sickness. He guessed. She had to tell him. It all fell apart after that.'

'Do you know where he was last Saturday afternoon?'

She looked at me like I'd just asked the stupidest question in the world and expected a smart answer.

'Was he at Goose Creek Bridge with Eve? Did he kill her? Is that what you're asking?'

It was, but I wasn't going to say so.

'I just asked if you knew where he was.'

'No, I don't.'

She didn't seem happy to divulge that piece of information. 'Mia . . .'

'He *didn't*. He wouldn't. Besides, Bobby already questioned him.'

'Oh?'

'Before the storm. The derecho. Fabrice told Bobby that he saw Eve the day she was killed at the bridge, but she was alive and well when he left her. He also said she was upset about something, but she wouldn't tell him what it was.'

That would have been the same day Eve wanted to see Quinn. She didn't want to tell Fabrice what was bothering her, but it seemed as if she wanted to tell Quinn about it.

Except now we'd never know what *it* was.

Mia didn't know about Eve and Quinn, and I wasn't going to tell her, either. 'Did Fabrice have any idea what was upsetting her?'

'Nope. He's a good person, Lucie.' Her voice was soft. 'I really like him.'

'Me, too.'

She gestured to a table behind her in the living room covered with a paint-spattered oil cloth. It was littered with tubes of paint, glass jars and containers with brushes poking out of them, sketch books, a tub of gesso, a hair dryer, and assorted items I either couldn't identify or figure out why they were there – a coat hanger, a bag of flour, a small hacksaw, a roll of duct tape. In short, it was the colorful, messy place where my sister was happiest as she created beautiful things.

'I'd better get back to work,' she said. 'I'm trying to finish a papier-mâché hat for Monty and without power I can only work during the day.'

'Monty? You mean Monty the Fox?' He had supposedly gone home with Carly and Richard Brightman.

She nodded.

'Why are you making him a hat – now?'

'Carly paid a ton of money for him,' she said. 'More than I ever expected. I told Grace I'd make him a hat as well. She said it was really sweet of me to offer, but you know, they give money to artists who need help. I figured doing this would be a way to help pay back people who helped me when I was starting out.'

'That's really thoughtful.'

'It's no big deal. I'm glad to do it. Do you want to see the hat? It's not finished yet, though.'

'Of course.'

I followed her over to her work table. She picked up a papier-mâché flat cap that she had painted a jazzy red and blue plaid. She was in the middle of applying fake jewels so it would be as blingy as the rest of Monty's attire.

'I'm almost tempted to add a visor,' she said. 'What do you think?'

'I think it looks terrific as it is now.'

She studied the hat from different angles. 'Maybe I'll leave it then. Either way, I need Carly or Richard to bring Monty back here to the studio so I can attach it properly.'

'Do they know about the cap?'

'They do. Carly says she's thrilled and can't wait to see it.'

'I should let you go back to working on it,' I said. Then, to get it over with because I knew it was going to hurt when I told her, I said, 'By the way, the wedding garden is completely ruined. And the summerhouse is destroyed. The storm . . .'

I stopped and our eyes met. Hers filled with tears.

'Oh, Lucie. I'm so, so sorry.' She set Monty's hat on the table and swiped at her eyes. 'I know how hard you worked on that garden, getting Parker Lord to design it and all. It was such a labor of love. You must be devastated.'

'We can replant, restore it. Everything will grow back. It's OK. I'm OK.'

My sister knew it wasn't and I wasn't. 'Not by Saturday it won't.'

'There is that minor detail.'

'What about the wedding?' she asked.

'I don't know. I haven't thought that far ahead. Maybe we'll move it to the courtyard or the Ruins. I'll talk to Frankie and we'll figure out Plan B.'

'Can I do anything?'

'Thanks, but I don't think so. Quinn and I are about to go to check out the vineyard,' I said. 'See how much damage we've got out there. Hopefully not as bad as Highland House.'

'Let me know?'

'Sure. Stop by the house sometime. Pépé would like to see you, too. Bring Fabrice. Like I said, he's almost family.'

'Thanks,' she said. 'I think he'd like that.'

She waved at Quinn from the front door as I stepped outside. He waved back and when I climbed into the Gator he said, 'What took you so long?'

'I told you to come with me.'

He gave me a martyred look.

'She's sleeping with Fabrice,' I said. 'She was at his place during the storm.'

'*Sleeping* with him? What happened to Eve? I thought he was sleeping with her. In fact, my money was on Fabrice to be the baby daddy.'

'Apparently when he found out she was pregnant, and her getting pregnant being rather . . . recent . . . that ended any romantic interest on his part. Although Mia said he was still helping Eve with her dissertation.'

Quinn put the Gator in gear and we drove out to the Merlot block behind Mia's cottage. 'So he's not the father. I wonder who is.'

'The other candidates who come immediately to mind are all married. We've been over this.'

'Richard, Jackson, Sloane.'

'Right. Of course, there's also Vance as a long shot,' I said. 'Who happens to be unmarried.'

Quinn shook his head. 'Doubtful it's Vance.'

'Something's going on between Vance and Landau's,' I said. 'We should stop by GSV later today and see how their cleanup is coming along since our guys are going to be there helping them out.'

'And do what? Ask Vance if he's the baby's father? Or if he killed Eve?' I knew he was going to stick up for his friend. 'He's not and he didn't. Come on, you like Vance, too. You don't believe he's guilty.'

'Of course I like him, but there's something funny going on,' I said. 'I guarantee you.'

'We can stop by if you want,' he said, 'but *I* guarantee you Vance is a straight shooter.'

The vineyard had fared better in the storm than we'd feared. A lot of the flowers were blown off – as expected – but we got off easy, considering. The courtyard was a mess, the wine barrels filled with plants overturned on their sides and flower petals from the hanging baskets scattered everywhere. The Villa didn't look too bad; fortunately we had moved all the chairs and tables on the terrace out of the way so nothing got knocked around by the wind. All in all, the derecho appeared to have been kinder here than it was at Highland House.

The Ruins were another story: they were hit hard. I caught my breath as the old house came into view. The chimney had toppled over and the stage was gone; it was supposed to be our dance floor on Saturday.

Quinn pulled up next to it and stopped the Gator. He reached for my hand, stroking it over and over with his thumb. He said nothing but that little gesture told me he knew how devastated I was. Ever since the Yankees burned the place during the Civil War, what was left of the house had stubbornly survived for another century and a half through *everything* until the derecho roared through last night and destroyed what remained with a scorched-earth ferocity.

After a few moments I took an unsteady breath and said, 'We're kind of running out of options for places to have our wedding. First the garden, now the Ruins. Maybe the courtyard after we clean it up . . .?'

Quinn turned to me, his eyes filled with tenderness and compassion and love. He pulled me into his arms. 'I'd marry you on the dark side of the moon, Lucie. I don't care where we get married. I just care *that* we get married.'

The floodgates opened and I choked back a sob. 'Me, too.'

'We'll make it work. I know you wanted the whole package, the wedding in that beautiful garden you just created, with our family and friends there, dinner at sunset in the vineyard and dancing here at the Ruins by moonlight. But it doesn't matter. It *doesn't*. You know?'

I nodded, still trying to regain my composure. 'Yes. I know.'

He was right. It didn't matter, really.

It didn't mean it still didn't hurt.

I pulled back from him. 'I'll talk to Frankie. Like I told Mia, we'll figure out Plan B.'

'We will. It'll be OK.' He ran a finger down my cheek, brushing away a tear. 'I promise.'

'I know,' I said and swiped at my damp eyes, 'which reminds me you're getting your wedding gift from me tonight.'

His eyes lit up like a kid who just got told Christmas was coming early. 'Oh, yeah? Why tonight?'

'You'll just have to wait and find out.'

'If I guess will you tell me?'

'Nope. No way. It's a surprise.'

He smiled and put the Gator in gear again. 'All right,' he said, 'I'll wait. But it's going to be tough.'

We agreed we'd split up the last of our derecho damage inspections: he took the winery, which, it seemed, had been an impregnable fortress during the storm, thank God. Plus we had a generator to keep most of the equipment and the cooling system running. So we were lucky. I wanted to see how the Villa had fared. That might be another story.

I wasn't expecting to see Frankie's black SUV in the parking lot. Like everyone else, she probably had no power and her home had taken a battering, but here she was anyway.

She was standing behind the bar when I walked in. The large room seemed eerily quiet, as though all the air had been sucked out of it.

'What are you doing here?' I asked.

'I wanted to see how bad the damage was. I've already been to the courtyard. We can get that put to rights pretty quick.'

I nodded and she saw the expression on my face.

She gave me a steady look and said, 'The garden at Highland House?'

She might as well have asked how bad it was, because she knew something had happened.

'Destroyed. The Ruins, too.'

'Oh my God.' She was stunned. 'I figured there was some damage, but I wasn't expecting *destroyed*. I'm so sorry, Lucie. You must be heartbroken.'

Or numb. Which was probably more accurate.

'Everyone's OK and everything that was damaged can be replaced, just like the courtyard.' I shrugged. 'We got off lucky, all things considered.'

'Except for the wedding.'

I thought of the notebook she'd carried around these last few months, the detailed planning and attention that had gone into every single moment of our wedding. Her labor of love for Quinn and me, a perfect celebration.

All. Gone.

'Which is why we need to figure out Plan B,' I said.

'Right,' she said. 'Plan B.'

'We might be without power for a few days.'

'I know,' she said. 'Which could be a problem. Have you spoken to Dominique since she's the caterer?'

'My phone doesn't work. Does yours?'

'Oh, jeez, no, of course it doesn't. Obviously you haven't talked to her. My Lord, I still can't believe it. No power, no nine-one-one, no *nothing*.'

'A tulip poplar came down and blocked the driveway at the house, so Quinn and I haven't been able to get out. Antonio is there now with a chain saw, so once the tree's moved out of the way we're planning to drive around and check on everyone. Did you happen to fill up your car with gas before yesterday?'

She shot me a worried look. 'No. I wish I had. I've got half a tank. I came through Middleburg on my way here. It's so weird. Everything's dark. Safeway has its doors open to let light in since it's pretty gloomy without electricity, but there's not a whole lot left on the shelves. And no refrigeration.'

I hadn't checked what we had on hand in the pantry or in the refrigerator back at the house. We probably could make do, but honestly . . . I never expected something this catastrophic.

'Quinn got caught in the derecho yesterday on his way back from the winery,' I said. 'A tree landed on the blue pickup. He was lucky, but the truck is totaled. Eli and I found him passed out in the driver's seat and the three of us walked the rest of the way to the house in the dark. I think he needs stitches for a gash on his forehead and maybe a CAT scan to make sure everything is OK.'

That got me an even more worried look and Frankie shook her head. 'Lucie, all the hospitals in the area . . . I heard on the radio as I was driving over that they're swamped.

Using generators, so they've got power, but they're turning people away from the ER unless it's life or death.'

A possible concussion and a deep cut wouldn't warrant being looked at. They were not life or death.

We really were on our own.

'I guess we'll skip the trip to Catoctin General then.'

'I would if I were you.'

'We're still going to drive over to the inn and check on Dominique.'

'Good, because the food for the wedding . . .' Frankie began.

'I know. Is going to spoil. Even what's in her freezer.'

'Depending on how long the power's out.'

'It might be a while. I think we should eat it before it goes bad.'

'It's food for a hundred and twenty people,' she said.

'I know that. So why don't we have an impromptu early celebration? Invite everyone who was coming to the wedding – we can stop by friends' homes, ask them to tell the others . . . word will go around like it always does, power or no power.'

'I've heard,' Frankie said, 'that there are zones here and there where there is actual cell phone service. So we might not have to do this totally by word of mouth or sending up smoke signals.'

'OK, great. Do you think we can get everything done in time to have it tomorrow night?'

'Contacting everyone *and* getting the food ready *and* getting tables rented *and* everything else set up? I think that's pushing it. There's still going to be a lot to clean up from the storm – branches and brush and downed trees and all. We're not going to have the help we usually have to pull this off. Everyone's going to be busy.'

If Frankie said no – and she could pull off anything, however impossible sounding – it was no. 'Well, then, Wednesday. At the latest. After that the food is . . .'

'I know. We don't want to give anyone food poisoning because something went bad. Wednesday we can do. Although it'll be whatever it will be,' she said. 'But I can tell you this: your wedding dinner will be unforgettable for a lot of reasons.

And if we can't get in touch with all your guests we can always do what they did in the Bible at the wedding feast for the king's son. Go out in the streets and invite a bunch of strangers.'

'Somehow I don't think lack of guests is going to be our biggest problem. Everyone's going to be down to eating the labels off cans of whatever is in their pantry.'

'You're probably right.' She reached under the bar and found a note pad and a pen on the counter, back in planner mode. 'I'll get in touch with a few people to help as servers. We should be able to pick up the tables, chairs, and table-cloths from the rental place early since I doubt anyone else is planning to throw a party for a hundred and twenty this week.'

'We can have it in the courtyard since it probably won't take too long to get everything put right there. It's supposed to be gorgeous for the next few days so at least we won't have to worry about the weather.'

'That's a blessing.' She tapped her pen on the pad. 'It just occurred to me we should talk to Dominique about this rather major change of plans.'

'We probably should.'

'You're going to see her today?'

I nodded. 'I'll talk to her, confirm everything is OK with her, and let you know.'

'Great.' She scribbled again on her notepad, absorbed in making yet another list. Bless her heart. Ditching all the plans she'd made, her lists and notes in that big thick binder, and starting over from square one with five days to go. Like it was no big deal.

'There's something else,' I said.

She looked up, saw the expression on my face, and said in a wary voice, 'Lucie? What?'

'Maybe we should just get married tomorrow at the dinner and it'll be done. Forget all the plans for Saturday.'

'No. No, no, no,' she said with rising insistence. 'There's an eternity between now and Saturday. We might have power by then. A lot could change.'

'I know, but—'

'We're probably going to have to make this up as we go along, but it's going to work out, I promise. Don't worry about a thing, Lucie. Leave it with me.'

'I don't know.'

'*Please.*'

She waited me out.

'OK,' I said. 'Thank you.'

So we would get married Saturday after all, no matter what. That was five days from now. Although other than eating the wedding dinner early before the food spoiled, Plan B was still a plan with no details.

That we had to figure out.

SIXTEEN

I t took longer than expected for Antonio, our crew, and the crew from Golden State Vineyard to cut up the tulip poplar in our driveway and get it moved out of the way, so Quinn and I didn't get by GSV until nearly three o'clock. By then the guys had moved over there to help with their cleanup. The sound of chain saws buzzing like an angry hive greeted us when we got out of the Jeep. Maybe when I thought about this storm later – because the derecho would be a storm you never forgot, one you talked about and reminisced about – I would remember the relentless, incessant noise of so many chain saws. But I would also think about the total silence when they stopped, the eerie lack of sound, no humming electricity, no bright lights, no *nothing* that made it feel as if we'd been cut off from the rest of the world.

Quinn parked in front of the winery, a large rustic building painted barn red with a distinctive mansard roof. I loved it – it was one of those grand old Virginia barns that dotted the countryside – but Vance had shown Quinn drawings of a new building because Sloane didn't like the barn one bit and wanted to tear it down. Apparently Sloane planned to replace the current winery with something totally over-the-top Hollywood: equal parts cobwebby French wine cellar and Disney castle, with a bit of Versailles château thrown in. Maybe it would look great on the bluff of a hill in Napa or on an estate in Bordeaux, but right here nestled against the foothills of the Blue Ridge Mountains it would look just how you'd think it would.

Vance was in the winery checking on the stainless-steel tanks, which were running thanks to their generator, when we walked in. He came over when he saw us, looking rougher than usual: two-day stubble, haggard expression, dead tired. Something in his eyes told me it was more than the derecho that was weighing on him. He was also grieving a loss.

Eve.

'Thanks for sending your guys,' he said.

'Thanks for sending your chain saws,' Quinn said.

'Did you have much damage?' I asked.

'We got off better than I expected considering it sounded like the end of the world when those winds blasted through,' he said. 'A couple of trees came down that your guys are helping mine cut up right now. This building took a beating, but it's going to be torn down anyway. The vines look OK, although we lost a lot of flowers. What about you?'

'We weren't so lucky. We're still assessing how bad it is,' Quinn said. I knew he wouldn't tell Vance about the tree coming down on the blue pickup. When he was in it. 'We had damage to a couple of outbuildings and our backyard looks like someone dropped a bomb in the middle of it.'

'Your backyard? Aw, jeez. Your wedding was going to be there. Is it . . .?' He was going to ask if it was salvageable, but the look on our faces must have answered his question. 'That's rough. I'm sorry.'

'The Ruins, where the dance floor was going to be, was destroyed, too,' I said. 'We're working on Plan B.'

'The Ruins, too? *Damn.*'

'It could have been worse. We'll figure out something else, like Lucie said.'

The two of us exchanged glances. It was time to shift the subject away from our shattered wedding plans.

'Did Sloane get out before the storm hit?' I asked.

Vance nodded. 'He and Isabella left Sunday afternoon. He's

been calling nonstop, but I don't think he plans to leave LA and fly back to Virginia. Besides, we've got everything under control. Him returning wouldn't change anything. Isabella, on the other hand, is on a flight that gets in tonight. She's in a total panic about the girls being here with no one but the housekeeper and the place not having any power. As soon as life gets back to normal she says she's ordering a whole-house generator.'

'She'll probably have to take a number,' Quinn said. 'Everybody and his grandmother is going to be in the market for a generator after this is over.'

'No fooling. It really was a hell of a storm. I've never seen anything like it,' he said.

'Us, neither,' Quinn said.

'What happened to your forehead?' he asked. 'That bandage.'

'Nothing. I banged into something in the dark last night.'

Vance looked at me for confirmation.

'Something banged into him. He's just being stubborn,' I said. 'As usual. I hope he doesn't have a concussion.'

'I'm *fine.*'

There was an awkward moment of silence while Quinn glared at me and I glared back.

'Don't mind us,' I said to Vance. 'A pre-marital difference of opinion.'

'Sure.' He smiled half-heartedly. 'Uh, Lucie, I was wondering . . . you, uh . . . Saturday . . .'

He wanted to know about Eve. I finished his sentence.

'Found Eve.'

'Yeah. I heard it was a pretty rough scene. Brutal.'

'You heard right,' I said. 'It was awful.'

He closed his eyes, looking so anguished my heart broke for him. When he opened them, I said, 'Do you have any idea who might have done it?'

He shook his head. 'I know I'm on Bobby's list of people to talk to, but he hasn't been around yet. The storm probably derailed all that. But when he gets back to it again, I hope he finds the bastard who did it and hangs him from the highest tree.'

I almost took a step backward, away from the intense heat

of the anger in his voice. Vance didn't kill Eve, not the way he was talking. In fact if the killer materialized right here in front of us at this moment, he looked like he'd be perfectly capable of throwing *him* off the bridge, because an eye for an eye was fair punishment.

'Did you know she was planning to leave Landau's after she finished her dissertation?' I asked.

'She told me.'

'Any idea when she decided to do that?'

'It wasn't that long ago – maybe a couple of weeks. Why do you ask?'

'I was just wondering if the timing of her decision had anything to do with the baby,' I said, 'rather than leaving after she got her degree.'

He looked as if I'd just punched him in the gut. In the poignant silence that followed, now I knew two things for sure: not only did Vance not kill Eve, he wasn't the baby's father. Because he hadn't been sleeping with Eve.

But he still loved her. And I wished with all my heart that I could take back what I'd said, that I hadn't been the one to inflict more pain on him, because he looked completely soul-destroyed.

'I thought you knew,' I said. 'I'm so sorry.'

'I did know. But not from her.'

'When was the last time you saw her?' I asked.

He avoided my eyes. 'When she and Richard were here the other day to talk to Sloane and me before they left to see the two of you.'

'Was Eve the reason you're backing Landau's about the diseased vines not being their responsibility? Because of how you . . . felt about her?'

'Lucie . . .' Quinn spoke up, a warning tone of voice.

'*No.* Not at all. But I agree with Landau's that the problems we're having with our vines have to do with climate change,' he said. 'It's an undeniable fact. It's *happening*, Lucie.'

He hadn't answered the question, but the message in Quinn's eyes was unmistakable. *Don't go there. Let it go.*

'Lucie, Quinn. Can I talk to one of you guys for a minute? In private?' None of us had heard Antonio walk into the winery but his timing had been perfect.

'I'll go,' I said and turned back to Quinn and Vance. 'Will you two please excuse me?'

Both of them nodded and I thought Quinn looked relieved that we were going to end this awkward conversation.

As soon as we were outside, Antonio said, 'Lucita, I think we're gonna be here a while cutting up trees. They got more damage than we do.'

'Vance said the damage was minimal.'

'I don't know why he'd say that when it's not.' Antonio looked uncomfortable. 'I mean, I can take you guys around and show you what's left to clean up if you want.'

'No, you don't need to do that, Antonio. I believe you. I just don't know why Vance would say something that's not true.'

Antonio's dark eyes narrowed. 'Yeah, well, that's not the only thing he told you that's not true.'

'What are you saying?'

'When I came in a moment ago I heard him say him and Eve Kerr were getting along good the last time they saw each other.'

'That's right.'

'He lied.'

My heart constricted. No need to ask if he was sure because he was.

'Antonio, how do you know?'

'One of the guys who works here – a new kid, doesn't speak much English – told us when we were taking down one of the big trees.'

'Told you what? What did he say?'

Antonio shrugged. 'Well, since he doesn't understand English too good, he couldn't tell what they were talking about. But he knows shouting, people yelling at each other, angry, when he hears it. And that's what the two of them were doing.'

'He has no idea what they were arguing about?'

'It didn't seem like he did. He brought it up when one of the guys started talking about *la rubia que era muy guapa* who died. The real pretty blonde.'

'What about Sloane? Was he angry, too?'

'What are you talking about?'

'Vance said the last time he saw Eve was when she and Richard came over to talk to him and Sloane.'

'Nah, that's not right. The kid said it was only Vance and Eve. Just the two of them, no one else.'

'Are you serious? He's *sure* about that?'

'Why would *I* lie?'

'Sorry, Antonio. I don't doubt you, honest. But it's just that Vance's story is completely different.'

'I can ask the kid again if you want.'

'Yes, please. Could you also see if he can remember anything else about their argument? Any words?'

'Sure.' Antonio hooked his thumb over his shoulder. 'Look, I'd better get back to work. It's gonna be a while before we get these trees cut up.'

'Be careful.'

'I will.' He turned to go and then stopped. 'They can't both be right, you know. Someone's lying.'

'I know.'

'I don't think it's the kid, Lucita.'

He left.

Neither did I.

When I walked back into the winery, Quinn said to me, 'Is everything all right?'

'Yes, fine. Antonio wanted us to know he'll be here for a while. He says you have more damage than we do, Vance.'

He looked nonplussed. 'News to me,' he said. 'I'll go check things out. All we really need to do is clean up the most urgent stuff so the road through the vineyard isn't blocked. Once we get power again and things are back to normal we can take care of everything else.'

He walked Quinn and me out to the Jeep.

'So is the wedding still on?' he asked after we had both climbed in. 'Once you figure out Plan B?'

'We've figured out one part of it already,' Quinn said.

'It's turning into a multi-day affair,' I said. 'The wedding dinner is going to be on Wednesday. We're trying to get the word out to everyone who was invited.'

'Why Wednesday?'

'Because if we don't have power for a few days, everything

that needs to be refrigerated, even frozen, is going to go bad,'
I said.

'Good reason.'

'Can you make it?' Quinn asked. 'Six o'clock?'

He hesitated. 'I'll try. With the boss being gone, there's still
a lot to do around here.'

He was ducking us. It was a lame excuse. I could have
cajoled him that he still needed to eat, so he could take a
quick break from his chores and join us.

But I didn't. He wasn't coming on Wednesday. I knew it.

Antonio just told me Vance flat-out lied to us. It didn't take
a genius to figure out that he wouldn't want word to get around
that the last time he saw Eve Kerr they'd had a huge shouting
match. And then someone killed her.

Vance was hiding something. I just didn't know what it was.
Yet.

When we reached Mosby's Highway, Quinn said, 'Let's see if we
can find one of those zones where you can get cell service.'

'I suspect the dead giveaway will be all the other
people who were looking for the same thing and found it
before we did,' I said. 'They'll be hanging around, phones
clamped to their ears. Or else in their cars.'

He grinned. 'Why didn't I think of that?'

'What did you and Vance talk about while I was with
Antonio?'

'What do you think?'

'Eve.'

'He didn't kill her.'

'I know that. But he lied to us.'

'What are you talking about?'

'Antonio told me just now. He told me one of the guys
who works at GSV overheard an argument between him
and Eve. They were shouting at each other and it was just the
two of them.'

Quinn's head swiveled away from the road so he was
looking right at me. 'Is he sure?'

'Very.'

'What were they arguing about?'

'Unfortunately, the kid who overheard them doesn't speak much English. Antonio said he'd talk to him again, push him a bit and see if he can get anything out of him.'

Quinn was silent, back to concentrating on his driving.

'There's probably a logical explanation,' he said. 'Vance is a solid, stand-up guy.'

'Who has something to hide,' I said. 'I like him, too, Quinn. I don't think he killed Eve any more than you do, and it doesn't sound as if he was the baby's father, either. But he still loved her. I think there is – or was – something going on between him and everyone at Landau's. Even if Vance didn't kill Eve, somehow he's mixed up in what happened to her.'

He didn't answer me, just started worrying his lower lip with his teeth, which meant he was upset.

'I know you would like me to be wrong, but you don't think I am, do you?' I said after a moment.

He turned toward me again. 'No,' he said. 'I'm afraid I don't.'

'He's your good friend, Quinn. Maybe you can talk to him. Find out what it is. Help him do the right thing – especially if he knows something that might have to do with Eve's death.'

'Yeah. Maybe. I'll see what I can do.'

He sounded less than enthusiastic, and I knew it was because he didn't really want to know Vance's secret, in case it had something to do with the reason Eve wanted to see *him* that last day. Quinn didn't want to get mixed up in the middle of God-knew-what.

And Vance sure as hell didn't want anyone to know what he was hiding, either.

SEVENTEEN

We found cell service on the edge of Middleburg, at the turnoff on to The Plains Road. As I'd told Quinn, the scrum of cars pulled off to the side on both shoulders was a dead giveaway.

For the next twenty minutes the two of us sent group text messages to our wedding guests inviting them to a pre-wedding dinner on Wednesday and explaining the situation. That, in fact, it *was* the wedding dinner. When I wrote David to invite him, I asked how he'd fared in the storm. He replied right away from a café in Georgetown where they had power. He was fine, the carriage house he rented nearby was fine, but Pepco, the D.C. power company, had no idea when they would be able to turn the lights back on at his place. Maybe five days, maybe a week. And he said he'd see us Wednesday.

I left a voicemail checking on Kit, asking how she, Bobby, and Baby were doing. Then I called Dominique, who surprised me by answering the phone. The inn had no power, but it was located in another zone that had cell service.

I put the phone on speaker so Quinn could hear and asked if the inn had sustained much damage.

'We lost a couple of big trees, including the weeping willow out front,' she said. 'When it came down it destroyed the Japanese garden. And killed all the koi in the pond.'

We'd been listening to the all-news station on the car radio as we drove around, catching up on the latest information about the damage and devastation caused by the derecho. The stories kept coming in as everyone began assessing how bad it had been, including reports of a number of deaths, mostly from falling trees, but also a few collapsed roofs, and several heart attacks. In the big scheme of things, the loss of a few small fish shouldn't be that upsetting. Or a magnificent weeping willow.

But for some reason it hit me the wrong way, a little tragedy piled on top of everything else that had been lost or destroyed by this ferocious wind that had swept through with no warning like an avenging angel, catching us all off guard.

My eyes filled with tears. 'I'm so sorry. Especially about the koi.'

'Me, too.' Her voice caught. 'What about you?'

I told her. The garden and the Ruins both destroyed. Downed trees. The summerhouse gone.

'Oh, Lucie, *ma pauvre*. All your wedding plans . . .'

'It'll be OK.' Talking about it was like picking at a scab so the wound wouldn't heal. 'We're trying to make new plans. We're going to change the dinner and have it on Wednesday since no one knows how many days we'll be without power. I hope that's OK with you because we've already invited everyone.'

'It is,' she said, 'but any later than Wednesday and you'd be sailing on pretty thin ice.'

As only she could express it. 'Are you saying we should be OK for Wednesday?'

'Wednesday should be fine.'

'Great. Quinn and I found a zone where we can get cell service because there's nothing at the house or the vineyard, so we've been texting everyone about the change in plans. Right now we're just outside Middleburg on The Plains Road. Could we drop by to talk about a revised menu – since it's obviously not going to be what we originally planned?'

'*Bien sûr*. Come for supper. We're serving a cold buffet on the terrace. Leftovers, mostly. The chef and I got creative with whatever was still in the refrigerators.'

'Leftovers sound great,' I said. 'See you soon.'

I disconnected and Quinn said, 'I'm sorry about the fish, honey.'

My eyes filled. 'It's stupid, I know. Just . . . fish.'

He brushed away my tears with a finger. 'It's not stupid. There's so much going on right now – the derecho, the wedding.' He paused. 'And when all is said and done, there is still a murderer walking around somewhere.'

Middleburg was a ghost town when we drove down Washington Street a moment later. All the buildings were locked up and dark, and an unnatural stillness seemed to have settled over everything like a fine coating of dust left behind by the storm. The traffic light at Washington and Madison was dead. Quinn put on his turn signal even though there were no cars and made a left on to Madison, and another turn at the dogleg to Foxcroft Road where the inn was located.

I had tried texting Pépé to let him know our dinner plans had changed before we left the cell service zone, even though I knew he probably wouldn't get it.

When I checked my phone for the fourth time, Quinn said, 'If you're worried about Luc, I wouldn't be. What do you bet he and Persia are having a nice cozy dinner together on the veranda? If we were there we'd just be in the way. Those two can take care of themselves. Besides, you know she's sweet on him.'

I put my phone away and smiled. 'Just like every other woman of a certain age in Atoka and Middleburg.'

Quinn turned the final corner on Foxcroft Road and there was the inn, tucked into a bend in the road, as comforting and familiar as ever. And totally dark and quiet.

'Were you holding your breath?' Quinn asked.

'I know Dominique said it survived the storm, but I was still worried.'

'Looks like a lot of tree branches came down, especially on the roof.' He pulled into the parking lot.

The magnificent weeping willow had been cut up and the feathery branches moved to a corner of the parking lot, but part of the trunk was still defiantly standing, bloodied but unbowed. The koi pond, or what was left of it, was empty, I was glad to see. No dead fish floating belly up. We got out of the Jeep. Small branches and fresh green leaves covered the ground like a beautiful bright carpet except for the fact that in a few days everything would turn brown, curl up, and die.

Someone had propped the arched wooden front door open with a cast-iron doorstop shaped like a fleur-de-lis. Quinn and I stepped inside to the cool, dim lobby where Hassan, Dominique's Moroccan maître'd since she'd taken over owner-ship of the inn, stood behind his familiar lectern. Instead of the tuxedo he wore every night, he had on dark trousers and a white dress shirt unbuttoned at the neck. He looked elegant as always but, knowing Hassan, he probably considered his dressed-down outfit on a par with wearing sweats or gym clothes. I got kisses on both cheeks and Quinn got a handshake.

'Dominique told me you were coming,' he said. 'I'm glad to see you both are OK. *Quelle désastre, n'est-ce pas?*'

He glanced at the bandage on Quinn's forehead, but didn't say anything.

'It was bad,' I said. 'How is your home?'

He lived further west, in the little village of Bluemont at the edge of the Blue Ridge Mountains in a place called Snickers Gap.

'Bluemont did better than most other places. We had very little damage because we're located in the Gap. But like everyone else we don't have power,' he said. 'As for you . . . the wedding. I'm so sorry. I heard about your garden and the Ruins from Dominique.'

Quinn squeezed my hand.

'Thank you,' I said. 'We're making other plans. We'll be OK.'

'You will,' he said. '*Ce n'est pas la mer à boire.* Whatever new plans you make will be just fine. Better than fine.'

I smiled. It was one of my mother's favorite expressions: you don't have to drink the ocean. There was no magic wand to wave and our wedding would be the way we'd planned. As Hassan said, however it turned out, everything would be all right. Quinn and I would be married and it would be a celebration.

'We're moving the wedding dinner to Wednesday,' Quinn told him. 'While we still have a dinner to move.'

Hassan looked startled. Then he chuckled. 'All weddings are memorable, but yours, I suspect, is going to be unforgettable. And speaking of dinner, I was told to send you out to the terrace when you arrived. We've moved everything to the one off the main dining room. Just go through the French doors.'

The inn had a series of stepped terraces that ran alongside Goose Creek. We were well downstream from where Kit and I had found Eve, but I still shuddered when I heard the rushing sound of the creek as we stepped outside.

'You OK, baby?' Quinn asked.

'Fine.'

Dominique found us right away and we exchanged kisses. Like the rest of us, she looked weary and as if she hadn't slept much.

'Get something to eat,' she said. 'We'll talk afterward.'

The buffet was eclectic and surprisingly lavish. Caviar – red *and* black – smoked salmon, two kinds of pâté, home-made bruschetta on crackers, cold poached asparagus with Dijon lemon sauce, an assortment of cheeses, a cucumber and radish salad, tomato, black olive and feta salad, a green salad, and a plate of charcuterie. Two red wines: our Cabernet Franc – from older vines that were still healthy – and a California Zinfandel.

Later, when the two of us were sitting at a small table in a corner of the terrace and I was reading Quinn texts from guests who said they'd be able to come on Wednesday, Dominique joined us. She had a glass of wine but no dinner plate.

'Did you eat?' I asked her. She had always been rail-thin, and even though she ate *comme quatre*, or 'like four' as the French say, she burned it off with the energy of a wind-up toy that never ran down.

'I will. Later.' She tipped her glass toward Quinn's and mine. 'To no more derechos. Ever again.'

We clinked glasses.

'How are you doing, *chérie*?' she asked. 'I haven't had a chance to talk to you since . . . Saturday. I've been worried about you.'

She meant since Kit and I found Eve.

'I'm OK. Now. I wish Bobby had been able to find out who killed Eve before the derecho hit,' I said. 'The storm probably put a stop to the investigation. I'm sure they're concentrating on dealing with all the damage and helping anyone who was hurt. Plus they're stymied until the nine-one-one system is working again.'

'What time was it when you found her?'

It was an odd question. 'Around four thirty. When we first got to the bridge. Why do you ask?'

'Then the news must have gotten out very quickly.'

She was going somewhere with this. 'Because?'

'Because Vance Hall was in here a few hours later on Saturday night. The bar, not the restaurant.'

Quinn and I exchanged uneasy glances.

'What about it?' he asked.

'He showed up around eight o'clock and started drinking,' she said. 'My bartender got word to me and I told him to keep an eye on him, cut Vance off if he thought he'd had too much. I hadn't heard about Eve – I didn't find out until the next morning – but afterwards I wondered if Vance already knew about her when he came in here. Because he was drinking a lot.'

'Are you saying he was drinking because he was upset about Eve?' I asked.

'Possibly. I'd seen him in here a couple of times *with* Eve. Anyone could tell that he was heel over toes in love with her.'

'What happened on Saturday night?' Quinn asked.

We got the arched-eyebrow *it wasn't good* look. 'Otto James showed up. He had a couple of beers and then he and Vance had words. The bartender said Otto started it.'

'Words about what?' I asked.

'Apparently Otto told Vance, "I know what you did" and the bartender said Vance turned completely white and said, "You don't know what you're talking about and everyone knows you drink too much so why don't you shut up?"'

'What happened after that?' Quinn asked.

'Otto told him he had no intention of shutting up and he left. Vance stayed another twenty minutes or so and then he left, too,' she said.

'Do you think Otto was talking about Eve?' I asked. 'That he was implying Vance killed her?'

'I don't know,' she said. 'At the time I thought they were talking about something else since I didn't know she was dead.'

'Maybe they *were* talking about something else,' Quinn said.

'We were at GSV this afternoon. Vance was absolutely devastated about Eve's death,' I said.

'He didn't kill her, Dominique,' Quinn said.

'I don't believe Vance is capable of murdering anyone,' she said. 'In his heart, he is a good man.'

'Still, Otto's got something on him,' I said. 'I wonder what it is.'

On the drive home I said to Quinn, 'Maybe we should talk to Otto and find out what he knows that got Vance so upset.'

'I think we should leave that to Bobby.'

'Aren't you curious?'

'No.'

'Oh, come on. You just don't want to know what it is.'

'Why do you want to ask Otto?'

'You ducked my question.'

'It wasn't a question, it was a statement. You most definitely ducked mine. Why do you want to ask Otto?'

'Because I found Eve. It feels personal.'

What I didn't say was that I was also worried that somehow Quinn was peripherally involved in this as well. And that Eve had wanted him to know what was going on. Then someone killed her before she could tell him.

'I still think you should leave it to Bobby,' Quinn said.

'Who is probably dealing with derecho issues right now.'

'As is everyone else. Including us. Let Bobby deal with the murder, baby. He'll get to the bottom of it.'

'I'm sure you're right,' I said, to placate Quinn. 'He will.'

But now it seemed as if someone else knew what was going on.

Otto James.

I wondered what it was.

And how he'd found out.

When we walked through the front door to Highland House a few minutes later it was pitch dark except for a rectangle of flickering golden light coming through the screen door to the veranda. I tiptoed as quietly as I could and listened at the door to Pépé's deep, pleasant voice rising and falling as he told some story and Persia's quiet laughter and the cadence of her musical voice as she responded to him. I turned back to Quinn and put my finger over my mouth to shush him.

'They must have had dinner together. We should let them be,' I whispered. 'Besides, I promised I'd give you your wedding gift tonight.'

'We could take a bottle of wine upstairs and open it in bed,' he said.

'Uh . . . no. It wouldn't fit. It would be better if we got that bottle of wine and opened your gift outside.'

He looked puzzled, but he said, 'I'll get the wine. You get . . . it.'

I got the box from the front hall closet and carried it outside to the driveway. When Quinn joined me with wine glasses and a bottle of red, I had placed a couple of lanterns so the box sat in the middle of a pool of light.

'You got me a telescope,' he said, his face lighting up with joy.

'It's another Celestron,' I said, pleased that he was so happy. 'But the next generation. A very patient astronomer at the observatory in Great Falls helped me figure out which one to get. At least I hope it's the right one.'

He swept me into a hug and kissed me. 'It's great,' he said. 'It's perfect.'

'It's also some-assembly-required. Apparently it's not that complicated, although I don't know if you want to do it by lantern light.'

'It's portable like my old one. It shouldn't be that hard.'

He poured two glasses of wine and we sat on the front steps while he read the instruction manual with his telephone flashlight. 'This is easy,' he said. 'Plus I can run the controller on batteries since we don't have power. Looks like it came with them in the battery base.'

It didn't take him long to unpack, assemble, and align the finder scope. He used Venus as his point of reference.

'Come here,' he said after a few minutes. 'You've got to see this. The rings of Saturn. I think it's the most beautiful planet of all of them.'

I took a look through the eyepiece and, sure enough, there was golden Saturn surrounded by its silver and gold rings. 'It is beautiful,' I said. 'You can see it so much clearer than with the old telescope. The sky is lovely tonight, everything's so vivid.'

'There's a lot less light pollution, thanks to the derecho and the power being out everywhere.'

'The stars look amazing. I almost wish it were like this all the time. They seem so big and so much closer. You want to reach up and grab a fistful.'

'I know.' He sounded wistful. 'I wish we could. I've told you we're made of stardust, haven't I? Human beings, I mean.'

'No, and that sounds like poetry, or else you're teasing me.'

He switched places with me and peered through the eyepiece once again. 'I'm not teasing. Humans are created from the exact same elements as the stars and planets and asteroids. Every atom in every person can be traced back to the Big Bang that began the universe. Stars that exploded five billion years ago are part of all of us.'

'It still sounds like poetry, except for what you said about humans and exploding stars. Which sounds kind of disgusting.'

He raised his head from the eyepiece and grinned. 'It's a big messy world out there. And this is the best wedding gift you could have given me.'

'When I saw your face this morning after we found out the summerhouse was destroyed, I was tempted to tell you then. You looked heartbroken.'

'I was,' he said. 'I knew I'd buy another telescope, but it would never arrive in time for the supermoon and the eclipse.'

I cocked my head. 'I hear a car on Sycamore Lane. Probably Eli.'

But it was Antonio, not my brother. He pulled into the circular drive and parked next to Quinn and me.

When he got out, he gestured to the telescope. 'Did you get this from the summerhouse? Man, I thought everything in there was *flattened*.'

'The one in the summerhouse probably is flattened,' Quinn said. 'This one is my wedding present from Lucie.'

That got me an approving look from Antonio. 'My wedding present from Valeria was a new suit,' he said. 'Which I'm wearing to your wedding. The same one I wore to my own.'

'Practical,' Quinn said. 'You married a practical woman.'

'Not much you can do with a suit. Except wear it.'

'You'll be the second handsomest man at the wedding,' I said, and Antonio grinned.

'What brings you here?' Quinn said. 'Everything all right?'

'Everything's fine with me,' he said. 'Not so much with Vance Hall, though.'

My pulse quickened. 'The kid who overheard him arguing with Eve told you something?'

'It was like pulling teeth, but, yeah, finally he did.'

'What did he say?' I asked.

Quinn had gone into the house and returned with a beer,

since Antonio was a beer guy after hours. He handed it to Antonio who opened it and said thanks.

'They were arguing like I told you. But it was Eve who was mad. She was yelling at Vance,' he said.

I glanced at Quinn, who looked impassive. 'Go on,' I said.

'As near as I can tell, the kid said she was asking him: "Why did you do it?" And "Why didn't you tell me?" That kind of thing.'

'Do what?' Quinn asked.

Antonio shrugged. 'Beats me.'

'You never found out what "it" is?' Though it was more information than we'd had before, it was a letdown to be tantalizingly close to an answer.

'Nope.' Antonio drank his beer.

'And he's sure Eve was the only one who was shouting?' I asked.

'He didn't say too much about Vance. Just "*la chica loca*."'

'The crazy girl.'

He nodded. 'Crazy angry.'

'Doesn't sound like they were talking about a baby,' Quinn said. 'She wouldn't be asking him why he did something and didn't tell her. So that's off the table.'

'I think we already knew that,' I said. 'Whatever he's involved in, Eve knew about it – or found out right before she died. Otto might have found out about it, too.'

'Presuming "it" is the same thing,' Quinn said.

'What do you bet *it* is?' I said. 'Vance was keeping a secret that finally got out. And someone – who wasn't Vance – murdered Eve Kerr.'

'The timing of those two things happening together could be a coincidence,' Quinn said, though he didn't sound convinced it was.

Neither was I. 'You know what Bobby always says about coincidences,' I said.

'I know,' he said. 'There's no such thing in a murder investigation.'

EIGHTEEN

I discovered a couple of bars on my cell phone when I turned it on after breakfast the next morning, along with a call and message from Bobby Noland. We still didn't have power, but the return of cell service felt as if we had just emerged from traveling around the dark side of the moon.

Bobby's message surprised me. He was planning to stop by the vineyard today because he had a few more questions for us. Which I figured meant he was back to working Eve Kerr's murder investigation. But why did he want to talk to Quinn and me?

More than likely he was a step ahead of us. He'd probably already found out what Otto James knew about Vance and for some reason that made him circle back to Quinn.

And me.

Which I found unnerving. On both counts. Not to mention that I was dying of curiosity.

'I wonder what he wants to ask us,' Quinn said, echoing my thoughts. 'You're sure his message said both of us? Not just me?'

'It's Bobby. He said "you guys" so I assume he means both of us.'

He showed up while Quinn and I were cleaning up the garden in the backyard, trimming broken branches and picking up others that littered the lawn. Antonio and the crew had already been here, hauling away the remains of the arbor under which we were supposed to get married and working their chain-saw magic with the enormous saucer magnolia that had come down. I was glad I hadn't been there when they cut up the tree. It would have felt like being at the funeral of an old friend. A *very* old friend. That magnolia had graced our garden for a century. It hurt to lose it.

I went inside when Bobby arrived to get a pitcher of Persia's sweet tea and three glasses. When I joined him and Quinn on the veranda they were sitting at the glass-topped table making small talk about the Nationals' baseball games being moved to other cities because of the derecho and trash talking in general since Quinn felt his California roots required his allegiance to the Giants forever and ever amen, and Bobby was a diehard Nats fan.

I handed Bobby a glass of tea. 'You didn't come here to talk about baseball, did you?'

'No. But it was a nice diversion.'

'Is this about Eve?' Quinn asked.

'Indirectly.'

Quinn and I exchanged glances. 'So?' I said.

'Did Jackson Landau ever offer either of you money to keep quiet about problems with his grapevines?'

It was the last thing I expected him to ask. I said with complete conviction, 'No, no way. Never.'

'What exactly do you mean?' Quinn said and my heart stopped beating.

'Just what I said,' Bobby told him. 'Should I take your answer as a yes?'

There was a long, uncomfortable silence while I stared incredulously at my fiancé. Bobby's eyes darted between the two of us as he waited Quinn out.

Finally Quinn said, 'It wasn't Jackson.'

'*Quinn?*' I said. 'What the . . .? Was it *Eve*?'

'No. It was Richard,' he said. 'And he was pretty subtle about it. Honestly, I wasn't even sure I was reading him right.'

'Why didn't you tell me?'

I couldn't figure out how I felt just now. Horrified? Angry? *Betrayed?* Especially with Bobby sitting there, taking in this new development and not saying a word, not reacting.

'You weren't here,' Quinn said. 'You were still in France. Your father had just hired me. Literally. I'd been the winemaker for a couple of weeks. The last damn thing I wanted was to get involved in another scandal – if that's what this was. I shut Richard down pretty fast – and then he acted like he'd never brought up the subject and that I had completely misinterpreted him. It never came up again. I mean *never*. And if it had, I guarantee you he would have denied it.' He paused and added, 'And then he would have pointed to my reputation, to what had happened in California. It would have boomeranged right back on *me*.'

He looked ashamed at having to admit to Bobby that this painful chapter of his past was still a vulnerability, still his Achilles' heel. My anger softened and receded.

'What made you ask us this now, Bobby?' I wanted to shift Bobby's laser-focused spotlight off Quinn.

'Like I said, it might be relevant to Eve's murder.'

And just like that the puzzle pieces started slotting into place.

'You're asking us because we're not the only ones, are we?' I said. 'That's the dirt Jackson has on Vance Hall. Or maybe it's Richard who's behind this. That's why Vance is taking Jackson's side and claiming the reason so many local vineyards have diseased vines is because of climate change. Jackson bought and paid for Vance's complicity. Or, at a minimum, paid him to keep quiet.'

Bobby's eyes narrowed. 'What makes you think Vance took bribes from Jackson?'

'Antonio told me one of the Hispanic workers at GSV overheard Vance and Eve arguing. According to Antonio, who talked to the worker, Eve was shouting at Vance and saying, "Why didn't you tell me?" Then Dominique told us last night that Otto James confronted Vance in the bar at the inn on Saturday and told him, "I know what you did" like it was some kind of threat. If Vance was taking kickbacks from Landau's, all that makes sense.'

'Was he?' Quinn asked. His face was ashen. 'Taking kickbacks?'

'I'm really not at liberty to say.'

'That means yes,' I said.

'It means I'm not at liberty to say.'

The silence between the three of us was painful. I loved Bobby like a brother. Vance was a friend and he and Quinn were really tight. Both of them were coming to our wedding.

'Does what we just discussed help you in any way to find Eve's murderer?' I asked finally.

Bobby finished his glass of sweet tea and pushed it to the center of the table. 'The official answer is that I'm not at liberty to say,' he said. 'But, honestly – and this stays right here – I think it's related, but I'll be damned if I can figure out how.' He got up. 'You two get any insights, call me, OK? Because whatever is going on, it has something to do with Jackson. And him and Richard and Eve selling you guys grapevines that they knew – at some point – were going to die.'

'It doesn't seem as if Eve knew,' I said. 'Don't you think?'

'What do you mean?' he asked.

'If she was yelling at Vance and asking him why he didn't tell her – don't you think that sounds as if she had no idea about the bribe money?'

'Hard to believe she wouldn't know, as tight as those three were,' he said, 'but I guess it's possible.'

I looked at the man I was about to marry. Now we knew why Eve had been so upset with Vance before she died. I'd bet good money she'd met Fabrice who helped her with her dissertation *after* she met with Vance, not before. What was still a mystery was this: why did she want to talk to Quinn that last day?

What did she want to tell him?

'We'll be in touch if we come up with anything,' Quinn was saying.

'Besides,' I said, 'aren't you coming tomorrow?'

Bobby frowned as if he were trying to figure out what I meant.

'We're having the wedding dinner a few days early,' I said, 'in case we don't get power back before Saturday. Didn't Kit tell you?'

His face cleared. 'She did. Sorry, it slipped my mind. It's been pretty busy.'

I gave him a hug and said, 'See you tomorrow. And good luck with everything.'

He said thanks and left. Quinn and I looked at each other.

'I'm sorry,' he said. 'I never meant to deceive you or keep anything from you. Richard was so adamant that I misread him that I just let it go.'

'I understand.'

'By the time you came home, it was ancient news. Your father had just died. There were so many other issues we had to deal with.'

'I know.'

'Are we OK?'

I wanted to say *yes* or *of course we are.*

'I hope so.'

Five days until our wedding and we had just had a conversation where I learned Quinn had kept a secret from me that I should have known about years ago. Even if it hadn't seemed important when I first came home, it had become an issue in the last few weeks.

So why hadn't he told me?

And where were we going to go from here?

Quinn left for the winery shortly after Bobby took off, saying he wanted to see about derecho cleanup in the fields. In truth I knew he needed to clear his head because he didn't object when I said I wanted to keep working on the garden. We had taken a look at the summerhouse and concluded that we'd need to get the Bobcat for cleanup and a dumpster. So that project was for another day.

Before he left, Quinn came over and put his arms around me, resting his chin on the top of my head. 'We'll talk tonight in bed, OK?' His voice was soft and low in my ear. Tender. Gentle. 'I know you have a lot of questions and I have some explaining to do.'

Already I felt better. We always resolved everything – a disagreement, a misunderstanding, a rare out-and-out shouting argument – when we were in bed. First we talked it out and then we made love. It worked every time.

After he was gone, I made a half-hearted effort at continuing to clean up. Pricked my thumb so badly on a spiky thorn from the crimson Othello rose bush in the rose garden that it bled like crazy for five minutes. Went inside and got another glass of sweet tea and a Band-Aid. Thought about listening to music or an audio book on my phone as a distraction until I remembered I needed to save the battery.

Finally I gave up.

I had too many questions and too few answers. There was one place, though, where I might get at least a few answers. From someone whose finger was on the beating pulse of

everything that went on in Atoka and Middleburg. Or, to be
more accurate, her velvet-gloved fist was wrapped around the
nexus of relationships and goings-on, with a little delicious
gossip thrown in for good measure.

I got the keys to the Jeep and drove over to the General
Store.

To see Thelma Johnson.

Like every place else in town, the General Store had no
power. Someone – Thelma, by the looks of the handwriting,
spelling, and content of the message – had taped a homemade
sign to the two gas pumps out front that read: 'Curtesy of the
Derecho We're Plum Out of Gas.' The front door was propped
open so sunlight streamed in through the doorway as well
as the large plate glass window, but if you looked deeper
inside, the light turned milky and the gloominess gave
everything the faded look of an old watercolor.

Although once I walked in there wasn't much to see. The
shelves looked as if they'd been ransacked. The large vitrine
where Thelma kept all the fresh-baked goods delivered daily
from a bakery in Leesburg was empty, as were the three coffee
pots – Plain, Fancy, and Decaf – she always kept going. Usually
when I entered the place the sleigh bells she hung on the door
handle jingled and then I'd hear the muted chatter of the
television in the back room where Thelma would be watching
her beloved soap operas. Recently she'd fallen in love with
the Spanish telenovelas, especially because she found the
dark-eyed, dark-haired male heart throbs 'as sexy as all get
out.' Though the sensual, voluptuous women weren't half-bad,
either. Even though she didn't speak a word of Spanish, she
loved to explain to anyone who dropped by what she believed
was happening, which – Thelma being Thelma – was probably
even spicier than the actual plot.

I called her name and her reedy voice answered from a
corner of the store.

'Lucille? Is that you, honey? I'm over here.'

Over here meant she was sitting in her favorite Lincoln
rocker next to the pot-bellied stove, which kept the place toasty
warm in winter. Other rocking chairs were pulled into a little

circle – 'mine' was the Bentwood rocking chair – where
Thelma liked to hold court, sharing the latest news the Romeos
had brought her or else interrogating one of her guests in a
way Quinn insisted would make her an attractive candidate
for any country's intelligence-gathering operation. Thelma
could get you to admit things you didn't even know you knew.

I walked down empty aisles until I found her sitting in her
chair with one of her soap opera magazines on her lap.
Thelma's age was a more closely guarded secret than the
nuclear codes, but it was definitely north of eighty, or as she
liked to say while vamping like an aging Broadway diva,
'I know I'm not as young as I look.' She dressed with the
carefree sexy verve of a teenager who managed to get out
of the house for a hot date before her parents caught her and
sent her upstairs to change into something *more respectable
and less short, tight, and revealing, young lady.*

When I saw her just now my steps faltered because for
the first time she looked shockingly old and frail, despite the
sleeveless paisley mini-dress and bright red sling-backs. I
hoped she hadn't noticed my hesitation, but her thick trifocals
were in her lap on top of the magazine, so she probably
hadn't. I'd always thought of Thelma as ageless, or maybe
I hadn't thought about her age at all because she was such
an institution. Her General Store was the glue that held Atoka
together, the place everyone went in good times and bad, to
share news, to find out what was happening, to just *be there*
for each other. I could probably count on the fingers of both
hands the number of times over the years – decades, actually
– I'd been in the store and didn't know everyone else who
was there – my neighbors, my friends.

Thelma closed her eyes and pinched the bridge of her
nose with a thumb and a forefinger as if she were trying to
exorcize a bad headache. 'Sorry, child,' she said. 'I just need
a moment, but do come set a spell. How are you doing? I
heard all about the damage to your garden and the Ruins, and
that you and Quinn are fixing to make other arrangements.
I just don't know the details.'

She didn't say *yet*, but she might as well have done
because she planned to grill me until she found out.

I opened my mouth to ask how she knew so much already and then closed it. Someone had told her, although Thelma also liked to say that she became 'aware' of things – just *knew* them – because of her 'extra-sensible psychotic perception.' She also had a highly sensitive Ouija board that communicated with folks who occasionally returned to have a little chat with her from The Great Beyond. Among them my mother and father.

Which always freaked me out.

'Are you OK, Thelma?'

'I'm fine,' she said, opening her eyes. 'Just a bothersome headache is all. Those winds the other night were turrible, child, just turrible. That's what brought it on.'

'Can I get you something? A glass of water?'

'No, thanks, I've taken a pill. It'll start to work soon.'

I took my habitual seat and said, 'Is your apartment OK? Any damage?'

She lived above the store. It seemed to have fared well enough so I hoped that meant her home was fine as well.

'A tree branch came down and poked a hole right through my roof – in my bedroom, if you can imagine. It's in the back so you can't see it from the parking lot, but the Romeos, bless their hearts, have already taken care of it. A nice young man came over today and put a trampoline over the hole, you know, one of those big blue covers they always use. He'll fix it for good once we get past this durn derecho.'

'That must have been scary.'

'Well, I, uh . . . had a guest in for the evening. So it wasn't as bad as it might have been.'

'Oh.'

She hadn't specified the gender of her guest, but I could tell by the coy way she'd brought it up that it had been 'a gentleman caller' as she probably would say. For some reason I started blushing furiously as if I'd stumbled on her and her friend having sex. She'd also put her glasses back on and was now looking me over.

'You don't need to look so scandalized, Lucille. You young people don't have a monopoly on passion and romance and having carnival relations. I've met some very fine friends on places like Matchstick dot com and the like.'

First of all, 'carnival relations' was way more than I wanted to know, but more alarming was her discovery of 'Matchstick dot com.'

'*You're dating online?*' My hands tightened on the arms of the rocking chair. 'Thelma, do you think that's wise? I mean, it could be dangerous for . . .'

'Someone my age?'

'I just mean that someone could take advantage of you.'

She winked and said, 'I wasn't born yesterday, or even the day before. I can handle myself just fine. Even if my date turns out to be a real Casablanca.'

She looked as if she'd actually relish the prospect of 'a real Casablanca' showing up to take her out somewhere. I felt the color leave my face. The wrong man, the wrong situation, the wrong . . . everything. Some stranger. With Thelma, who would be by herself. She was naive, trusting, vulnerable . . . lonely.

'I understand what you're saying, Lucille,' she went on. 'I'm not going to take any risks or be taken in by some good-looking fellow who thinks he's the catnip's pajamas. Besides, I haven't stopped thinking about Eve, that poor lamb, ever since I heard what happened to her. She was strong and beautiful and had her whole life ahead of her. The last time she was in here she was so full of plans for her future, a fresh start somewhere new. Her and her baby.'

She had dropped that bombshell into the middle of a conversation about her dating habits like a boulder falling into a still pond.

'Wait a minute, what?' I said, aghast. 'You *knew*? You knew Eve was leaving Atoka *and* that she was pregnant?'

''Course I did.'

'How . . .?' My brain had been stuck on Thelma dating men who thought they were Casablanca or the catnip's pajamas and all of a sudden she'd revealed she knew all about Eve's baby and her plans to leave town.

'People tell me things, Lucille. You know that. I've always told you I'm like the Orifice of Delphi, that goddess everyone used to go to in Delphi, which is in Ancient Greece in case you didn't know, if they wanted to talk about their problems and gain wisdom.'

It wasn't the first time Thelma had compared herself to the Oracle of Delphi. Though Orifice was probably more accurate. Things just flowed out of her mouth. Like just now. To be honest I was shocked Eve had told Thelma – who was known for *not* being the soul of discretion – about her news and her plans. I asked how she'd found out.

'She didn't actually tell me,' she admitted. 'But she was buying ginger ale and crackers and peppermint tea – all the usual things a woman takes when she's got morning sickness. Plus the day she was in, she was as pale as a sheet.'

'So you guessed?' That sounded more like it. You couldn't put anything over on Thelma.

'I did.'

'And?'

'It just all came out, Lucille. She wanted to leave, get away from here, and raise her baby somewhere else. Probably back in California by the way she was talking.'

'Did she say who the father was?' I asked.

'No.'

'Did you ask?'

She looked indignant. 'Not outright. I know how to be subtle, child. But, let me tell you, she clammed up on that subject. She wouldn't give him up for love or money.'

'Do you know if *he* knew? The father?'

'Not for sure. But if you ask me, she was wrestling with herself about whether or not to tell him. So maybe he didn't know.'

'Do you think she might not have wanted to tell him because he was married?'

'She wouldn't say. I think she might not have wanted any more to do with whoever he was – she'd soured on him. So if she told her baby's daddy, well, then, he'd know he had a son or daughter out there somewhere and she'd always worry that he might try to find the child someday. *And* her.'

'So you think the father was still interested in her?'

'Well, it would explain why she was worried, wouldn't it?'

'Who do *you* think it was, Thelma? You must have some ideas.'

She steepled her fingers and gave me a sly look. 'Oh, I do.'

I waited.

'First, though, I'd like to know who *you* think it was, Lucille.' She'd turned the tables. As usual.

'I don't know,' I said. 'I don't know if I *want* to know, because I wonder if whoever it was might not have been happy to learn her news – if she told him. I'm worried maybe he was the one who pushed her off the bridge.'

Thelma took off her glasses and polished them on the hem of her short dress. 'That worries me, too,' she said.

'Except it doesn't make sense. If you believe the father was still interested in her, then why would he kill her?'

'Maybe because she'd found somebody new.'

'So it was a crime of jealousy? Anger?'

'Maybe.'

'Who would be capable of something like that, do you think?'

I hoped she wasn't going to say Fabrice. Who was now sleeping with my sister.

'Eve had a face like a poker chip, Lucille. She wasn't giving up any names.'

Thelma wasn't giving up any names, either. 'So,' she went on as though it were not a huge non-sequitur, 'I see you changed the plans for your wedding dinner to tomorrow night.'

She'd been anything but subtle. Dropping the subject completely. Maybe, like me, Thelma didn't want to imagine that someone she knew could have committed such a violent crime.

'We did. Are you coming?'

'Of course. I wouldn't miss it for worlds. I just wish your sainted mother was here to see you get married. In fact, I was thinking of having a little chat with her tomorrow.'

On her Ouija board.

It always unnerved me how Thelma could be so casual about the way she claimed to summon the spirits of people she knew who had passed away. Like they were dropping by for a cup of her Fancy coffee and a donut or a croissant.

'Uh, OK. And, um, what about Eve? Have you spoken to her yet?'

She shook her head. 'Of course not. I can't.'

'Why not?'

'Well, because she's not *there*. She's not over to the other side yet and she won't be until she's at peace.'

'You mean until Bobby Noland finds out who killed her?'

'Exactly. Eve wants *revengeance*, Lucille. For her and her baby. And she's gonna get it. Mark my words.'

Revengeance. A true Thelma word. Revenge *and* vengeance. If Thelma was right, what she was saying was that Eve herself was somehow going to play a role in finding her killer. And her baby's.

From beyond the grave.

NINETEEN

Thelma wouldn't elaborate on that last comment, about Eve's supposed role in helping find her killer. But when it came to otherworldly matters, Thelma believed with the faith of a child that she had a special ability to communicate with the dearly departed – and an obligation to pass on their messages to the rest of us.

As I was leaving, she got up from her rocker and walked me to the door, laying her hand on my shoulder. Her grip was surprisingly strong.

'I'm afraid that Eve's death is going to cause a lot of heartache for a lot of folks, Lucille, especially once Bobby finds out who killed her,' she said.

'Why do you say that?'

She tapped her temple with her index finger. 'My extra-sensible psychotic perception. I just *know* things.'

'Thelma, *what* things?'

She gave me a grim smile. 'You've got a whole box of Pandoras just waiting to get out when you have a gorgeous woman like Eve Kerr, who had every man in two counties wrapped around her pinky finger, goin' and gettin' herself pregnant and not telling anyone who the baby daddy is. Plus you have rumors buzzing around about big problems her boss Jackson Landau is having with his business – serious, ugly stuff. Then someone up and kills Eve. You put that all together and you got yourself one doozy of a scandal when it all comes out in the wash.'

I drove home and thought about Thelma's box of Pandoras and potential doozy of a scandal and wondered, for the thousandth time, what Eve had wanted to tell Quinn that had roped him into her life hours before she was murdered. But, as David had said the other day when he came over to photograph me, now we'd never know and it was time to let it go.

I was trying, but it was easier said than done – especially the more we learned about Eve's last days.

In bed that night – after stargazing with the new telescope – Quinn and I talked by candlelight about what had happened between him and Richard when my father was still alive and running the vineyard and I was living in France.

He was sitting up, propped against the pillows, and I was in his arms, my head resting on his chest. He stroked my hair absently as he talked. Two half-full glasses of Malbec sat on his bedside table. Somehow I didn't think we were going to get around to drinking them.

'So tell me,' I said. 'What happened?'

'Sweetheart, don't forget, it was six years ago. I don't know if I remember exactly who said what to whom.'

I lifted my head and looked him in the eye. 'Give it your best shot.'

He gave me a guilty grin and kissed my hair. 'I'll try.'

'I'm sure you'll remember more than you think you will.'

'OK, OK. So, the way it happened, as I remember, was that Richard came over one day – Eve wasn't working with him and Jackson back then – to take a look at some vines your parents had bought from Landau's. I think it was Riesling. There was a problem with yellowing leaves and Richard wanted to see for himself what was going on. Back then he was a lot less cynical than he is now and he really wanted to make things right,' he said. 'A real Boy Scout do-gooder, all earnest and sincere.'

He'd been twirling a lock of my straight dark-brown hair

around a finger as he spoke, making a big corkscrew curl over and over.

'Go on.'

He shrugged. 'So, we're talking and he's examining the leaves and all of a sudden he says something like, "You know, we could really use your expertise." So I said, "What do you mean?" And he said, "You could keep us updated about problems like this so we can get a handle on them when it's still early." So I said, "Sure, be happy to give you a call whenever something comes up," because all of a sudden I've got this university professor who's an expert on vineyard diseases on speed dial and he's plugged in to the nursery your father does business with.'

'Sounds like a good offer,' I said. 'Sounds reasonable.'

'Sounded like a terrific offer to me.'

'Then what?'

'Then he said, "Well, of course we'd pay you to make it worth your while." And I said, "What do you mean?" And the wheels are spinning and I'm wondering why he wants to pay me to tell him there's a problem with some of the vines they sold us when I'm happy to tell him for free as long as he's willing to fix what's wrong. Or at least diagnose it so we can fix it before things go south.'

My alarm bells had started going off as well. 'So what did he say to that?'

'He said, "Well, we'd just want to compensate you for giving us an early heads-up, saving us problems down the line by letting us get out in front of something." And then he said, "Obviously we wouldn't want this to get around, you understand," so I said, "Want *what* to get around – you paying me or problems with your vines?"'

'And he said?'

'And he said, "Well, both." So then we kind of looked at each other and sized each other up and his face got real red and he said, "Look, I think you might be getting the wrong idea here." So I said, "I'm not sure *what* idea I'm getting." So he said, "I thought you might be interested is all. Forget I brought it up."'

'Then what?'

'He left pretty soon after that and I tried to forget about it. Then I *did* forget about it. The last thing I needed was another scandal. Already I was on probation with Leland. I *needed* this job. The next time I saw Richard he acted like nothing had happened – all friendly and back to being the Boy Scout, so I thought, "All right, you want to play it this way, I will, too."'

'So you kept your mouth shut?'

'I did. Until now.'

'Until now. So if you had taken money from Richard with the ostensible reason of helping Landau's deal with problem vines, then eventually . . .'

'Then eventually I probably wouldn't want to bite the hand that fed me,' he said. 'Would I?'

'If this exchanging of money for "expert advice" had been going on for, say, six years, well, then, yes, it would be sort of complicated,' I said. 'It would be hard to call out Jackson and Richard for a problem like we're having now.'

Quinn reached for the Malbec. I sat up and he handed me a glass. We were going to drink it after all.

'And if Vance is taking money from Jackson and Richard, it would explain why he's standing up for them, why he's defending them,' I said. 'Because it's payback time.'

Quinn took a big gulp of wine. 'You can't discredit the idea that Vance genuinely believes the problems we're having are due to climate change. And we don't *know* that he's taking money.'

'Come on. If it walks like a duck.'

'It could still be a goose.'

'Is that what you really think?' I asked. 'That he's *not* taking money from Jackson? After what Bobby asked us today – and the conversation we're having now about you and Richard six years ago?'

It took him a long while to answer. Almost too long.

'No, it's not what I really think,' he said at last, though it sounded as if he was reluctant to admit it. 'I think it's . . . possible . . . he's been taking money from them.'

'Probable.'

'OK. Probable.'

'Which leads us right back to Eve,' I said, 'who wasn't

working at Landau's when Richard approached you about money.'

'Right, but what are you getting at?'

'Based on what Antonio told us, it sounds as if she'd only just found out about the hush money and confronted Vance about it that last day.'

'OK.'

'What do you bet Sloane doesn't know anything about this, any more than Harry Dye probably did when he owned the vineyard?' I said. 'And what do you think Sloane would say – or do – to Vance when he found out? *If* he found out. The problems we're having now with black goo aren't some minor thing. It's a lot of money, hundreds of thousands of dollars.'

Quinn finished his wine. 'If Vance didn't want Eve to talk . . .'

I finished my glass too. 'It would be a motive for murder.'

'It would,' he said, 'but I think we both believe – especially after we saw Vance today – that he didn't kill her. Goddamn it, Lucie, he *loved* Eve.'

And love, pushed to an extreme, can turn into ugly, possessive jealousy.

I took his wine glass and set both glasses back on the nightstand.

'So where does that leave *us*?' he asked. 'That's all I really care about. Making everything right between you and me.'

'We're OK,' I said. 'We're good. I wish you had told me sooner about Richard, but you didn't. We need to forget about this and move on. Besides, we made each other a promise when you moved in and so far we've always kept it.'

He smiled and took me in his arms. 'Never let the sun go down on your anger.'

'Right,' I said as he laid me back against the pillows. 'We have another deal, too. We make love after every argument. I don't want that to change.'

'Me, neither. And it seems to me this argument is over, don't you think?' He slipped on top of me and bit my earlobe.

I wriggled under him and closed my eyes. 'Mmmm, I do.'

'Then let's move on, baby.'

*   *   *

On Wednesday everyone took a break from the routine of derecho cleanup and vineyard work to get the courtyard ready for our wedding dinner that evening. We still had no power, but it was slowly coming back on in D.C. and a few close-in places in Virginia and Maryland. The announcers on the all-news radio station said we might – *might* – have power out in the far western region of Loudoun County where we lived by the end of the week, but no guarantee.

Power or no power, we were committed to going ahead with the wedding on Saturday, although no electricity and water was getting to be really, really old and more tedious with each passing day. Still, we could have the ceremony in what was left of the garden in our backyard – under a pretty gauzy canopy Frankie was designing in place of the rose arbor – and move the reception and the band to the courtyard. I wasn't sure how it was going to work with the noise of the band's outdoor generator competing with their music, but they assured us they'd done this before and could deaden the generator's sound so it didn't seem as if a jet engine was idling nearby.

Frankie had worked her usual miracle to transform the courtyard, which had been mostly put to rights, into a beautiful spring garden for tonight. She'd bought eight enormous terra-cotta olive jar shaped pots from Seely's Nursery – she would have bought more if they'd had them – and filled them with the downed branches of redbud, azalea, wisteria, and rhodo-dendron, placing them around the courtyard perimeter. She also rounded up a dozen vintage-looking wrought-iron lanterns – from where I don't know, since stores had long since sold out of lanterns, candles, flashlights, matches, fire-starters, and batteries – and placed them along the low stone wall that overlooked the vineyard. In between the lanterns she set milk glass vases of pink and white peonies, more casualties of the storm. As for the dinner, we decided it made more sense to rent rectangular tables and make two long rows so we could eat family style, rather than the round tables we'd originally planned on. We also changed the meal to a buffet instead of being served by waiters and waitresses from the inn. I'd lost track of how much time Frankie had spent working on seating arrangements – as well as having place cards designed by a calligrapher – so when I asked her who should sit where tonight, she pointed to a small table she'd placed perpendicular to the two rows so it looked like a 'T' and said, 'You two are going to sit there, along with Kit and Antonio so you can see all your guests. Everyone else can find their place cards on the table where the guest book will be and sit wherever they like.'

We were in the middle of setting out the folding chairs on either side of the tables. Frankie had twisted her strawberry-blonde hair into a knot and used a chip clip to keep it in place. A lock of hair had come down and was hanging in her eyes. She swiped at it with her forearm and managed to tuck it behind her ear. She looked up at me from across the table as she set another chair in place. Both of us were grimy, sweaty, no makeup, dirty hair, and in serious need of a shower. We could not have looked less like we were preparing for a wedding, or at least part of a wedding, in a few hours.

'I'm sorry all your careful planning seems to have gone for nothing,' I said. 'You spent so much time on every detail, especially the seating plan – and now it's just, "What the hell, sit wherever."'

Something in what I said, or maybe the woeful expression on my face, made her burst out laughing and then she couldn't stop, her laughter bubbling over until I joined in, too. There hadn't been much to laugh about lately and I didn't even know why we were laughing. Except that it felt good.

Overdue.

'Well,' she said, finally wiping tears from her eyes, 'maybe I did go a little bit overboard and this is my comeuppance. Not everything needs to be planned to the nanosecond.'

I thought of the binder that had grown so big and thick she needed to lug it around in a tote bag. 'A little spontaneity is a good thing sometimes.'

'I'm glad you think so. Because we're probably just going to wing it and see what happens,' she said. 'But one thing's for sure: no one is going to forget this wedding.'

She was probably the third person to say that to me in the last few days. At least she hadn't made the other obvious comment: Because all our original plans had been destroyed in a single night by a storm so violent it was one for the record books.

Frankie had found a hotel in Reston that had power and an available room, so she rented it for Quinn and me so we'd have a place to shower and change before the dinner. It was a good forty-five-minute drive east toward Washington, plus our return trip to Atoka meant we'd be dealing with rush-hour traffic leaving D.C. But to be back in the world of lights and electricity and sounds like fans and air-conditioning and hotel lobby music and just plain *normalcy* felt wonderful and strange.

We took a long, luxurious shower together and then I made Quinn wait in the bedroom while I got dressed in the bathroom. When I opened the door and stepped out, he stopped fiddling with a button on his shirt collar and stared.

For a moment he didn't say anything and I thought maybe the dress – a long, low-cut spaghetti-strap dusty-blue lace and chiffon concoction that skimmed my figure so it showed off all my curves – was a bit too sexy, too revealing, not what he would have expected me to wear. Then he said, '*Wow*. You look sensational. Absolutely gorgeous.'

Now I was blushing like a teenager on a first date. 'I'm glad you like it. And you look pretty fabulous yourself.'

'Thanks,' he said. 'It's nice to feel clean again. And every man at that dinner tonight is going to wish he was me once he sees you.' He hadn't taken his eyes off me. 'Although I think you're missing something.'

I looked down to see what I'd forgotten. 'Pardon?'

'Close your eyes.'

I obeyed and a moment later he was standing behind me and draping something around my neck, which he clasped in the back. He kissed my bare shoulder and said, 'OK, you can open your eyes now.'

He walked me over to the full-length mirror hanging on one of the closet doors and stood behind me. A pendant consisting of a row of half a dozen European cut diamonds alternating with oval-shaped dark blue sapphires hung around my neck on a heavy braided white gold chain. Clearly something old. And very beautiful.

I touched it. 'How lovely. I love it.'

'It belonged to my *abuela*, my grandmother, just like your engagement ring did,' he said. 'It's my wedding gift to you. My grandfather gave it to her when they got married so it's quite old. It's actually a pin, but Frankie suggested hanging it on a chain so you could wear it as a necklace. She also told me your rehearsal dinner dress was blue – I was hoping you'd wear it tonight so the sapphires would go with it.'

'Now I know why Frankie talked me into buying this dress.' I threw my arms around his neck and kissed him. 'I love it. I love you.'

'I love you, too,' he said. 'And now that we're all dressed and cleaned up, should we go home and welcome our guests to our wedding dinner, Mrs Almost-Santori?'

'That sounds like an excellent idea.' I slipped my arm through his. 'I think we should.'

The dinner was fabulous in every way right up until the end. Although we hadn't specified a dress code, since no one had running water unless they had a generator because we were all on wells, the women wore flirty summer dresses or sun dresses and the men wore dress pants and open-necked collared shirts or polo shirts. Everyone was hungry and plenty of jokes went around about who was down to eating whatever was left in the pantry and announcing what it was. Ramen noodles, breakfast cereal, peanut butter, tuna fish, canned fruit. Someone even had leftover Halloween candy.

David was there in his official capacity as wedding photographer, but I managed to persuade him that he needed to sit down and eat dinner with us as well.

'Are you up for a trip to the Goose Creek Bridge tomorrow morning?' he asked. 'The weather is supposed to be gorgeous, so I thought I'd come back out here and take my photos then. I'm working on another Civil War project.'

'I'm not sure I'm ready . . .'

'I'll show you photos from tonight if you do. Don't you want to see them? Otherwise, you might have to wait until after your honeymoon.' He gave me an evil grin.

'That's bribery.'

He grinned some more. 'I'll pick you up at ten o'clock.'

Frankie joined us. 'I think everyone's here,' she said. 'With the exception of Bobby Noland and Vance Hall. We should probably announce that the cocktail hour is over and dinner is served.'

'I'm going to take a few more photos before everyone sits down,' David said. 'Will you two excuse me?'

'Vance might not be coming,' I told her after David left. 'He said he's got a lot going on at GSV with Sloane out in LA. And Kit told me Bobby's working tonight, but he expects to be by later. So we should go ahead without him, too.'

'I'll tell Hailey,' Frankie said. 'She's in charge of the waitstaff tonight.'

'Is something wrong with her?' I asked. 'She seemed a bit out of sorts this evening.'

'I know, I thought so, too. I'll talk to her.'

'You won't need to find her,' I said. 'She's on her way over here.'

'Lucie,' Hailey said as she joined us, 'I've been meaning to tell you that you look absolutely dazzling tonight. Everybody is saying so.'

'Thank you,' I said. 'Thanks to Frankie, Quinn and I actually got to take a shower at a hotel in Reston, which helped with the dazzle. But thank you for the lovely compliment.'

'Lucky you, a real shower. I'm still doing sponge baths. By the way, the reason I came over is that Dominique says dinner is ready to be served.'

Frankie nodded. 'There's a dinner bell on the buffet table. Can you ring it, please?'

'Yup.' A bit curt.

'Is something wrong?' Frankie asked.

'What do you mean?'

'You've seemed upset this evening, or like something's on your mind,' I said. 'Frankie and I were concerned.'

'You mean grumpy? Irritable?' She looked contrite. 'Sorry. It's been miserable at work these past few days. Everyone's out of sorts and ready to bite each other's heads off. Especially Richard. I didn't mean to bring it here.'

'Because of Eve's death?' I asked.

'That's part of it. The other part is that he and Jackson had a big argument the other day. I didn't hear it, but I did hear *about* it. It sounded epic.'

'Before Eve was killed or after?' I asked.

'After. But Richard and Eve were going at it *before* she was killed.'

Who hadn't Eve been arguing with before she died? First Vance. Now Richard. 'What were all these arguments about?'

Though I had a pretty fair idea by now.

'Listen, you two, dinner's going to get cold.' Frankie laid a hand on each of our arms. 'And this is a wedding celebration, not an interrogation room at the Sheriff's Office. We have one hundred and twenty hungry guests to feed. Can you talk about this later . . . if you even have to talk about it, you being the bride and all, Lucie?'

I gave her a guilty grin, and Hailey said, 'Of course. Sorry.'

But later, after everyone was served and all our guests were eating and there was a pleasant hum of conversation, Hailey stopped by our table and leaned down so she could speak softly in my ear.

'All of the arguments were about the problems with dying vines in your vineyards, Lucie. Yours and everybody else's. I don't know any details, but what I heard was that Eve was mad at Richard because she said he was lying to people. And then Richard and Jackson were arguing about Eve, about something she'd found out,' she said. 'That she'd become a liability.'

'A liability?'

'Don't quote me, but something like that.'

'Lucie?' Frankie touched my shoulder. 'It's time for you and Quinn to cut your wedding cake. Or rather your cupcake. Hailey, can you make sure the champagne flutes are filled and the staff is ready to serve them?'

The wedding cake had been one of the early casualties of the derecho. Frankie had come up with cupcakes as an alternative and found a bakery in Georgetown that could not only make them and decorate them for us in time, but would also deliver.

It was after the toasts and speeches and everyone was eating cupcakes that Bobby showed up at our table. He looked like he'd had the day from hell. Quinn got up and got a chair for him and signaled for Hailey to bring Bobby a beer.

'What is it?' Kit asked.

'I've just arrested Richard Brightman for the murder of Eve Kerr,' he said. 'He's in jail and being held without bond.'

TWENTY

R ichard Brightman had pushed Eve Kerr off the Goose Creek Bridge and left her there to die. Bobby's news shocked us all into silence, the savagery of her death, the revelation that someone so close to her had killed her and walked away, leaving her to drown after brutally hitting her. Someone all of us knew and had worked with for years.

'How did you find out?' I asked.

'You're sure it was Richard.' A statement rather than a question from Kit, who knew her husband wouldn't have made an arrest in a murder investigation without having an absolute iron-clad, airtight case that no defense lawyer could dispute.

'Damn sure. We found the murder weapon in the trunk of his car,' Bobby said. 'Wrapped in a towel. There was blood on it and our tech lifted a couple of good, clean fingerprints. Richard's. We tested the blood and, no big surprise, it was Eve's. Plus Win Turnbull confirms that hammer we found is consistent with the wound that killed her – or almost killed her. No idea why Richard left it in his car, why he hadn't gotten rid of it – for a smart guy it was a stupid thing to do. But we had a search warrant, so we found it right away. Manna from heaven.' He took a long, deep slug of beer. 'I hate this expression, but it works for this case. Slam. Dunk.'

I glanced over at Hailey, who was putting empty wine and champagne bottles into their original boxes so they could be brought back to the winery. Since Bobby had arrived, she'd been casting furtive glances in our direction, so she knew something was up. She caught me looking at her looking at

us and mimed drinking a glass of wine, asking if we wanted
another drink. I shook my head.

But it wouldn't be long before this news got out. Besides,
Kit had already pulled out her phone.

'I need to call the Metro desk and update them,' she said.
'At least we'll get it on the Internet since it's too late for
the print edition.'

She got up and walked over to a quiet corner of the
courtyard.

'What did Richard say when you arrested him?' Quinn asked.

'I can't go into detail, but the short answer is not much.'

'You mean he didn't say, "You've got the wrong guy" or
"Let me explain?"' I said.

'Nope. Just "I want my lawyer." The usual. We're, ah, also
testing his DNA.'

'To see if he's the father of Eve's baby?' Quinn asked and
Bobby nodded.

'Did you ask him if he was?' I said.

'I told you, he didn't say much. We're gonna find out
sooner or later, anyway.' He finished his beer and set the
glass on the table.

Quinn pointed to his glass. 'Another one?'

He held up a hand. 'That's my limit. Thanks. It's been a long
day. Sorry I missed the wedding dinner, but this couldn't wait.'

'Were you surprised?' I said.

'That it was Richard? Not really. He'd been high on our
list of suspects from the get-go. Disappointed, yes. Mad as
hell, absolutely. No jury is going to let him off easily because
of the way he killed her and that gives me some satisfaction,'
he said. 'But I still don't feel good about it. It's not going to
bring Eve back.'

Kit had returned from making her phone call. 'Thank God
we've got cellular service again. I dictated something and
they're putting it on the website right now.'

'The word is going to go around like wildfire,' I said.
'Once this gets out.'

'I know,' she said. 'I wonder how Carly's doing. She must
have been absolutely destroyed when she found out.'

'Carly's pretty tough,' Bobby said. 'I think she'll pull through.

She wasn't there when we cuffed him and took him away, so at least she didn't have to watch that scene.'

Frankie joined us and placed a hand on my shoulder. 'Your guests are starting to leave, Lucie and Quinn. Bobby, I prepared a plate of food for you to take home since I'm guessing you haven't eaten considering the day you had.' She held up her phone and turned it sideways so we could see what was on the display. A banner headline from the *Washington Tribune.*

UNV Professor Arrested for Murder of Vineyard Expert Eve Kerr.

'Well, that didn't take long,' Kit said.

'I overheard a few folks talking about it already,' Frankie said. 'Some people are tethered to their phones, even with no power.'

'We should say goodbye to everyone before this really gets around,' I said to Quinn as we stood up. 'This wedding is unusual enough without throwing in Richard being arrested for murder as our guests' parting memory.'

As it turned out, we were too late. I didn't say goodbye to a single person who didn't already know what had happened and felt the need to express some sentiment or opinion on the subject, especially since I'd been one of the people who found Eve. Shock, sadness, along with the usual prurient conjecturing about whether Richard and Eve had been having an affair, had she dumped him for someone else, and what do you bet he was the father of her baby. Oh, yes, and poor, poor, Carly. How can she face anyone in town after this?

When Quinn and I said goodnight to Mia – who was clinging to Fabrice's arm – she said, 'Carly was supposed to come by the cottage tomorrow. I attached Monty's cap to his head and called her earlier today to say she could stop by whenever she wanted to pick him up. She told me she'd see me tomorrow morning.'

'Was that before . . .?' I asked.

She nodded. 'Maybe I'll take him over to her. I might wait a day or two, though. It's going to be so weird to see her after Richard.'

She didn't need to finish.

'That's probably a good idea,' I said.

'I wonder how she's doing.' Fabrice shook his head. 'Finding out your husband is a murderer. Someone you loved. Slept with every night. Someone you thought you knew.'

'If it were me, I'd probably still be in shock,' I said. 'Or denial.'

'If it were me, I'd leave town,' Mia said. 'Start over some place where no one knew me. Change my name.'

David joined our group, camera bag slung over his shoulder. 'Change your name to what?' he asked.

'Not me,' she said. 'Carly Brightman.'

'What are you talking about?'

He had to be the only person at the dinner who hadn't heard the news. I told him.

'Jesus,' he said. 'That's awful. I'm glad Bobby found out who killed her, but, wow, what a shocker. The guy who is her close colleague and buddy.'

'We're all still reeling,' I said. 'And you look like you're ready to take off.'

'That's what I came over to tell you. I need to get back to D.C. and finish up some work tonight. I'll pick you up tomorrow at ten, since we're still on for that.' He leaned down and said in my ear, 'At least there won't be any ghosts to haunt you now that Eve's killer was found. Maybe you can lay it to rest.'

I nodded. 'Maybe. I hope so. And thank you.'

Thank you, David, for trying to give me back my sanctuary – the place you and I first met – to make it feel like a refuge again.

We exchanged kisses and then he kissed Mia and said goodbye.

'What's tomorrow?' Mia asked.

'He wants to take photos at the Goose Creek Bridge and he asked me to go with him.'

'Won't that be creepy? I mean, well, you know. *Now?*'

'That's why he asked me. So it won't be.'

'He's a good guy,' Quinn said.

'He is.'

Quinn and I stayed behind with Frankie, Hailey, and the waitstaff to help with cleaning up. Mia vanished like smoke, taking off with Fabrice, which was not really a surprise. We told Eli and Sasha to scoot and take Pépé and Persia home and get Hope and Zach off to bed because we had enough people to finish what was left to do. After they were gone, it grew quiet.

The necklace of lanterns along the courtyard wall flickered in the soft darkness, bronzing the silhouettes of anyone caught in the gilded light. A breeze had sprung up, scented with the elusive sweet smell of the flowers still left on the vines. The almost-full moon, soon to be a supermoon, had risen earlier and was now a large silver disc in a star-scattered sky.

I thought about Carly Brightman and the family of Eve Kerr, people who were broken and hurting because of what Richard had done. I hoped Eve's family, her parents and brother and sisters, would find peace and solace, but I knew it would take a long, long time. As for Carly, how had she not known, or even *suspected*, her husband might be guilty? She worked in the intelligence business where she'd been trained to suss out the difference between truth-tellers and liars, cons and phonies, deceivers and the merely mentally unstable. She must have had *some* idea.

'Honey?' Quinn's voice behind me, hands on my shoulders, arms circling around my neck. 'We're all done. Let's go home.'

We had decided not to go back to the hotel in Reston even though it was ours until the next morning. We both wanted to sleep in our own bed in our own bedroom, the lack of electricity and water notwithstanding. After we undressed by candlelight, we made love – this time with an intensity that brought a swift, satisfying release after the stress and anxiety of the past few days, the storm, the quick re-arranging of tonight's candlelight wedding dinner, and finally Eve's murder and Richard's arrest – all the pent-up emotions we had needed to work through that left us exhausted and spent when we were done.

For the first time since the derecho, I slept deeply and dreamlessly in Quinn's arms and I did not stir again until morning.

David brought two café au laits and two slices of lemon-strawberry pound cake from Baked and Wired in Georgetown to our photo date at the Goose Creek Bridge.

'I'm sorry the coffee is lukewarm,' he said, 'but with no electricity out here for the last few days I figured it might be an improvement on what you've been drinking.'

'It is,' I said. 'It's great coffee. Thank you.'

For the last half-hour he had been taking photos of the bridge in the dappled sunlight with me watching him work as I sipped my coffee. The creek was still running fast a few days after the derecho, but it would slow down to a trickle once summer came and brought with it the withering heat and oppressive humidity we always had. In the past few days, it seemed like more honeysuckle was in bloom because the cloying, sweet scent, like jasmine-tinged vanilla, was even more overpowering than it had been the last time I was here. The day Kit and I found Eve.

David clambered down the embankment and waded into the middle of the creek – it was only up to his calves and he had rubber boots on – so he could shoot photos of the bridge, and especially the arches, from below. I got up from my seat and moved out of the range of his viewfinder.

'What's that?' I asked, peering down at him.

'What's what?' He lowered his camera.

'I think there's something under the log next to where you're standing. Something shiny. I caught a glimpse of it but now it's gone.'

He twisted around and looked behind him. 'Under this log?'

'Yes.'

'Where?'

I pointed. 'In between where those two branches are joined. Whatever it is looked like it was caught or hung up on a branch.'

He sloshed back to the embankment, climbed up the slope, and handed me his camera. 'Hold this while I take a look.'

He waded back into the creek and stuck one hand into the water, shifting one of the branches I'd pointed to. 'Damn. The water's really cold.'

'Sorry. Thanks for doing this.'

He bent down and, when he straightened up, he held the object I'd seen between his thumb and forefinger.

A woman's wristwatch.

A sports watch, with a large circular face and what was now an extremely sodden leather strap with a missing clasp.

My voice came out in a croak. 'Oh my God, it's Eve's.'

'Are you sure?'

I nodded. 'That's the spot where we found her body. Her watch probably came off when she was lying in the creek. Maybe it got caught on a branch and just ripped off her wrist. It must have gotten wedged under those logs. Nobody saw it the other day, but since then we've had the derecho and all that wind. Everything must have shifted.'

David clambered out of the creek again and handed me the watch. I held it between my thumb and index finger like he had done.

'What do you want to do with it?' he asked. 'It's completely dead, of course.'

'We need to turn it over to Bobby. I'll call him and maybe we can take it to him when you're done here. He's definitely going to want it, even though he's already arrested Richard.'

'I just need a few more shots,' he said. 'Besides, maybe you can let the band dry out a bit if you set the watch on the parapet in the sunshine.'

'Sure,' I said. 'Take your time.'

But when I laid the watch on the parapet and wiped some of the grime off the cracked face I could just make out that it had stopped at 5:03. Had Eve been alive then, or was she already dead?

The only person who knew the answer to that was Richard.

I wondered how much talking he would do now that he was lawyered up.

'Lucie,' David said, 'you know what? I'm good. I don't need any more photos. You seem a bit freaked out by finding Eve's watch.'

I stared at it. The watch wasn't ticking, doing some telltale heart mind-bending weirdness, but David was right. Finding it was upsetting.

'All right,' I said. 'Maybe I should call Bobby now and we can give it to him.'

Get rid of it.

'Sure. Call him and I'll drive you wherever.'

Bobby's phone went to voicemail so I left a message about David and me finding Eve's watch in the creek and telling him I'd have it at the winery so he could come by and pick it up or send a deputy to do so.

I was about to put my phone away when it dinged that I had an incoming text. From Mia.

I read it and groaned.

'What's up?' David asked.

'Do you think you could drop me off at Mia's cottage? She says Carly is on her way over to pick up Monty the Fox and she asked if I'd be there as a back-up. She feels kind of strange about seeing her now that Richard's been arrested and charged with murder.'

'Sure,' he said. 'Your wish is my command.'

I texted Mia back and told her I'd be there in a couple of minutes.

'What am I going to do with the watch?' I asked.

'I can give you a cloth I use for cleaning my lenses that you can wrap it in since the strap is still wet. Maybe stick it in your pocket until you get back to the house?'

'I guess so.'

'You're not going to want to flash it around in front of Carly and Mia and tell them what you found. Especially not Carly.'

'I *know* that.'

'It'll be OK, Lucie.'

I took a deep breath as he signaled for the turnoff to Sycamore Lane.

'I know. It just feels strange.'

Carly's little two-seater convertible was already there when David pulled into the drive in front of Mia's cottage. He kissed me on the cheek.

'Can't wait to see you Saturday when you're the beautiful blushing bride.'

'Thank you. See you then.' I kissed him back. 'And thanks for this morning.'

'For part of it, at least. You're going to be able to go back there, right? To the bridge?'

'Maybe not right away. But eventually.'

'Well,' he said, 'that's something. And good luck with your meeting with Carly. I hope it's not too strange or awkward.'

'At least we'll get it over with, get past the initial . . . awfulness. She probably feels pretty alone and isolated now. I would, if I were her.'

'You're a good friend, Lucie. You'll help her.'

'Thanks.' I got out of the car and watched him drive away.

When I knocked on the door and walked into the cottage, Mia and Carly had their backs to me, the two of them bent over Monty the Fox who was reposing on Mia's table, newly resplendent in his bejeweled flat cap.

'. . . looks terrific,' Carly was saying.

They turned around when I closed the front door.

Carly looked worn-down. Her face – without a bit of makeup – was gaunt-looking under her suntan.

'Carly,' I said, 'I'm so sorry. I don't know what to say. If we can do anything for you . . . whatever you need. We're there for you. Don't forget it.'

'That's so kind, Lucie,' she said. 'You don't know how much I appreciate it. I'm still just . . . reeling.'

She raised a hand to tuck a strand of hair behind her ear.

Which is when I saw the pale outline on her tanned skin where her watch had been. A big watch like a sports watch. Circular face. Thick strap. I'm guessing leather.

The watch David and I had found in Goose Creek a little while ago, which I had just assumed was Eve's. Except now I knew it wasn't.

It was Carly's.

Eve's murderer.

TWENTY-ONE

Never try to con a spook.

Carly's eyes hardened. She'd seen me staring at her wrist. I kept smiling as if nothing had changed, nothing had happened, and I hadn't seen what I just saw

– that circular patch of pale white skin – and put two and two together.

But she *knew*.

In the meantime, Mia, relieved to have me here as her backup, especially now that I had addressed the elephant in the room – Richard's arrest for Eve's murder – was effusively offering sympathy and understanding and friendship as I'd just done.

'Oh, Carly, we *get* it, we're just so *sorry* about what happened. But, like Lucie said, if there's *anything* we can do to help all you need to do is ask.'

Carly turned to her with a smile. 'That's so kind. It means so much.'

'Of course.'

To me she added, 'You didn't need to make a special trip to come by to console me, Lucie. I *know* what you're thinking right now, believe me. Mia said you were out with David taking photos at Goose Creek Bridge.'

The hair on the back of my neck stood up. 'That's right.'

The silence in the next few moments seemed to last an eternity, as if I were watching in slow motion as a beautiful handblown vase fell to the ground after it had slipped out of my hands. Knowing I couldn't stop it from shattering into a million razor-like shards and that there would be no way to repair it or make it whole.

Ever.

In those moments I watched Carly realize she hadn't gotten away with the perfect crime: her disappointment, her shock, her *anger*. All the while she was watching *me* try to come to grips not only with the brutality and cruelty of how she'd murdered Eve, but the cold-blooded way in which she'd framed her husband for the crime. Eve and Richard must have been lovers and I'd bet my life he was the father of her baby. Carly, a career woman who had not wanted children – though Richard had been desperate to be a dad – had found out somehow. And she wanted to punish Richard.

So she sought the ultimate revenge. Killing her husband's girlfriend, the mother of his child, and making him pay as if he'd done the deed himself. Richard would have known exactly what happened when Bobby produced 'his' murder weapon with its irrefutable proof – Carly had obviously transferred Richard's prints to the hammer, something she'd know quite easily how to do in her line of work. Leaving Richard to wrestle with the soul-destroying dilemma of whether to turn on his wife or accept his fate, which most definitely meant time in prison, because, at the heart of it, he'd betrayed Carly, cheated on her. He was responsible for her rage, her hurt. So in a bizarre, twisted way, maybe he'd feel it was a justified punishment.

I didn't know. I didn't *want* to know.

'Where is it, Lucie?' Carly asked.

Like I said, you don't con a spook. It didn't stop me from trying, maybe buying a bit of time. I'd left that voicemail message for Bobby. Maybe he'd call *right now*. Say he was on his way. We could end this before anything else happened.

'In the creek.'

And not about to burst into flames in the pocket of my jeans or glowing so vividly that you could see it from outer space.

'What's in the creek?' Mia's eyes darted between the two of us. She'd figured out that something was wrong.

When neither of us answered, she said, 'Lucie? Carly? What's in the creek? What's going on?'

'You tell her.' I wasn't doing this. It was on Carly.

Carly gave me a look of fury and spit out the words. '*My watch.* Dammit, I swear I saw it float downstream.'

Mia, my beautiful, blonde, angelic and occasionally naive sister, looked puzzled. 'Your watch?'

Our eyes met and hers grew wide. There were questions in hers; the right questions. I barely nodded and saw everything click into place, the pieces fit together.

Now she knew, too.

'Lucie.' Carly's voice was hard and cold. 'If you weren't so damn skinny it wouldn't be obvious that you're lying through your teeth and there's something in the pocket of your jeans. I'm guessing it belongs to me.'

'Not any more. I told you. I called Bobby and he's on his way here. It's over, Carly.'

'I really don't want to do this, but you need to give me the watch.' With one swift motion she pulled a revolver from a holster underneath her navy blazer. I hadn't realized she was carrying concealed, a dumb mistake on my part, living in Virginia all my life.

'What are you going to do?' I asked, though I didn't want her to answer that question. 'Shoot us both? Because that's what you're going to have to do to get out of here. And then what? Bobby *knows*, Carly. He knows David and I found your watch. How far can you run?'

'Give me the damn watch, Lucie. I'm a crack shot and I'm warning you.'

I didn't doubt her. 'And if I give it to you, then what? You're still going to shoot us?'

She aimed the gun at me and Mia screamed. I could feel the shot whistle past me and behind me, glass shattered, sounding like an explosion.

'Give me the damn watch or next time I'll put a bullet in your knee and you'll never walk again. That one was just a warning, to let you know I'll do it.'

She started to raise her arm once more, but before she could aim the gun at me Mia picked up Monty and swung him hard, whacking Carly in the back of her head. The blow caught her off guard and she stumbled forward, losing her balance. Mia hit her again and this time she went down, groaning as she struck her head hard on the corner of Mia's work table. My fierce tiger sister was on top of her in an instant, her knee in Carly's back as she wrenched her arms together none too gently and gripped her wrists. Monty, who was now in two pieces, had lost most of the jewels that had been on his beautiful coat and his new flat cap. Colored stones rolled around the floor like marbles.

'Get the gun, Lucie. Quick, before she comes to. I'm not sure how long we have.'

I nearly slipped on a fake ruby before I picked up the gun from where it had slid across the floor. I put the safety on and tucked it into the waistband of my jeans.

'There's duct tape on the table,' Mia said. 'Bind her hands first, then her legs while I hold her.'

'Thank God you have a well-stocked art studio.' I found the tape.

'There's scissors if you need them, but you should be able to tear it off the roll.'

'I hope she doesn't wake up. She's strong and she knows martial arts. Be careful, Mimi.'

'You have the gun,' my sister said through gritted teeth. 'If she tries anything, shoot her.'

I bound Carly's hands and felt her stirring.

'Don't move,' Mia hissed at her. 'Lucie's a good shot, too.'

Getting her legs taped together was harder because she started to fight me, to kick, but Mia was able to help since Carly's hands were bound, so between us we managed. When we were done, we rolled her over so she was lying on her back. A huge red and purple bruise had appeared above her right eye, which she must have gotten when her head hit the table.

'Let me go, goddammit,' she said. 'They both had it coming. She deserved what she got and so did he.'

'Now it's your turn,' Mia said as I pulled out my phone and dialed 911.

'You don't know who you're dealing with. You don't know what I can do to you.'

I tore off one more piece of duct tape and placed it over Carly's mouth.

'I can't listen to this,' I said.

TWENTY-TWO

May's full moon, called the Flower Moon because it occurred during a season when so many flowers were in bloom, was unusual because it would not only be a supermoon, when the moon was at its closest to earth, but it would also produce an astronomical event known as a Blood Moon. For approximately half an hour, beginning at three thirty on Friday morning, a lunar eclipse would take place and the moon would glide through Earth's shadow blocking any light from the sun and gradually turning a deep shade of blood red.

Quinn and I talked about the Super Flower Blood Moon, as it was being called, over dinner that night with Pépé and Persia when they joined us on the veranda for a cold buffet of wedding leftovers. The two of them had decided to leave the moon-viewing to us – rare though it might be – since it took place at such an ungodly hour. Persia said she needed her beauty sleep to be ready for our wedding less than forty-eight hours later, and Pépé said he was certain I wanted him to be awake when he walked me down the garden path to the canopy under which Quinn and I would be married. Staying up half the night would probably guarantee he'd be asleep on his feet on Saturday.

'It will be especially good for the two of you to see this moon just before your wedding,' Persia said to Quinn and me, as we sat around the table after dinner.

I took a guess at what she meant. 'Because it brings good luck?'

I had lit the pillar candles – now two chubby white stubs – since it was growing dark. Pépé had refilled everyone's wine glasses. Quinn got cigars, matches, and ashtrays for himself and Pépé.

Persia shook her head. 'Because the combination of a supermoon *and* a blood moon is considered to be a perfect time for renewal. For making a fresh start. It's also an excellent time to make life-altering decisions and changes.'

'I think we've already made those decisions and changes,' Quinn said, lighting his cigar and puffing on it until the tip glowed like an orange mini-moon. 'We're getting married. That *is* life-altering.'

'Yes, but that is not the type of change I am talking about.' Persia wagged a finger at him. She was smiling, but her voice was firm. She wasn't joking.

'And what type of change would that be?' I asked.

Persia believed in the power of spirits and practiced a Jamaican form of faith and spiritual healing known as Obeah. I didn't really understand it, except that it was an Afro-Caribbean blend of theology and mythology with some similarities to Voodoo – though its followers didn't worship a god or gods. I found it – and Persia's unshake-able faith in the spirits – fascinating and a bit magical.

She was also a devotee of astrology.

'This eclipse occurs in the fire sign of Sagittarius,' she said. 'It is a truth-seeking zodiac sign that will stop at nothing to obtain and gain knowledge. The Blood Moon is going to force you to confront issues you haven't wanted to deal with, force you to make decisions about anything you have been trying to ignore.' She gave us both a wise, knowing look. 'I believe you two have such a situation in your life at the moment. This moon tonight gives you an opportunity to resolve that issue before your wedding on Saturday. Which you should do.'

Quinn and I glanced at each other. *How did she know?*

Because the one thing that still festered, the only thing we hadn't dealt with, because we *couldn't*, was the subject of what Eve had wanted to tell Quinn that last day before she died. Now it would never be resolved, this niggling, irritating little sore that would not heal, even if it remained below the surface.

Unless we allowed it to heal and move on.

'Then I guess it's a good thing we're going to get up at three a.m. and wait for the Blood Moon,' I said.

Persia smiled an inscrutable smile in the candle-lit semi-darkness. A curl of smoke from Pépé's cigar drifted behind her so she looked almost as if she had come here out of a dream. 'Yes,' she said in her wonderful lilting voice. 'Yes, my loves, I guess it is.'

Before we went to bed to catch a few hours of sleep, Quinn had dragged two of the wicker chairs from the veranda and set them in the middle of an open space in the backyard where we would have a clear view of the moon. The Adirondack chairs we always used had been destroyed in the derecho, along with the summerhouse.

The alarm went off at two forty-five. Both of us groaned but we got up and got dressed though I was still half-asleep. While Quinn set up the telescope on the lawn, I made two mugs of green tea and brought them outside. The cool night air jolted me fully awake as if someone had thrown a bucket of cold water over me.

'We're going to have some clouds by three thirty,' Quinn said as I handed him his tea. 'I've been checking the weather.'

'Will we be able to see anything?'

'I think so. I hope so.'

I sat in one of the wicker chairs and drew my legs up under me, cupping my hands around the mug to warm them. 'At least we'll have time to talk about those life-altering changes Persia told us we ought to make.'

'In spite of what she said, I think we've already had enough life-altering changes in the last week to last a long time,' he said. 'Don't you?'

'Yes,' I said. 'The derecho being the biggest one.'

'I've been doing some reading,' he said. 'The all-knowing "they" in weather-land said we should be expecting more severe events, maybe even more derechos. Because of climate change.'

Which was going to make our lives even trickier, more complicated, if we couldn't plan for them in the same way the derecho had caught us off-guard. What were we going to do? Keep trying to dodge bullets?

'Regardless of whether Jackson and Richard sold us vines they knew were diseased, I think Richard and Eve were right the other day when they said we need to think about planting varietals that will work better in the climate we've got now,' I said. 'Josie's been beating the same drum.'

Quinn had been looking through the eyepiece of the telescope as I said that. He straightened up and looked at me.

'And where are we going to find the kind of money to do that?'

'I don't know. We'll figure out something. We always have,' I said. 'We'll have to adapt. Or else we won't survive.'

'Hey,' Quinn said. 'Come over here and take a look. It's starting.'

Quinn and I weren't expecting Vance Hall when he showed up at the winery later on Friday morning. We'd gone over there, as usual, to check on everything after getting a few hours of sleep, but after that we were going to spend the rest of the day preparing for the wedding on Saturday.

'You look like a couple of miles of bad road, buddy,' Quinn told him. 'What's going on?'

'I've turned in my resignation to Sloane,' he said. 'But before I leave Atoka I need to make some things right.'

'So you came here,' Quinn said.

'I came here.'

'Let's go over to the Villa,' I said. 'I think we could all use a cup of coffee. We're not open yet, so we have the place to ourselves. We can sit out on the terrace and talk there.'

We made awkward small talk in the kitchen while Quinn found the bottled water and made coffee on the camping stove we'd been using. I got out three scones left over from yesterday and a couple of individual foil-covered packages of jam.

'Are you still coming to the wedding?' I asked Vance. 'Because we'd really like you to be there.'

'Thanks,' he said. 'I'll try.'

Which meant no.

We took our coffees and the scones outside and sat at one of the picnic tables where we had a view of the vineyard, including our dying Cab Franc vines. The weather was glorious – sparkling sunshine, sharp blue sky, the gentle caress of a warm breeze – as it had been every day since the derecho. Tomorrow was supposed to be just as beautiful, as if Mother Nature decided we'd been punished enough. So she was giving us a week of perfect weather as if asking forgiveness for all the destruction she'd caused.

'Did you have to quit?' Quinn asked.

'I preferred to quit rather than being fired,' Vance said. 'Sloane was gracious enough to let me do it that way. But I'm not expecting a glowing reference.'

'You were taking money from Jackson, weren't you?' I said. 'Or was it Richard?'

'Either,' he said. 'Both. Does it matter?'

I thought it did, but I kept my mouth shut.

'Eve didn't know,' Quinn said.

Vance closed his eyes as if the sun was suddenly too bright and too hot for him. When he opened them he said, 'Not until right before she died.'

'Which was why she was arguing with Richard,' I said. 'And you.'

His laugh had no mirth. 'So you found out about that shouting match she and I had, did you?'

'Yes.'

'Who told you?'

'You were overheard. Apparently Eve was doing the shouting.'

'She found out about the money,' he said. 'The payoffs or whatever you want to call them. Hush money. Bribes. Take your choice. She was furious. She'd already given Richard holy hell.'

'Originally it was supposed to be money for helping Landau's get out ahead of any problems, wasn't it?' Quinn asked. 'Then it turned into something else.'

'How do you know?'

'Richard came to me with the same proposition and I turned him down. In a manner of speaking.'

'You're a noble guy, Quinn,' Vance said, but it didn't sound like a compliment. 'When was this?'

Quinn glanced at me. I sat there, mute, waiting to hear where this was going.

'Six years ago. Right after Leland Montgomery hired me,' he said. 'Was that when you were approached? Who came to you?'

'Richard. Also six years ago.' He rubbed his forehead with his hand as if he was trying to massage a migraine. 'I had no idea thirty pieces of silver weighed so much.'

'What did Eve say that last day?' I asked.

'She was going to blow the whistle. Put a stick of dynamite under Landau's. She said she didn't care if – when – it went boom because she knew she was doing the right thing. Later when you told me she was going to have a kid, I figured that had something to do with it. She'd changed. She didn't want to be part of something she knew was wrong, turn a blind eye.'

'She asked me to stop by her place that last afternoon before she died,' Quinn said. 'She said she wanted to talk to me about something.'

'Is that why you were late to the Chardonnay blending?' Vance asked. 'Because you were with her?'

'*I got there too late.*'

Vance's face flushed. 'Yeah, of course. By late Friday afternoon she was with Carly at the Goose Creek Bridge. Carly had just found out about the baby. Caught Eve walking out of her obstetrician's office Friday afternoon as she was leaving her own doctor for some check-up. She put two and two together and confronted Eve. Man, was she livid.'

'How do you know all this?' I asked.

'Small town. Isabella was also leaving a doctor's office with one of the girls. She heard them. Came to me. Wanted to know – indirectly – who the father might be.'

Of course. *She keeps Sloane on a tight leash.*

'The baby was Richard's?' Quinn asked.

He nodded. 'Carly wanted Eve to leave town and never come back, never see Richard again. And not destroy Landau's as her farewell gift.'

'Carly told us at Foxes on the Fence last Saturday that she knew Eve wanted to leave Landau's, give up her research work with Richard once she got her PhD,' I said. 'She said she was angry because Eve owed both Jackson and Richard for everything they'd done for her.'

'Yeah, well, she lied,' Vance said in a flat, hard voice. 'Besides, she knew Eve was dead.'

'Because she'd killed her,' Quinn said.

'Because she'd killed her.'

'She wanted to talk to Quinn about something that day,' I said.

'I know.'

'You *know*?' Quinn asked. 'You know what she wanted to tell me? Though I bet I have an idea what it might have been. *Now.*'

'Go on,' Vance said.

'She wanted to ask me what it was like to be a pariah, after what happened to me in California,' Quinn said. 'I bet she wanted to know what her future might look like, because everybody knows whistleblowers aren't universally beloved or highly thought of. You stick your neck out, think you're doing the right thing, and wham. You're the bad guy and everyone else is a victim.'

Vance pointed a finger at Quinn like it was the barrel of a gun and pretended to shoot. 'You got it. She told me she was going to talk to you, find out how you managed to hang on to your career and start over some place new.'

'You could have told me why she wanted to talk to me, buddy,' Quinn said, and a river of bitterness ran through his words. 'You could have told me sooner than this.'

Vance's eyes flashed. 'Not without being up to my ass in alligators I couldn't. *Buddy*. Plus I didn't know she never got around to talking to you.'

'She didn't,' Quinn said. 'So now you know.'

Vance stood up. 'I ought to be going. Thanks for the coffee. And good luck tomorrow with your wedding. I'll see myself out.'

After he was gone, we were both silent for a long time, staring out at the vineyard. I wasn't sure whether I felt relieved or numb. But when Quinn finally turned to look at me, there were tears in his eyes.

I had never seen him cry. Ever.

'I could have saved her,' he said and his voice broke, 'if I'd gotten there sooner.'

I went over and knelt next to him.

'Don't.' I pulled his head down on to my shoulder. 'Let her go, Quinn. *Let her go.*'

Then I held him as he sobbed for the loss of Eve Kerr, the beautiful golden California girl whose death had torn him up. I don't know how long we stayed on the terrace, but when he finally pulled himself together dry-eyed, I knew he had forgiven himself at last for something he couldn't have stopped.

And that he had found his way back to me again.

TWENTY-THREE

The power came back on Saturday morning just after nine o'clock. Quinn and I were in the bedroom when we heard Persia shouting, 'Hallelujah! Praise be!' downstairs from the kitchen along with the quiet explosion of the heating and air-conditioning system kicking in from the basement as well as half a dozen angry beeps and squawks from devices and equipment that wanted you to know they needed to be reset. Our phones began ringing – Frankie, Dominique, Eli, Mia, Kit, Antonio – everyone overjoyed to be back in the real world and asking if we had power again as well.

'I want a nice, long shower,' I said to Quinn. 'A real one. With hot water.'

'Let's take one,' he said, so we did.

The return of water, electricity, lights, air-conditioning, refrigeration, and the ability to use a stove and oven happened too late to rearrange plans for the wedding ceremony and the buffet of salads and cold dishes we'd decided to serve in lieu of a sit-down dinner, but at least the band could forego needing their generator. Still, Frankie told me she and Dominique had a few ideas they thought they could pull off, additions to the buffet menu, little extras. When I asked her to elaborate, she said, 'You'll just have to be surprised. Because I think we're going to be surprised as well. It depends whether we can make things happen so fast.'

Frankie and Dominique, Superwoman squared. I had no doubt they'd make anything happen if they wanted it to. The only caveat was that Frankie wouldn't be at the house when I got dressed. Secretly I didn't mind not having that part of the preparation so tightly scripted if she wasn't there to keep me on schedule.

Besides, in the new order of post-derecho planning we had decided to keep everything simple, natural, or as Dominique said, 'We'll just row with the flow.' As it turned out, I liked this more relaxed, casual vibe. It felt comfortable and more like *us*, starting with the laidback rehearsal dinner last night, which had turned into a couple of pizzas from a Leesburg pizzeria, a few bottles of wine, and a case of beer as everyone gathered on the veranda after a quick run-through with Eli of how the ceremony would go. Today would be more of the same: relaxed and easy-going.

'It'll just be Mia and Kit helping you,' Frankie said to me now. 'Can you manage?'

'We'll be fine. I'm sure between the three of us we can figure it all out. We've all gotten dressed up before, put on makeup, done our hair. We can do this.'

'Well, of course you can.'

'Good,' I said. 'So, don't worry. No fussing any more, remember? Plan B means no fussing.'

'Right,' she said. 'No fussing.'

Around one o'clock Quinn disappeared, going over to Eli and Sasha's place where he would stay until Antonio joined him and they all came back to Highland House, to the garden, just before the ceremony at four. Before he left, he took me in his arms and kissed me.

'I'll see you soon,' he said. 'I can't wait.'

Kit, Mia, and David arrived next, almost at the same time.

'How's Bobby?' I asked Kit.

'Still beating himself up for falling for a stupid setup. If it hadn't been for you finding Carly's watch . . .'

'I'm sure the truth would have come out sooner or later.'

'You tell him that,' she said. 'I've tried. But not today. Today you're getting married and that's all that matters.'

Persia did my hair, fixing it in a loose French braid. I did my own makeup. Frankie had given me an at-home manicure yesterday afternoon before the rehearsal, painting my nails with the delicate pink Gossamer polish we'd chosen an eternity ago, before the derecho, just before Eve and Richard came over to see Quinn and me for what turned out to be the last time.

I wasn't sure how comfortable I'd be with David in the bedroom taking pictures of me getting dressed with Kit and Mia, but as he'd reminded me he'd worked with hundreds of models before, with and without clothes on.

'Your call,' he'd said, 'but I'd like to photograph you getting ready. All of it, or most of it – if you're willing.'

So I'd agreed. 'OK, all of it.'

He was discreet and remained so much in the background that I nearly forgot he was there except for the rare occasions when he'd give directions.

'Tilt your head a little more to the left.'

'Look at Kit, please.'

'You look absolutely gorgeous. Another one just like that.'

He was great, as I knew he would be, putting all three of us at ease, especially when he showed us photos on the preview screen that none of us had realized he had taken.

'Wow,' Kit said. 'These are stunning.'

'Thank you. It's easy when you have beautiful subjects.'

Kit blushed and Mia said to him, 'I saw the book you gave Lucie on the Confederate monuments. I was wondering if you'd consider exhibiting some of those photos at The Artful Fox, the gallery in Middleburg where I work part-time, maybe as part of your book tour. They're incredible, David. Powerful.'

'You left out "controversial,"' he said.

She looked up at him and smiled her most angelic smile. 'The owner of the gallery is known for being controversial. She likes to stir things up, make people think. It would be a great exhibit.'

He looked at me.

'You should do it,' I said.

'Then I'm in.'

'Excellent,' Mia said. 'I'll talk to the owner and she can get in touch with your publicist.'

'Your flowers are here,' Persia called from downstairs. 'Shall I bring them up?'

Quinn had picked the flowers for my bouquet himself from a flower farm in Bluemont. I had no idea what to expect, but when I saw what he had chosen I had to bite my lip to keep the tears back. It was beautiful, messy, feminine – all the flowers I loved in shades of pink and white: roses, peonies, ranunculus, calla lilies, with green-and-silver dusty miller woven through it all.

The men had calla lily boutonnieres, so I pinned David's

on myself. Then I walked down the spiral staircase with Kit and Mia holding the train of my dress to where my grandfather waited for me below.

I heard Kit murmur, 'I knew we should have brought more tissues.' And then she sniffled.

'You look just like your mother,' Pépé said in a husky voice, kissing me on both cheeks. 'You are beautiful, ma belle.'

I pinned on his boutonniere. 'And you are very handsome. I'm glad you stayed so you could give me away today. Just like you gave Mom away.'

The door to the veranda opened and closed and Frankie walked in. She had seen my dress before when we found it at a consignment shop in Georgetown, but her eyes still widened. 'Lucie, oh my God, you look *stunning* . . . and Kit and Mia, you both are lovely,' she said and then she stopped. 'Wait a minute. Why is everyone crying?'

'Because . . . we're . . . so . . . happy.' Mia choked back a sob.

Which made all of us start laughing and then Frankie fussed, in spite of the no-fussing rule, because my mascara had run and she thought I looked like someone who belonged at a Kiss concert.

Sasha arrived with Hope and Zach, my flower girl and our ring bearer, and then it was time for Pépé to walk me down the garden path after Hope and Zach and Kit preceded us to where Quinn and Antonio and Eli were waiting.

Quinn never took his eyes off me, and when Pépé placed my hand in his, my husband-to-be said in my ear, 'I've been waiting all of my life for you.'

'I've been waiting all of my life for you, too,' I said.

He bent and kissed me until Eli finally cleared his throat and said under his breath, '*Mawage is wot bwings us togevah today.*'

We pulled apart and I shot my brother a look. He winked and grinned. 'The kiss comes *after* I pronounce you man and wife. *After.* We practiced this last night.'

'Sorry.'

'So are you ready?'

Quinn took my hands. 'We are,' he said, and I nodded.

'Then let's begin,' Eli said.

ACKNOWLEDGMENTS

*B*itter Roots was written entirely during the pandemic in 2020 and early 2021, which meant I traveled nowhere and met with no one in person as I was researching this book. It felt strange, a total disconnect – as if I were writing in a vacuum. Research has always been one of my favorite parts of writing, not just for the information I learn and the people I meet, but from the energy I get from those experiences: it fuels my writing.

Still, I owe thanks to several people who were kind enough to answer my questions and share their expertise with me by email or over the phone. Lucie Morton, one of the country's top viticulturists and internationally known ampelographer, as well as the inspiration for Josie Wilde, explained Vine Decline, climate change, and the devastating impact these issues are having on the wine industry to me (especially the problems California faced in the 1990s). Rick Tagg, winemaker at Delaplane Cellars in Delaplane, Virginia, answered all my vineyard and wine-related questions and told me all about wine barrels with patience and humor as he has done for the past thirteen years. Our friendship is very dear to me; I can't imagine how I would have written this series without his help.

Photographer Brian Rose (introduced to me by Donna Andrews, my long-time writing buddy and up-the-street neighbor) sent me an early copy of *Monument Avenue Richmond: Grand Boulevard of the Lost Cause*, his moving book of photographs of the Confederate monuments as they were being defaced and pulled down in Richmond, Virginia in the summer of 2020. Now a New Yorker, Brian also sent me his essay about coming to terms with the role the monuments played in his life growing up in southern Virginia.

Artist and friend Rosemarie Forsythe offered suggestions for designing Monty the Fox for Foxes on the Fence, which is a real event and fundraiser that takes place each May in Middleburg.

Thanks to Donna Andrews, John Gilstrap, Alan Orloff, and Art Taylor, the talented group of writer friends I've met with every month without fail for the last ten years, for comments, observations, and thoughtful critique on early drafts of this book. I miss our in-person meetings, but at least we've got Zoom.

Strictly speaking it was pastry chef Mary Bergin who said that every woman should have a blowtorch in the kitchen; a remark she made many years ago while caramelizing sugar for crème brûlée (to drizzle over a chocolate Bundt cake) on Julia Child's PBS show 'Baking with Julia.' Julia, who was oohing and ahhing over the concoction, told Bergin, 'Oh, Mary, every*one* should have a blowtorch in the kitchen.' To which Bergin replied, 'No, Julia, every *woman* should have a blowtorch in the kitchen.' Later the comment became the title for one of Julia's cookbooks, and ever since then it has been associated with her.

At Severn House, thanks to Kate Lyall Grant, publisher and my editor, who was so wonderfully supportive of this series. I will miss her greatly, though I know she's excited about a new opportunity with a new publisher. Thanks, also, to Natasha Bell and Michelle Duff for all that they did to make sure books got to reviewers and bookstores during the crazy pandemic days.

As always, thanks and love to my agent Dominick Abel, who makes it all happen.

Last but never least, so much love and gratitude to my husband, André de Nesnera, who captured my heart the day we met and still owns it completely more than forty years later.